A SHADOW FALLS

BLOODLINES LEGACY
BOOK TWO

USA TODAY BESTSELLING AUTHOR
ROSE GARCIA

DEDICATION

For everyone trying to find their place in the world.
Don't lose sight of who you are, no matter how hard others
might try to change you.

THE FAE REALM OF

FAEVENLY

TORCH LAKE

STRONG HAVEN RUINS

MOTHERS RIVERS

SUMMIT RANGE

GREEN FALLS

SAND LUFF

THE GREAT COVE

THE MORNING SEA

PROLOGUE

Manny only wanted everyone to be safe. He ran his fingers through his thick dark hair, his stomach clenched so tight it felt like a fist. After all the heartache and loss, he didn't know if they could take much more. He, Gabriela, Leaf, and Gidna had left Strong Haven. They sought refuge in the Sublands after Julio's untimely passing and built a new life in Sandhaven, the smallest village in the region. They kept to themselves, far away from any remnant of their former lives, while the Kanes set their sights on destroying the Stromms. Or maybe it was the other way around. Not that it mattered. He and the others were finally free from danger, or so he had thought.

"Manny, did you hear me?" Lady Sonia asked.

He pinched the bridge of his nose and lowered himself onto the plush chair in the small living room. "What do you mean, Gabriela is still at risk?" He lived alone. Gabriela and Leaf lived not far from him. Maid Gidna stayed even closer. To the villagers, they were simple Sublanders. No one knew of their connections to House Strong or even House Kane. Only the steward of the Sublands, Rook Cailean, and his most trusted allies, siblings Verona and Adrius, knew their true identity. How could they be at risk here?

Lady Sonia swept her long, dark cape behind her and sat across from him. "My sisters and I are not sure. We fear it has something to do with the spirit of the aquoise stone that lives within her."

"What?" Manny's mouth fell open as tingles of fear skittered down his spine like a vicious swarm of ants. He leaned forward, fists pounding his legs. "I knew that damn thing would hurt her! I knew it!"

After they had defeated Draven the Witch, the last piece of aquoise in all of Faevenly transformed from a jagged-edged rock into a floating blue haze that shot itself straight into Gabriela's chest. He hated that it was there. But he kept reminding himself that Gabriela's and Julio's magic caused the phenomenon. If it came from them, then it had to be okay.

Lady Sonia reached out and squeezed his hand. Her touch sent a soothing wave through him, but the feeling didn't last. "My friend, we do not think it will harm her." She held on for a few long seconds before releasing his fingers. "However, we fear it could be used as a means to find her."

His brows shot up. "Like a tracker?" He jumped to his feet. His thoughts zigzagged in a dozen different directions, imagining the dangers lurking around them. "That's way worse, Sonia. Way worse! What if the Kanes are on their way?" He glanced out the row of small rectangular windows carved into the stone walls. He lowered his voice. "What if they've known where we are this whole time, and they've been waiting to strike?"

She rose to her feet. "They do not know anything. I assure you."

He had no idea how she could know that, but he trusted the wise witch. She had never let them down before. "But we have to do something." A nervous laugh escaped his lips. "We can't simply sit here, right?"

She folded her hands together, her movements slow and purposeful. Her calmness felt misplaced, like a dam holding back a flood. "We can. And that's why I'm here. I want to remove the aquoise from Gabriela and store it somewhere safe—somewhere no one can get it but us—should we need that level of power again."

"Yes," Manny blurted. Gabriela would be safe without that thing inside of her. "Let's get it out. Immediately!"

He burst out the door, and Sonia followed, matching his frantic pace. She'd expected no less from the emotional human. It was his nature—unpredictable and theatrical.

When they arrived at Gabriela's and Leaf's home, Lady Sonia repeated the same information. Leaf cut her off before she could mention her plan to remove the aquoise.

"Take it out." The tall fae's sharp blue eyes narrowed, his nostrils flaring. "Now!"

"Yes! Exactly!" Manny added, his voice rising.

"Leaf, please." Gabriela wrapped her arm around him and pulled him close. "I'm sure that's why Lady Sonia is here."

Lady Sonia bowed her head. Gabriela was the calm, thoughtful one, while Leaf was the rash, impulsive one. Their love had seen many challenges and would see many more. "It is, my princess."

3

"See," Gabriela said to her mate, rubbing his arm. "She's here to help." She cast a reassuring look at Manny. "You can relax, Uncle Manny."

"Relax?" Manny paced in front of the fireplace, rubbing the back of his neck. He blew out a breath. "Fine, I'm relaxing." The air remained thick with the earthy scent of aged wood and faint smoke clinging to the mud-brick walls. He stopped his circling and faced Lady Sonia. "So how do we do it?" A tiny ember held on to the remnants of wood, a flickering reminder of the Sublands' cold nights. "Will you"—he waved his arms—"do a witchy spell or something?"

"Or something," Sonia said, her voice steady.

It had not taken long for Lady Sonia and her coven sisters to devise a plan. That was the easy part. The hard part would be implementing it—or convincing Gabriela and the others to agree.

"Let's hear it," Manny said.

"The princess will use her magic to expel the aquoise from her body and infuse it into another object," Lady Sonia explained.

"It won't work." Gabriela shook her head. "I've tried getting it out of me several times before, and I can't do it."

Lady Sonia and her sisters foresaw this response. "This time will be different." They knew the difficulty Gabriela had controlling her unpredictable human magic and the volatile nature of the aquoise itself.

Leaf's eyes narrowed. "It will?" Always the suspicious one, a trait Sonia had come to admire and even count on. For Gabriela's safety, the former guard needed to remember his ultimate role in his mate's life.

4

He was her fiercest protector and greatest love. "How so?"

She lifted her chin, knowing her explanation would not be well received. "Because this time, Gabriela will be dead."

"Whoa!" Manny froze in place as if he'd hit an invisible wall. "Have you lost your witchy mind?"

Leaf moved Gabriela behind him, his voice low and tight. "Explain yourself."

It was the reaction she had anticipated, especially since Gabriela's death would also mean Leaf's. Their souls were bound as one. "I will place the princess in a state of death using this potion." She pulled a small, dark vial from the inside pocket of her cape and held it out. "When her heart stops beating, the aquoise will float out of her and funnel into Leaf's sword." She motioned to the sword hanging at the tall and lean fae's waist. "When the aquoise has transferred to its new host, I will awaken Leaf and the princess. Then I will take the sword for safekeeping."

Silence hung thick, suffocating and dire, as if everyone in the room was facing their final breath.

Leaf broke the tension. "The risk is too great. There must be another way."

Manny jumped in. "I agree with Leaf. What if she doesn't wake up?" His brown eyes welled with tears, and his bottom lip trembled. "We have to find another way."

"There is no other way." Gabriela stepped forward. "Is there?"

Everything Sonia and her coven had seen spelled certain death for Gabriela and Leaf. But the act of removing the aquoise would not be the culprit. Their ending would come later. Still, the aquoise played a great role in their as yet unconceived child's survival and the ultimate healing—or destruction—of Faevenly.

Sonia took Gabriela's small, delicate hand. "There is no other way." Her eyes softened. There was so much of Celyse and Julio in the young princess. Gabriela had inherited her father's human witch abilities, keen empathy, and profound understanding. From her fae princess mother, she had an intuitive connection to nature, athletic prowess, and graceful elegance. She was the best of them. Gabriela and Leaf had weathered many storms together, but Sonia knew their time would not last.

She removed her cape and hung it on the hook by the bedchamber door. She motioned for Gabriela to lie down. Leaf dragged a wooden chair over. He sat beside his mate, scooting as close to her as possible. When she was but seconds from handing over the potion, a vision gripped Sonia's mind. Gabriela, on the same bed, drenched in sweat, a pregnant belly, blood around her legs. Sonia's body shook as she forced herself to remain composed. The princess could not know what she had seen.

"Sonia?" Gabriela asked, sitting up. "Is something wrong?"

Something was most definitely wrong, but the vision belonged to a time not yet written. Sonia pushed it away and painted a reassuring smile on her face. Today was not about that moment. Today was about the aquoise. "All is as it should be, my princess," she said, her voice steady but her heart racing with the uncertainty of what was to come.

Leaf raised a brow, his eyes never leaving Gabriela. He leaned closer, his voice low and earnest. "We can face whatever comes our way. You do not have to do this."

Gabriela cupped his face in her hands. "I love you. But I do need to do this." She kissed him. "I will be fine."

"Wait," Manny said, his voice tight. He wrung his hands, his eyes darting between Gabriela and Leaf's onyx sword leaning against the foot of the bed. "*Mija*, are you sure?"

"Yes, Uncle Manny." Gabriela's tone was calm, her resolve unshaken. "I trust Sonia, and I trust what's happening here."

Always doing the right thing. Sonia had expected no less from Gabriela. "You honor me." She bowed her head to the princess, her voice softened with the depth of their shared history. "If there is nothing else to add, let us begin."

Manny moved to the foot of the bed. Leaf edged closer to Gabriela, his hand brushing hers in a silent promise to stay by her side. An uneasy hush fell over the room, the weight of unspoken fears settling over everyone like a thick fog. Sonia harbored her own fears but knew this was the only way.

She handed the small vial to Gabriela. "Please drink this in its entirety."

Gabriela took the vial with a steady hand, uncorked it, and swallowed the liquid in one swift motion. "There's no going back now," she muttered, settling onto the bed. Leaf placed his sword across her chest. The vessel that would hold Gabriela's power. Gabriela wrapped her hands around the hilt. Leaf's hands covered hers, his fingers trembling.

With a nod, Sonia drew in a deep breath and held her hands above Gabriela's chest. Closing her eyes, she spoke in a low voice. "Concentrate on your blue energy power, princess. Envision it inside of you. Cover it with your thoughts. As you fade from this world, ask the power to leave your body and enter the sword."

"Okay," Gabriela replied in a whisper. "Leave my body and enter the sword."

Sonia held her hands over the princess for a few long seconds before calling forth the deadly magic she and her sisters had placed in the vial. "Bind her spirit, halt her breath, until I call her back from death."

When Sonia spoke the final word of the spell, the room seemed to tighten, the air thickening with unnatural stillness. Gabriela's lips parted with a soft gasp, her knuckles whitening as she gripped the hilt. Her vibrant, tan cheeks drained of color as life slipped from her body. Her hands went limp. The invisible thread between her and Leaf tugged violently. His body slumped over beside hers.

Everything fell quiet as a silence heavier than stone blanketed the room.

"Oh my God," Manny uttered. "*Dios mio.*" He shot Sonia a terrified glance, his voice rising. "Hurry." He made the sign of the cross from his human religion, his hand shaking as it moved from his head to his chest and shoulder to shoulder. "Get it out of her so you can bring them back!"

"It's alright, Manny." Sonia placed a steadying hand on his shoulder. "I have done my part. The rest is up to the princess."

A second later, a blue light flickered from Gabriela's chest. The ember-like glow grew, pulsing until it enveloped her and Leaf's hands. The light danced across their skin in graceful pirouettes, gathering into a concentrated orb at the center of Gabriela's chest. With a faint hum, the energy pulsed one last time before rising, lifting from her body as though drawn out by an unseen force.

The blue light hovered midair, shimmering like stardust in the room. It swirled toward the sword, embedding itself in the blade. Like a stream cutting into river rock, it fused with the black onyx metal. The air crackled with lingering magic, then all fell still again. The luminous blue glow was now etched into the sword's edge.

"Now, Sonia." Manny tugged at the sleeve of her dress. "Wake her."

She placed her hand on Gabriela's cool forehead. She closed her eyes. "Awaken her spirit, restore her breath, bring forth the light, and banish death."

Stepping back, Sonia fixed her gaze on the princess's eyelids and waited for movement.

"Please, please, please," Manny whispered. His fingers trembled as he reached out and touched Gabriela's cheek. "Wake up, *Mija*."

The princess's eyelids fluttered open as if in response to her uncle's plea. She blinked, looking around. "What happened?"

Leaf's body jerked with a sudden twitch before he sat up. A tear glistened in his eyes as he cupped Gabriela's face. "You did it."

Sonia allowed herself a small smile, the relief of the successful spell washing over her. "Yes, you did." She motioned to the sword. "The aquoise is now in the blade."

Everyone in the room seemed to hold their breath as the weight of Sonia's words sank in. All eyes were on the blade. It shimmered in the dim light, alive with new power. Sonia waited, although her thoughts churned. They had no idea what this meant or what was coming. And they did not need to know.

Leaf cradled the sword like a fragile yet dangerous newborn star. "Now what?"

Sonia extended her hands. "Now I take it and store it in a safe place, where it will remain until the stone's power is needed again."

She wrapped the sword in a velvet sheath she had packed in her bag, then strapped it to her back. No one must find it until the time was right. Pulling her cloak over her shoulders, she bade farewell to her friends. She left Gabriela and Leaf's home on foot. Her steps were slow because she knew Manny would be rushing after her.

Behind her, sandals slapped against the gravel. Each hurried step crunched louder as Manny closed the distance. "Sonia," he breathed. "Wait. We need to talk."

"Of course." She steadied herself, admiring the human for his tenacity. Manny always had good instincts and never left things unsaid.

"There's a lot you're not telling us." He pointed at her as if scolding a child. "I can feel it."

She took his rough and weathered hand. "Like I said to the princess, all is as it should be." She squeezed. "I assure you."

He narrowed his eyes. "You're not going to tell me, are you?"

"Please, Manny." Her voice softened, careful to give him something without revealing too much. "When there is something you need to know, I will tell you."

He rubbed the back of his neck. "I don't like it, Sonia. Not one bit. But fine, we'll do things your way." He let out an exasperated sigh. "Answer me one thing. Is she safe?"

"She is."

For now.

She parted ways with Manny, heading down the gravel path. She glanced back as she turned the corner. She caught sight of the human before he slipped from view. "I will be back," she whispered to the wind, her gaze lingering on the darkening horizon. "When the shadows fall."

CHAPTER ONE

The Sublands felt like another world, a place where Avalynn didn't belong. Sitting atop the red, craggy butte, the oppressive weight of the barren expanse pressed down on her, the dry air clawing at her lungs. Her chest tightened with each breath, her eyes burning as she squinted against the searing dryness. The red, rocky Sublands stretched in every direction like a barren sea of rust. How could anything exist in this quiet, desolate place?

Not long ago, life surrounded her in Summit Range. She found it in the rustling trees, chirping birds, and the hum of wildlife. She had wanted to go back there and save Mateo. She, Manny's family, and Lady Sonia had devised a rescue plan. But his new station in life had delivered a fate she could not undo. The note Manny had received might as well have been a dagger.

I know who I am, and I am staying at the palace. I will see to the peaceful banishment of the Sublands.

Mateo

A wave of shock and sorrow crashed down on her, threatening to pull her under. She had believed she could infiltrate Stromm Palace and save him. That she could stop the banishment of this place that was her new home. But those beliefs had been shattered in an instant. What had she been thinking? The words in his note were sharp, slicing through the fragile threads of her hope. He had learned his name and had chosen them. The Stromms. The very people he despised. Her heart ached. Despite everything they had shared, she faced the bitter realization that she had lost Mateo.

But then another feeling niggled at her, shallow and insistent. She missed her former station in life. She longed for the warmth of her bed with its thick furs and woven blankets that had wrapped her in comfort. She missed the indulgence of fresh fruit and honeyed bread served at dawn and the hearth's crackle in the evening as shadows danced across her room's marble floors. She especially missed her luxurious warm bath after a long day. She sighed. It all felt like a distant dream now. In the Sublands, every edge was jagged, every breath an effort, and every moment a reminder of what she had lost. And what Mateo had gained.

Stormshroud's snout nudged Avalynn's hand, then

nestled beneath her palm. Lady Sonia had said the wolf-beast was bound to the Strongs. Did the wolfbeast sense her melancholy? Or was she only missing Mateo? She missed him too. She leaned against her new companion. How could Mateo have done this? How could he have betrayed his wolfbeast and his family and friends?

She swallowed hard, the truth sinking in her gut like a stone plunging into the sea. She knew how because she had betrayed him first. She knocked him down just before crossing the finish line with her kill. Who was the villain now?

"I'm so sorry about everything," a small voice said.

Avalynn turned. A petite girl with long white hair and large green eyes approached. Her white dress and blue slippers made her look almost regal, like a princess, like her sister, Lily. A stab of sorrow needled her heart. Was Lily okay? Did she miss Avalynn? Or was she too dazzled by Mateo to care?

"Thank you, maiden," Avalynn murmured.

The girl moved closer. "May I sit with you?"

Avalynn motioned to the red rock and dirt next to her. "Of course."

When the girl neared, Stormshroud shifted to Avalynn's other side. The wolfbeast sat on her haunches and narrowed her eyes. Her muscles tensed as if she was readying herself to pounce. Did the girl mean her harm? Small and slender as she was, Avalynn didn't think so. But she moved closer to Stormshroud just in case.

The maiden lowered herself. "My name is Abigail."

"I am..." Avalynn hesitated, unsure of who she was

anymore. "Avalynn. I am new here." No house. No family. Only the clothes on her back, a new sword left at Manny's home, and a cross necklace from her birth mother. And that streak of white in her long brown hair that symbolized her transformation.

The girl began playing with the blue ribbon around her waist. "I am new here too, but I'm only visiting. I'm not from here."

Not from here? She didn't think the region saw that many visitors. "Where are you from?"

"The human realm."

Avalynn's breath caught. Her heart skipped as the words sank in. She looked closer. The soft fullness of her face, the rounded ears peeking through the pale, thin hair. Avalynn resisted the urge to touch her own ears. Since her transformation, they were not as sharply pointed as most fae. Still, they were not rounded.

There were many fae with human blood in the Sublands. Yet the maiden looked like a full blood. And there were definitely no newcomers. All the portals had been destroyed at the end of the Strong era.

"You're from the human realm?" she asked.

Abigail stopped fiddling with the ribbon around her waist. "Yes. I have traveled far to see you." Her eyes were shadowed with an intensity far beyond her years. "To warn you."

A chill skittered down Avalynn's spine. The wound from the shadowblood's claws at her back seemed to flare up, throbbing and fresh as if it had never fully healed in the Green Falls waters. "Warn me about what?"

The maiden scooted closer. "Some prophecies are meant for breaking."

Time seemed to halt as Avalynn recalled the prophecy she'd read in the note from her part-fae, part-human mother, Gabriela. It had been stored in a box and safeguarded by Lady Sonia, who'd been disguised for years as her maid and friend, Nia.

In the twilight of transformation, there will arise like a mighty storm, one born of the union between realms. With a sword of blue in hand and the heart of a champion, this Only One will restore peace to Faevenly and forever unite the bloodlines.

The words had clung to her like a destiny she could not escape. But now, this human girl suggested a different path.

"One more thing," Abigail said. "I must warn you about your realm. It is—"

A gravelly crunch sounded. Stormshroud growled, her ears shooting upright. Avalynn jumped to her feet. She scanned the area but saw no one. Whipping back toward Abigail, she found her gone. A chill ran through her, sending a shower of goose bumps across her skin. A spirit. Lady Sonia had said her human magic allowed her to see them. But she couldn't deal with that now. Or the girl's cryptic warning.

Someone was coming.

She scanned the area for a weapon. Rocks were scattered everywhere, but none of them were small enough to grab. She balled her hands into fists, her pulse quickening.

Stormshroud planted herself in front of Avalynn, baring her teeth. "Get ready, girl," Avalynn whispered, her voice low and steady. After everything she'd faced in the hunt, she expected anything—foxes, elk, maybe a bear. What kind of creatures roamed these lands? Instead, a petite figure with long brown hair stepped out from behind a boulder.

Her bow and arrow drawn, Camilla aimed at Avalynn's head. "Camilla?" Avalynn kept her fighting stance firm. "What are you doing?"

Camilla's expression darkened as she pulled the arrow tighter. "You betrayed my brother and so have betrayed my family. For that, I cannot let you live."

Stormshroud growled, stepping forward, ready to attack. Avalynn's heart pounded, but she raised a hand to stop the wolf. "Stormy, back."

Stormshroud paused but kept her body tense, her muscles primed to pounce.

"You have poisoned her against us," Camilla spat, looking at Stormshroud, her voice filled with pain. "How dare you."

Avalynn's voice softened, steady but pleading. "I'm sorry. I didn't mean for that to happen." She stayed still, knowing the slightest movement might unleash the arrow. "I deserve your anger. But I promise you I want Mateo back as much as you do. I only did what I did to protect him and help the people of the Sublands."

Camilla's aim wavered. Was she getting through to her?

"If we had crossed the finish line together, my father —" Avalynn stopped. She swallowed hard. He wasn't her father. She had to remember that. "The High King would have found a way to execute Mateo anyway. And he would have imprisoned me. Or executed me too. I thought I could help him—and the Sublands—if I was the sole victor. If I stayed alive."

Camilla's gaze hardened. She repositioned her arrow. Uh-oh, Avalynn had said the wrong thing. Camilla snarled. "Raised a Stromm. It's who you are. You deserve to die."

Avalynn's chest tightened, a quiet dread settling in her bones. The words struck home. Camilla was right. She'd grown up in the palace of their enemy, where Sublanders were lesser and unworthy. And Avalynn had believed it. Like them, she was capable of cruelty.

The memory of Mateo's face etched with betrayal as she crossed that finish line without him was seared into her mind. The truth gnawed at her, raw and undeniable. After everything they had been through, everything they had shared, she had done the unthinkable. Her justification made little sense now. Even though she was a Strong by blood, being raised at the Stromm Palace felt like a stain she would never be able to wash away.

Avalynn lowered her hands. Stormshroud let out a low whimper. Could the creature sense her guilt? Did the wolf know that she was surrendering to whatever fate the Sun, Moon, and Stars had planned for her? That she was willing to go to the Passing Place and leave Faevenly for what she had done? It was an honorable destination.

"Do what you will," Avalynn said. "I accept the consequences of my actions."

A rock careened through the air and struck Camilla's hand. "Oww!" Her bow clattered to the dirt.

Two figures burst into the clearing, elbowing and shoving each other. One had long silver hair. The other wore red braids.

"Stop, Gareth! Let her have her revenge!" the silver-haired one hollered.

Avalynn stepped back. Stormshroud barked and circled the brawling pair. Gareth's name she knew. The other must be Lirien. They were Mateo's friends.

Gareth grunted as he slipped his arm around Lirien's upper body, lifted him, and slammed him into the dirt. With his knee on Lirien's chest, Gareth worked his hands fast and furiously. She didn't know how to interpret his sign language but didn't have to. He was protecting her.

"I will not!" Lirien spat. "He's over there because of her!"

A warning yip from Stormshroud drew Avalynn's attention to Camilla, who was reloading her bow. She raised her hands in surrender. Gareth darted before her, planting himself in front of her like an oak tree. She couldn't see his hand movements from behind his thick frame, but she could see Camilla.

Tears welled in Camilla's eyes as her arm shook. "She is a Stromm, and Mateo is gone because of her!"

Avalynn's heart ached at Camilla's pain. Manny's and little Floriana's too. She knew what her betrayal had cost them, the family who had loved and raised Mateo. Every tear in Camilla's eyes and every hurt look from Manny reminded her that her choice shattered them. She wished she could undo it, take back every step across that finish line. Stay a Stromm while Mateo stayed a Vela. Could she have saved him that way? Freed him from the Stromm dungeon during the night? She would never know. All she could do was try to make it right.

Squaring her shoulders, she stepped forward. "I will do whatever I can to get Mateo back. And if I fail, you can take my life."

Camilla lowered her bow and arrow. Gareth turned to face Avalynn. He formed a three with his thumb sticking out and his pointer finger and middle finger sticking up and brought them down on the thumb in a closing motion while shaking his head, his mouth forming an "ooh" shape with the lips.

Lirien pushed him. "Let Camilla decide."

Silence fell over them like a blanket. The whisper of wind stirred the sand. The stillness felt heavy, almost sacred, as if every desert creature held its breath awaiting Camilla's decision. In that vast quiet, Stormshroud pressed against Avalynn's leg. Her warm fur was comforting and grounding amidst the hanging tension.

Avalynn had fallen in love with Mateo. Somewhere between their shared battles and quiet moments, her heart had slipped into his hands. The memory of his smile, the warmth of his body next to hers, and the intense fire in his eyes. All of it pierced her heart and singed her soul. She could not ignore the truth. Like blood and breath, her love for Mateo was a part of her.

She could not leave him to the mercy of the Stromms. Whatever the cost, she'd see him free and hold him in her arms once again. And if she failed, her life would be forfeit, just as she had promised. She was okay with that. It was over without Mateo anyway.

Camilla's gaze locked onto Avalynn, fierce and unwavering. "Fine. I accept your offer."

CHAPTER TWO

Mateo had no idea who he was anymore. He walked the perimeter of the bedchamber, staying close to the walls. For days, he refused invitations to celebratory feasts. He ignored requests to attend palace meetings. He isolated himself in the confines of his quarters. His only interaction with the outside world came from Maid Penny's food deliveries. He needed time to process, to think. He wore his simple green pants and the long-sleeved black shirt he'd brought from the Sublands. The High Queen had left a new wardrobe for him, but he couldn't bear to wear any of it. Even if her tears at his return had stirred some sympathy within him, he wanted nothing from her.

His gaze lingered on the stack of garments sitting on the wood dresser. The fine embroidery, the gilded threads, the perfumed fragrance—it all felt wrong to him. He didn't belong in them any more than he belonged in the palace with its gold and marble. He stretched out his fingers, then curled them into fists. He repeated the motion as the walls seemed to press in. The silence in the chamber remained heavy, like iron chains. It wrapped tighter with every passing second. His heart weighed heavy too.

He wanted answers. Who had switched Avalynn and him at birth? And for what purpose? He slowed his restless pacing. Did it even matter? He might be a Stromm by blood, but in his heart and spirit, he was a Vela. The truth was immutable. No one could ever change that. His true family lived in the Sublands—Manny, Camilla, Floriana. Even Gareth and Lirien. Little Poppy too. He needed to return to them. Bloodlines and devious designs be damned. He'd confront the queen at daybreak.

A tightness settled in his jaw as his thoughts turned to Avalynn. He had once wanted to go to her, to protect her. But those feelings had eroded with each step he'd taken in these quarters. Her face haunted him, that resolute look she'd worn as she knocked him down. She was a foot from the finish line and hadn't even glanced back. She had ripped his heart out with that single move and condemned him to death.

For all her talk of wanting to help him and the Sublanders, she'd thrown him aside the second victory was in reach. He should've known she would. And he couldn't forget it. She wasn't a Stromm by blood, but that act had proven she was more of a Stromm than he would ever be. She was in the Sublands now, but she belonged here. Here, in this palace, where betrayal came as naturally as breathing.

He stopped in front of the row of large windows and

pulled back the thick purple drapery. Pressing his forehead against the cool glass, he tried to calm the fire of rage burning inside him. In the distance, pale morning light crept over the jagged mountain peaks. It cast a wash of silver and pink across the forest below. Wisps of mist hung low among the tall pines. They trailed down the trunks before vanishing into the meadowland.

Not long ago he was out there, a mere Sublander fighting for his life. Now, he stood in a palace surrounded by luxuries. A palace that only highlighted what his family and friends lacked—embroidered garments, silver-platter food, healing seeds. All sickeningly hollow. But then a thought struck him, sudden and sharp. It sank deep, anchoring itself in his mind.

He was a Stromm by blood. In this place, he held power he could never claim as a Vela. It was a power he could wield for his true family. The ones who raised him and loved him. He'd already requested healing seeds and food to be sent to the Sublands, but he could do so much more. With every resource at his fingertips, he could reshape their future. He'd start with the removal of the banishment decree. He wouldn't leave for the Sublands, not yet. Not until he'd wrung every possible benefit from this gilded cage. For the first time since coming here, the palace felt less like a prison and more like a tool. He'd bleed it dry before he left.

Mateo pulled the whittled wooden cross from his pocket. He rubbed it between his thumb and forefinger. "Faith is a warrior." Tucking it away, he yanked the curtain closed and spun on his heels. He marched across the floor, his boots striking the marble like a warning call.

He jerked the door open and came face to face with Maid Penny.

Dressed in a pale yellow dress and with flowers tucked into her short brown hair, she held a tray of juice and fruit. She curtsied low. "My lord, dawn's blessings upon you." She righted herself and nodded toward her tray. "I have your morning juice and fruit and your schedule for the day, should you desire to leave your bedchamber."

Oh, he desired. He grabbed the tray and set it on the floor with a clank. "Take me to the king and queen. At once."

Her eyes widened, her lips parting in surprise. She hadn't expected that, and neither would they. "Yes, my lord." She clasped her hands in front of her slim waist and added, "Please, follow me."

She walked beside Mateo, her quick, short steps barely keeping pace with his long strides. He slowed as they neared the door to Avalynn's former bedchamber. Part of him wanted to step inside, to see if her sweet, floral scent lingered. But he pushed the thought away. If he didn't matter to her, then she didn't matter to him.

They passed the stairwell, rounded a corner, and entered the royal wing. Even more gold flecks dotted the marble floors. Garish. Obscene. But not as offensive as the floral garden that'd been violated for the pleasure of their majesties. The powdery scents of rose and jasmine hit him like a perfumed ambush. They passed rows of windows crammed with flower-filled vases. He wanted to hurl each one to the ground, splatter the arrangements in the dirt. Maybe later.

At last, they stopped before a floor-to-ceiling, wood-carved double door. Etched into the rich, dark wood was a scene. It came from the Summit Range Forest. Tall mountains, thick pine trees, and deadly forest animals were perfectly carved. How many servants lost fingers perfecting this monstrous display of wealth?

Maid Penny lifted her trembling hand to knock. Her face tightened with dread as though she feared summoning a cyclone. Mateo stopped her. "Thank you, Penny. I can knock. You may go now."

Her narrow shoulders eased. She managed a small, grateful smile before dipping her head. "Yes, my lord." Turning, she hurried away, eager to leave him to the task.

He knocked three times. A pause, then two more.

The door creaked open to reveal Marina, the queen's personal attendant. Thick and tall with a bumpy face that suggested troll ancestry, she nodded. "My lord prince," she said in a deep, resonant voice. Bowing, she stepped back and swung the door open wide. "How may I assist you?"

"I need to see the king and queen."

"Of course." She nodded. "I will notify your sires that you request an audience." *Sires*. The word hit like a cheek slap. She led him into a sitting area. "Please wait here."

A black velvet couch faced a large fireplace with a thick wooden mantle. A small fire crackled within, warming the room's bold, opulent colors. The floral scent from before still lingered, now mingled with wood and spice. Mateo clasped his hands behind his back, staying on his feet. Should he demand the immediate removal of the Sublands banishment? Or push for more food and healing seeds first?

Before he could decide, the High Queen entered from the room's rear. She glided in with a practiced elegance, chin lifted and posture impeccable. Her day gown whispered against the floor in layers of deep midnight blue and silver. A crease marred the High Queen's usually smooth brow as her gaze swept the room, steady yet shadowed by an urgency she couldn't mask. She brought a hand to her chest and held it there.

"I am so pleased to see you, my son." Her voice was honeyed, almost mocking.

Mateo's jaw tightened as he offered her a slight nod. She hadn't bothered to visit him in his bedchamber. She only came to inform him they'd notified the Sublands of his decision to stay. Her demeanor now suggested something was amiss. News from the Sublands, no doubt. Maybe something about Avalynn.

"Please, my son. Sit with me."

She perched on the edge of the sofa cushion. He chose an oversized wooden chair across from her. "I hope I am not visiting too early," he said.

"Not at all. I am so glad you are here." She angled herself toward him, her expression turning grave. "There is troubling news."

The king entered behind her. His brow furrowed, his nostrils flaring as the queen spoke. "The results of the Summit Range Hunt are being challenged," she said.

Mateo's stomach dropped. He pressed his back against the chair, muscles tensing as his mind raced. "What do you mean?"

The queen glanced at the king, then fixed Mateo with a pointed gaze. "House Lind and House Brunt claim that since you have been revealed as a Stromm, and, as you were not the victor, that Summit Range is the loser. They demand an audience to discuss the matter."

His thoughts spiraled through the implications. If their challenge prevailed, then Avalynn was the victor. The Sublands had won. They would not be banished. A surge of joy lit within him, but stark realization followed. He was still the loser.

His gut twisted. Of course, the Linds and Brunts wanted his head. Why wouldn't they? Both of their hunters died in the hunt. Eiric Lind, through his own folly, and Finnian Brunt, when he was taken by the dragon. Mateo wasn't out of the woods yet.

"But you are the highest authority in Faevenly. The High King and Queen," he said, his voice sharp. "They cannot make such a demand."

The queen leaned forward and clutched his arm. "They cannot, and they will not." Her voice softened, her eyes glistening. "We will do whatever we must to protect you, my son. We have just found you. We will not lose you again."

The king stepped forward. His large hand clamped down on Mateo's shoulder like an iron grip. "Your mother is right. We will defend you with everything we have. House Lind and House Brunt will pay for challenging House Stromm."

Mateo opened his mouth to speak, but the king's words stunned him, forcing his voice back. They had no idea he had planned to reject their claim, refusing them as his blood. That he had designs to draw every resource he could from them before returning to the Sublands. But this? He hadn't expected this—a promise to defend him, to rally around him with fierce familial loyalty.

For a moment, he faltered. Did he belong here after all? The thought churned in his stomach, clashing against everything he'd been ready to throw at them.

"Hold your thoughts," the queen said. "Your father and I have something we've been wanting to give you." She rose from the sofa and disappeared into an adjoining room.

When she returned, the queen wore a loving smile. Her eyes gleamed with a rare warmth. The cold, calculating, and sinister air she normally carried had softened. It revealed a striking beauty. Her almost tender expression unsettled him. In her hands, she held a small red box.

"For me?" he asked, his voice low. The last thing he expected was a gift.

"Yes, my son." She lowered herself on the sofa. "For you."

He took it, holding it for a moment before lifting the lid. Inside lay a gold chain with a round pendant. He scooped it out, his chest tightening as he held the piece. One side bore the letter S for Stromm. The other was engraved with a mountain peak, the banner of House Stromm.

He felt the weight of it—the pendant, the emblem, the life they wanted him to claim. A part of him rebelled, rejecting the notion that this simple object could bind him to them. And yet, he couldn't deny the strange pull it exerted.

"Your mother and I had necklaces fashioned for all of us," the king said, his voice steeped in tradition. "Including your sister, Lily. A symbol of our true family. We would be honored to have you wear it."

The queen extended her hand. "May I slip it over your head?"

He didn't want to wear it. Every instinct told him to refuse. But the hope in the queen's eyes held him still. He couldn't bring himself to disappoint her. "Yes, you may."

Her hands were steady as she eased the chain over his head, adjusting it so the pendant rested on his chest. With her fingertips pressed to the precious metal, she whispered, "There. Where it belongs."

The weight of the necklace settled around his neck. The pendant positioned against him like a brand. Part of him wanted to tear it off, to reject this token symbol from a family that had only claimed him when it suited them. A family that, days ago, would have seen him dead.

Yet another part, a part he hated to admit, felt a connection he couldn't explain. The queen's hands had lingered over the pendant as if it were a gift she'd waited a lifetime to bestow. He couldn't shake the tangled feeling of belonging and betrayal bound in that gilded chain.

What would the Velas think of him now? He didn't want to know.

The queen sat back, then folded her hands on her lap. The line on her forehead returned. "No one will take you from us. Not again."

The king moved to the fireplace, slamming his fist on

31

the mantel. "The Linds and the Brunts will see their end for daring to threaten a Stromm."

So, this wasn't just a family heirloom he'd been given; it was a shield. A token designed to protect him from the Linds and the Brunts and anyone else who might come for him. He had come here to save the Sublands, but now, once again, he had to save himself. Why must his life always be a struggle for survival? Could it ever mean something more?

The queen's voice softened. "My son," she said, the words lingering like a foreign phrase he struggled to accept. He was her son. Would he ever get used to that? "There is a heaviness about you. Is there something you came here to say?"

Mateo nodded. "There is," he said, steadying himself. Save the Sublands first, himself later. That would have to be his plan. "I want the Sublands banishment revoked. Right away."

The king's brows drew together. His mouth stretched into a thin, disapproving line. He positioned himself closer to Mateo, his stature looming like a storm-laden mountain. "Recognize the claim of our enemies? That is foolish!"

Before Mateo could respond, the queen chimed in. "Your father is right. The Linds and the Brunts, and anyone else, would see that as an official recognition that the Sublands are the victor. Where would that leave us?" She touched his knee, her expression firm but cautious. "Where would that leave you?"

Mateo saw the wisdom, but he wasn't here to play it safe. He had to act. Beginning with putting the king in his place. No one spoke to him like that. He eased himself up off the chair, meeting the king's gaze head-on. "You threaten me, I threaten you."

The queen jumped to her feet. She pressed her hand against the king's chest to calm him. "Enough, enough." Her voice softened as she turned to Mateo. "Please. We are on the same side, remember?"

"Are we?" Mateo didn't back down, keeping his stare locked on the king.

The king stepped back without a word while the queen filled the silence. "Of course we are." She adjusted a stray strand of her long dark hair, her gray eyes softening. "My son, your father and I give you our word that the Sublands will not be banished. We will announce it in due time." She took his hand and held it. "They raised you well, and we will honor your loyalty to them. But let us first deal with this more pressing matter... your safety. You must prepare for the arrival of the Linds and the Brunts."

Her words were all he had to go on. He was grateful for her agreement to spare the Sublands. But Manny, his sisters, and his friends needed help now. He tipped his head. "Thank you for agreeing to reverse the banishment. In the meantime, I would like more healing seeds and food sent to my family right away."

The queen flinched at the phrase "my family," as if it struck an emotional blow. But her composure remained intact. "Supplies will be sent."

With a flick of her fingers, Marina came into the sitting room. The queen issued the order Mateo had requested, and the troll left the room with a bow. The queen turned her attention back to him. "And now you prepare, yes?"

Mateo hesitated. His instincts nagged at him, warning of dangers he couldn't yet see. He wished Manny were here to guide him. His father always knew the right thing to do. His hand brushed against his pants pocket, finding the hard edges of the cross hidden within. Fool. His father was with him already. The words his father used before he left the Sublands sprang to mind. *"Stay true to who you are.... but do not trust anyone. Fae are cunning, manipulative, and devious. They cannot lie, but they do not have to."*

For a moment, he considered his loyalty to his birth family. But loyalty meant nothing here. He was, and always would be, an outsider. His real family in the Sublands needed him to be a force that could shift their future. He had no choice. Their survival meant he needed to pull whatever power he could from this cold, foreign palace and bring it to those who needed it the most. To do that, he needed to play the part.

"Yes, mother," he said, finally meeting her pleading gaze. "Now I will prepare."

CHAPTER THREE

High Queen Lysandra Stromm had her son right where she wanted him. Every smile she offered, every tear-filled glance, every touch of his arm, his knee, his hand... everything she had said and all the things she didn't say... it all landed perfectly. And with that pendant around his neck, he would step into his destiny whether he wanted to or not.

Lord Prince of House Stromm, next in line for the throne of Faevenly.

He would forget the Sublands and the lesser-born human who had raised him. Over time, Mateo would even grow to despise them. Whatever hold they had on him would be severed, like a blade slicing through the flimsiest ribbon. Her heart swelled at her plan, every piece falling into place as it should.

"That went well," Sylrick, her mate and king, said. He sat on the sofa. He crossed one leg over the other, his gaze still on the door Mateo had exited.

"Yes, it did." And no thanks to him. This was all her and Raelor. The crystal-eyed witch had been in the sitting room, advising them on the necklaces he had fashioned, when Mateo knocked. It was an unexpected visit, but most welcome. The sooner her son wore the pendant, the better.

Raelor entered the room, hands behind his back. "Impeccable timing by the young prince." His long silver hair hung loose down his back, glinting against his usual all-black attire.

The past struck Lysandra as she observed him. Over one hundred years ago, Raelor had appeared at the gates of Stromm Palace, claiming he could help end the Kanes. At the time, she had only heard whispers of crystal-eyed witches—most notably Draven. He had served House Strong and met a tragic end. Would Raelor surpass Draven's strength? Be even stronger than the elusive Lady Sonia, who had allied with the Strongs?

And if Avalynn was truly the Only One, how would Raelor measure against her?

There were many witches in Faevenly, each of varying powers. So when Raelor arrived, she had demanded proof of his abilities. With an eagerness to please, he demonstrated a potion that killed an elk with a single drop. He even choked a sheep in mere seconds with his mind.

He wasn't a soul-sucking vampiric witch, but Lysandra hadn't needed that. Raelor's talents had been what her rising house required most.

It was Raelor who had slain the Lords of House Kane after the Kanes wiped out the Strongs. That left the

Stromms to step in and rule Faevenly. She admired his loyalty and counted on his brilliance for many things. Now, he would help her reclaim her son and elevate Stromm Palace to even greater heights.

Her lips curled into a smile. "Yes, Mateo's visit came at the perfect time."

Everything was falling into place. The pendant Mateo now wore wasn't a mere gift. Forged by Raelor himself, it pulsed with dark shadow magic. It would protect her son from Avalynn's abilities. If she had any. It would also extinguish the light of the Sublands within him. Over time, the pendant would strip away all ties to his past and amplify his Stromm bloodline.

Lysandra longed for that day. Surely it would come sooner than later. When it arrived, Mateo would embrace her and thank her for showing him his true self.

Raelor sat in the chair near the fire. He folded his hands neatly on his lap. "What of this business of reversing the Sublands' banishment? It is an unwise move, my queen. I advise against it."

The king leaned forward, smashing a fist into his open palm. "Raelor is right. We have to end that province —and that lowborn Avalynn too. If she is the Only One, the descendant of Celyse Strong and the human witch Julio, she could be our undoing. And if the sword of power truly exists, then we are in trouble."

Lysandra remained composed, her thoughts turning. Such small minds, stuck on prophecy and ignoring strategy. Her fingers brushed the chair's armrest where Mateo had sat. She savored the lingering warmth of his presence, a reminder of how far she had brought him and how much further he still had to go. Mateo was hers, no matter what rebellion simmered in his mind. Soon, he would see it too.

"I told you," she said. "House Stromm will come out on top." She turned her gaze toward the king, her devious smile cutting through the tension. "Banishment will not befall the Sublands."

The king growled, nostrils flaring. "They are dangerous! Filled with human-blooded fae that are ruining our realm!"

She waved him to silence, her patience wearing thin. She did not need brute strength from him. Not yet. "They will not be banished. They will be destroyed," she declared, her menacing words leaving no room for negotiation. "Wiped off the face of Faevenly."

Avalynn's presence, and any sword of power she might possess, along with the meddling Sublanders, required total annihilation. Nothing else would do.

"The entire province?" The king stayed forward and licked his lips. "How?"

"Dragons." Her single word sent a ripple through the room.

Once thought extinct, a pair of dragons had been spotted in the outer realm, along the edges of the Strong Haven ruins. Engrendorn had perished investigating the appearance. Not surprising, given that fae who traveled into the Wild North never returned. They didn't know much about the beasts other than they responded to the pyrosia flower. They had used it to lure the dragons to the hunt. But only one dragon took the bait, and only one hunter was killed. Such disappointing beasts. If they had performed as expected, all the other houses would have been weakened and without their strongest warriors and heirs.

The king grunted. "If they had killed all the hunters like we wanted, we would not be in this mess."

She placed her hands on the armrests of the chair. He was right. She had expected much more from the winged creatures, but they had fallen short. "We need to learn more about the dragons, and more about pyrosia. There must be a way to use them, and the flower, more effectively."

Raelor stroked his chin, grunting his approval. "I will investigate both, my queen."

Investigate ... An idea sprang to her mind like a feral beast. Mateo was the key. She needed to activate her son with purpose, and this would be it.

"You will do no such thing, Raelor." She sat straighter. Her chest swelled at her own cleverness. "I will plant the idea with Mateo. Let him do the investigating. Let him be the hero."

"Are you sure, my queen?" Raelor asked.

"I am sure." Her smile widened, as sly as it was triumphant. "Mateo will think he is protecting all of Faevenly, including the Sublands. But he will be ensuring House Stromm's dominance."

Raelor laughed, his smile mirroring hers. "Most clever, my queen. I will leave the young prince to you."

She nodded, already envisioning her plan's success. She would handle her son and use Lily to assist her. Mateo's desire to serve as a protector would play into her hands. He would believe himself noble. Every move he made would only solidify House Stromm's power.

But there were still loose ends. She still needed Raelor and turned to him. "Take Bismore to the Morning Sea. No one can know our hand in bringing the dragon to the hunt. I fear the brainless brownie will not keep the information to himself."

"I will see to it, my queen," he said, dipping his head.

The king growled. "What of the Linds and Brunts?"

She tapped her long nails against the chair's wooden armrest. The rhythmic sound ticked like a clock. Would it be enough to say that when Avalynn finished first, she had done so for House Stromm? That Mateo's true identity, discovered only later, had no bearing on the outcome? No. That would be too simple. Too clean. She would need to devise a more intricate solution.

"Leave it to me," she said finally. She couldn't have the king or Raelor ruining things. "I will come up with something before their arrival."

"Yes, my queen." Raelor rose to his feet. Before leaving them, he clasped his hands behind his back and faced her. "Any challenge to the crown is treason, my queen. And treason is punishable by death."

She knew that and would not hesitate to employ Raelor to end both houses while they were here. "We will see if it comes to that."

A final nod and Raelor left the room.

The queen turned to her mate. She inched closer to him, her voice dropping to a venomous hiss. "I still want to know who was responsible for taking my son." Her hand rested on his knee, nails pressing just enough to remind him of her simmering fury. "I want someone's head."

The king growled low in his throat. "You will have it," he promised, his dark eyes narrowing.

Her door opened once again, and she turned to see Lily entering the room. The little princess usually had a skip to her step, but this morning it was nowhere to be seen. "There's my lovely little princess."

"Dawn's blessing, Mother, Father," she said. She sat on the sofa next to the queen, staying quiet while her gaze settled on the flames.

Lily had been close to Avalynn. Discovering her sister was not a Stromm had hit her the hardest. But over the days, with the queen's cajoling, Lily was finally seeing the miracle in Mateo's return. But still, she missed her sister. The sooner she got Lily invested in Mateo and their new family unit, the better. Now would be the perfect time to give her the matching pendant they'd all wear. While hers didn't contain any magic, its symbolism stood just as potent.

"Your brother, the prince, was just here." She eyed the king. "Your father and I gave him a gift, and we have one for you too."

Her eyes lit up. "You do?"

"Yes, my little love. We do," she said. "Let me get it."

She swept away to the adjoining room, then came back with a red box, the same as Mateo's. She handed it to Lily.

"I love gifts!" She quickly opened the box. Her eyes widened. "Beautiful gold!" She took it out and studied the pendant. "S for Stromm and our banner!"

The king took the chain and slipped it over her head. "It is a symbol of our powerful family. You, me, your mother, and Mateo. Nothing can break us."

"We are so powerful," she said with a smile.

"Mateo is one of us by blood," the queen said with a hard nod. "We must do everything we can to help him settle in here." The queen narrowed her eyes. "There can be no room for the traitorous impostor who invaded our home and tried to steal our name. Understand?"

Lily turned the gold pendant between her fingers, and the queen knew her mind was stuck on wealth and power. Like she wanted. "I understand, Mother."

"Good little princess," she said. "Now run along to attend your lessons for the day."

She sprang to her feet. She kissed the queen on her cheek and then the king. "I'm going to like having Mateo as a brother."

She smiled. "Yes, you are."

With Lily gone, Lysandra straightened, her mind churning. Someone had orchestrated Mateo's disappearance all those years ago. Someone had dared to steal her blood, her heir, and her future. That kind of betrayal demanded retribution. And when she found the culprit, they would pay the ultimate price.

The firelight flickered, casting shadows across the room. The darkness conspired with her thoughts. Lysandra would ensure that she cinched every loose thread and extinguished all threats. Her son returning to his proper place would be her greatest achievement.

As she lived and breathed, House Stromm's dominion over Faevenly would remain absolute.

CHAPTER FOUR

The rickety wooden bed groaned with every restless shift of Avalynn's body. A turn to the right. *Creeeak*. The worn planks protested beneath the thin mattress. A turn to the left. *Craaaack*. The sounds echoed in the small room, sharp and intrusive against the heavy silence.

She stilled for a moment, her heart matching the uneasy rhythm of the bed's complaints. But stillness brought no relief. The frame seemed to hold its breath, ready to betray her with the next inevitable movement. Even the faintest shift of her weight set it whining again, as though the bed itself shared her unease.

Could the others in the house hear her struggle? Or were they suffering along with her in their own uncomfortable beds? Doubtful. They knew nothing different. But Mateo now knew the difference. She imagined him stretched out on a pillowy mattress, enveloped in bedding so soft it felt like a cloud. The clean scent of soap and lavender would linger in Mateo's air. It would calm his mind and lull him to sleep.

She yearned for that soft bedding and delicate scent. She lay on a mattress hardened like lumped coal, scratchy sheets grazing her skin with every turn. The earthen smell of the room clung to her, a stark reminder of how far she had fallen from the comforts of her royal life.

Her thoughts turned to Camilla. No doubt she burned to make good on her promise to cut short Avalynn's life should she fail to get Mateo back. She probably even dreamed about it.

A wet nose nudged her clenched hand, cool and insistent. She loosened her fingers to let Stormy wedge beneath her palm. The wolfbeast's thick, warm fur was comforting as her hand rested on her head. She gave her a few absent-minded pats, then rubbed behind her ears. "At least you like me," she murmured, her voice soft and laced with sorrow.

She wasn't a Stromm and didn't belong in Summit Range. She wasn't a Vela and didn't belong in the Sublands. She was a Strong, the last surviving member, and belonged nowhere. But none of that mattered. She had pledged to save Mateo, and they had all agreed to start planning in the morning.

The image of Mateo knocked down to his knees replayed in her mind. Pain needled her heart, and a surge of tears clogged her throat. She should've never betrayed him. She should've crossed that finish line by his side. They should've faced the consequences together.

Stormy let out a low whimper, easing her front paws onto the bedding and resting her head in the crook of

Avalynn's neck. She wrapped her arms around the wolfbeast.

"I'm sorry, Stormy. So very sorry." She pulled up her blanket, wiping her eyes with its edge. She had hurt so many people. Even his childhood pet. "Please forgive me."

Her tears fell through the night—quickly at first, then slower and slower until she was utterly emptied. She had never been so alone, never felt so dejected. With her heart breaking and every muscle in her body aching, she surrendered to slumber.

A soft beam of light tickled Avalynn's eyelids. Morning already, and she had barely slept a wink. She stretched her arms, then propped herself up on her elbows. Stormy sat on her haunches on the stone floor, staring at her.

"Well, good morning, girl."

She swung her legs over the edge of the bed, her bare feet hitting the cool, rough floor. Judging by the haze coming in through the small windows, it was early morning. She paused her breathing and listened. Not a sound could be heard through the small home. Perfect timing for her to rise while everyone still slept. The more she stayed out of the way, the better.

She folded her rough fabric nightgown and placed it on the dresser. She ran her fingers through her long hair, then left it loose. She slipped on her black hunting pants and long-sleeved green shirt. Strange to think how the clothes had been soaked in rabbit guts not long ago. Now, they smelled like fresh water mixed with an earthy desert scent. Nothing like the floral perfumed soap she was used to, but at least they were clean. She threaded her brown belt through the loops. So much had changed in so little time. Her fingers paused at the buckle. What else was in store for her?

Avalynn peered at Stormy. "This is only the beginning, isn't it?" A head tilt told her she was right. Avalynn snorted. "You think you're so smart."

She headed for the small washroom everyone in the home shared. Pulling back the faded curtain, she stepped inside. The air hung warm and slightly damp, carrying the faint smell of dirt and dried sage. The space was barely large enough to turn around in but well maintained. A simple clay basin rested on a smooth wooden stand. Next to that, a matching pitcher filled with fresh water. A folded cloth lay neatly beside it, along with a small, hand-carved soap dish holding a sliver of lavender-scented soap—the one indulgence in an otherwise modest room.

No gold fixtures, no plush towels scented with fine oils, only a threadbare cloth draped over a hook in the wall. This was nothing like the grand washrooms of Stromm Palace. There, water cascaded from crystal spouts, and every surface shimmered with polished stone and gold flecks. This washroom was functional, nothing more. Yet, as crude as it was, it felt grounded and honest in its simplicity. An unadorned reflection of the Sublands and everyone who lived there. Avalynn needed to appreciate that.

She reached for the pitcher, her fingers brushing against its rough surface. She hesitated, struck by the thought that this had been Mateo's life. Her heart ached with those now familiar warring emotions of guilt mixed with longing. What would Mateo do when she showed up with the others to rescue him? *Don't think about that. Just focus on the task.* His reaction would be whatever it would be, and she would deal with it.

She made her way to the cookroom. She entered and froze. Manny sat alone at the table, his head in his hands. Oh no. Was he crying? She stepped back, ready to leave, when his head popped up.

"Avalynn?" He wiped his face quickly with his sleeve and straightened his hunched back. A weak smile flickered across his face. "Come in, *Mija*. I was just... resting."

She hesitated. "I didn't mean to intrude. I can go back to my quarters until everyone else wakes."

He waved her over with a smile. "It's okay. They'll be up soon." Deep lines were etched in his sun-kissed face. His long gray hair hung loose down his back. "I'll start the tea." He shuffled to the low brick hearth in the corner of the room where an iron pot hung from a hook.

Lady Sonia had said Manny was from the human realm and had been here a long time with the help of a potion she'd made to slow his aging. It didn't look like the potion was working anymore.

While he busied himself with the fire, Avalynn took a seat. "You have called me *Mija* and used a language I don't recognize."

He placed a scoop of shavings on the logs and rubbed the flint against a chunk of quartz. "It's Spanish. It's my native tongue from the human realm." Sparks landed on the pile, and he fanned them with his hand. "*Mija* means my daughter, but it's not only used for blood offspring. It's a term of endearment. Like calling someone dear." He placed sticks on the flame. "I call you *Mija* because you are dear to me. The granddaughter of my best friend, Julio."

Her throat tightened. She hadn't expected such an answer. "Thank you, Manny." He cared for her like a daughter despite what she had done. She didn't deserve it.

"No need to thank me for that," he said with a soft chuckle. "We are *familia*."

She cleared her throat. "So, today we make our plans to get Mateo."

"Yes, we do." He shuffled to the cabinets, retrieving wooden cups and a sack of herbs. "The day will be busy."

Would Camilla and Mateo's friends Gareth and Lirien join them? Lady Sonia? Or perhaps Lady Verona and the witch who had accompanied Mateo to the hunt? She tapped her fingers on the table. "Who will be planning with us?"

Manny set the wooden cups on the table. "That's up to Lady Sonia."

"I see." She wanted to tell him about the spirit girl she had seen at Spirit Butte. But his frail appearance stopped her. He'd been through enough already. She'd save the information for when she saw Lady Sonia.

Camilla entered the kitchen with Floriana trailing close behind. The little sister stayed close to the elder, stuck to her like ivy to a tree. Camilla worked her way around the cookroom, helping Manny with the tea and food while avoiding eye contact with Avalynn.

Floriana, however, snuck a peak. Their gazes connected, and Floriana frowned before turning away. Avalynn didn't blame her. She'd done the unthinkable and taken the only brother the young girl had ever known. Her promise to get Mateo back hadn't softened the anger. No matter what happened, they would always despise her.

They drank the minty tea and ate fresh fruit along with rosemary bread. The only sounds were muted taps of wooden cups meeting the table and the faint rustle of cloth as they shifted in their seats. When everyone finished, Manny began cleaning.

"Avalynn, get your things ready while I finish here," he said. "You and I will meet Lady Sonia at Spirit Butte. Camilla will stay home with Floriana."

Camilla shot Avalynn a death glare. She wanted to go but wasn't allowed. Good. The less she was around her, the better.

Avalynn sidestepped the eldest sister and returned to her quarters. She studied the small room. The only thing she had were the clothes on her back and the dark sword with blue etchings she'd brought back from the Passing Place. She raised her hands and studied her palms. She hadn't touched the sword since retrieving it. Partly from fear, but mainly due to uncertainty. Mateo needed her, and the entire Sublands needed her. Yet she had no idea what it meant to be the Only One, let alone wield a sword of power.

Inch by inch, she approached the sword. She reached

out timidly, then placed a finger on the cool blade. Right on the blue etchings. Nothing happened. With a shaky sigh of relief she gripped the hilt. She slipped the dark sword into its sheath and secured it to the leather harness Lady Sonia had given her. The straps crossed her chest and shoulders snugly, holding the blade diagonally across her back. She adjusted it so the hilt rested within reach above her shoulder. It was a part of her now, whether she liked it or not.

Stormy trotted into the room. Avalynn folded her arms and faced the wolfbeast. "Where have you been?" Stormy snorted and shook her head. Avalynn smiled. "At least one of us is having a good time."

She sat on the edge of the bed, ready and waiting. Her leg bounced. The Stromm Palace was heavily fortified, so getting in would not be easy. There was also the matter of Master Kragar. What would he do when he saw her? A vision of him with his red tuft flapping and a mad grin, charging her with an axe sprang to mind, and she shuddered. He wouldn't hesitate to end her.

A light knock on her door pulled her away from her morbid thoughts with a jump. "*Mija*, you ready?"

She rubbed her hands on her pants. "Yes," she said, but thinking no. She wasn't ready. Not at all. But that had never stopped her before. When she opened the door, she found Manny in black pants with a dark-red shirt beneath a brown cloak, his walking stick in hand.

He held out a matching cloak for her. "The days are warm, but the nights are cool in the desert."

She took it and slipped it over her head. "Are we going to be a while?"

He handed over a flask of water. "You never know with Lady Sonia. But we might. Best to be prepared."

Avalynn stepped outside Manny's tiny home. The cracked earth crunched beneath her boots, and the wind stirred the red dust. Spirit Butte loomed in the distance, its silhouette jetting out against the fiery sky. The stillness of the desert was striking. Only the whir of the wind and the occasional bird broke the silence. Vibrant colors painted the land, defying its harshness. But a weight hovered in the air, as if the land carried every villagers' burdens.

She adjusted the dark sword slung across her back beneath her cloak. The weight of it reminded her of the burdens she now carried. What burdens did Mateo carry now that he was a prince of House Stromm?

"The Sublands are beautiful, aren't they?" Manny said with a smile as he drew in a deep breath.

Would she grow to view this place as beautiful? She wasn't sure but didn't want to say that. "It's not what I had imagined." She had studied the province during her lessons when she was younger, but she had never visited. If she had, would her views of the Sublands have changed? She had been terrible to Mateo when he arrived at the palace. All of the royals had been. She deeply regretted it.

They walked for a while in silence. When Sandhaven Village was far behind them, Manny interrupted the stillness. "Is there anything you want to talk about?"

Anything? How about everything? So many questions swirled in her head, with one overriding all others. "Tell me about my family. My mother and father. What were they like?"

A chuckle escaped Manny. "Oh, yes. Gabriela and Leaf." He shook his head. "At the start, they hated each other."

She skipped a step. "They did?" Just like her and Mateo. They might have killed each other if not for the Enbarr, Silverhoof, coming between them. It was her father's horse, watching over her. She wondered where Silverhoof was now. Near the Sublands? Or back in the valley of Summit Range?

Manny sat on a flat rock. He opened his flask and took a drink. "Oh, they did. Like fire and fire, those two." He chuckled again. "They collided like two sparks."

She sipped her water, then sat beside him. "Why did they hate each other?"

He re-corked his flask and hooked it to his belt. "Leaf was the fiercest warrior in Faevenly and served the Strongs. He was assigned to protect Gabriela from Draven the Witch and hated her because of her humanness. Over time, those prejudices faded, and they fell in love."

Manny's brows drew together. The corners of his mouth tightened, pulling his face into a grim mask. The light that usually lit his eyes dimmed, replaced with a somber shadow.

"Their love was fraught with perils," he said. "There

were simply too many that wanted the Strongs eliminated. They think they succeeded, but they didn't." He brought his gaze to hers and smiled. "You're here. The Only One. You have the sword of power." He took her hand. "You can change things."

Avalynn's chest tightened as his words settled over her like a heavy cloak. *The Only One.* The weight of it pressed down, threatening to crush her. Her fingers trembled, and she quickly pulled her hand back. "I don't even know what that means," she admitted, her voice above a whisper. "What if I fail? What if I let everyone down?" She glanced at Manny, searching for reassurance, but the fear swirling inside her made it hard to believe any comfort could be enough. "I'm not like them. I don't feel... strong. Not strong enough for this."

Her gaze dropped to her lap, shame burning at the edges of her thoughts. For all the talk of destiny, she couldn't shake the feeling that fate had chosen the wrong person.

He grabbed her hands and held on tight, like an anchor steadying her in a raging storm. "*Mija*, you *are* strong enough. You are part human witch, part fae. You were raised by the Stromms and know their strengths and weaknesses better than anyone." His gaze shifted to the hilt of her sword, peeking through the opening of her cloak. "You carry a sword of power." He tapped the cross hanging around her neck. "And the symbol of faith of my human religion. Faith is a warrior, and nothing can stop you!"

Faith is a warrior, as Mateo had said. Her chest warmed, hope flickering for the first time since she'd come to the Sublands. The doubts and fears that had gnawed at her began to recede, replaced by a growing sense of clarity and strength. She felt the sword's presence at her back as if it were an extension of herself, ready to fight alongside her.

She was stronger than she'd given herself credit for, and Manny's words were the reminder she'd needed. She wasn't alone in this. She had the strength of two worlds behind her. With the sword's power and this thing called faith, she could change everything.

Manny's arms wrapped around her with surprising strength for his age. He held her close as if he could absorb her worries. The world outside the embrace faded away, and all she could feel was the deep, unspoken bond between them.

He had been there for her mother and father, and the mother and father before them—fighting, sacrificing, loving. And now, he was here for her. She whispered, "Thank you, Manny."

He pulled back and kissed her cheeks one at a time. He smoothed the hair away from her forehead. He nodded and slowly released her. "This is where I leave you."

"What?" She blinked, stunned.

He rose to his feet. "You will continue on your own to Spirit Butte. Lady Sonia's orders."

"But why?" She stood before him, a cold shiver trickling down her spine.

He placed his hands on her shoulders. "You will have to find that out for yourself." He shifted his cloak and readjusted the flask at his waist. "I will see you when you are finished, *Mija*."

She stepped forward, watching him walk away for a few long seconds before turning back to face Spirit Butte. Stormy circled her a few times, unsure of what was happening. But the wolfbeast finally positioned herself next to Avalynn.

"Well, girl." She blew out a long breath. "Let's go see what Lady Sonia has planned for us."

CHAPTER FIVE

Avalynn ascended the narrow trail, cloak billowing behind her. Stormshroud padded ahead, her black fur blending into the shadows, her movements fluid and confident. The trail twisted, and Avalynn clutched the edge of a boulder for balance. That was close. The climb stole her breath as the air thinned.

As they reached the flat plateau, the wolf paused. Her dark form with her white streak stood out starkly against the glowing horizon. She swiveled her ears forward as if sensing something unseen.

Avalynn stopped. "What is it, girl?" She turned in a small circle, scanning the rock. "Is it Lady Sonia?" She gulped. "Or another spirit?"

Stormshroud growled low and deep, a warning that vibrated through the air. Her sharp teeth glinted as her lips curled in a snarl. Avalynn moved closer to her companion, a prickling panic crawling up the back of her neck. She reached for her sword when Lady Sonia stepped into view from the trail. And she wasn't alone. The ladies who had escorted Mateo to the hunt were with her. The witch with red hair and the steward of the Sublands, who stood tall and imposing with a long dark braid and piercing blue eyes.

Lady Sonia gestured toward the women. "Avalynn, you remember Lady Verona, the steward of the Sublands, and Rhyka, witch and friend to Lady Verona."

Avalynn stopped reaching for her sword and moved her hands together in front of her. "Yes, I do." She nudged the growling Stormshroud and said with a nervous laugh, "I apologize for my wolf." Which one of them did Stormy not like? Was it both of them? "She's not used to strangers."

The witch stepped forward. She narrowed her black crystal eyes as a whispering wind tossed her wild, red hair. "She is a keen one. She growls because she understands what we are about to do to you."

Fear jolted Avalynn as the witch flung out her hands. Stormshroud howled like a spirit wrenched from the Passing Place. The haunting cry halted as the wolf collapsed to her side, rigid as stone. "Stormy!" Avalynn fell to her knees. She touched Stormy's neck. The steady thump of her heart pulsed against her fingers. She glared at the witch. "What did you do to her!"

Lady Sonia and Rhyka moved back while Verona advanced. The steward drew the sword that hung at her waist. "We got your beast out of the way so we could test you. The Only One."

Fear tightened in her chest, the weight of it pressing against her ribs as she rose to her feet. They wanted to test her with an ambush? "I thought we were meeting to plan Mateo's rescue?"

The witch smiled. "Test first, plan after."

"Fine," Avalynn said, her fingers trembling as they wrapped around the hilt of her sword, but she drew it nonetheless. The blue etchings of the dark blade glinted in the dim light. Even though Stormy's collapsed body lay close by, she forced herself to focus on the threat in front of her. If they wanted a fight, she'd give them a fight.

"It is a fine blade," Verona said.

"It is," Avalynn replied, hoping she could do it justice. The air around her teemed with tension. She squared her shoulders. She lifted the blade. "If you think I'll just roll over, you're mistaken." She had never bested Kragar. Could she best Lady Verona?

Verona answered with a shifting of her blade. "I expect no less."

A blur of movement and Verona lunged, her sword swinging through the air. Avalynn barely had time to react. Her blade clashed against Verona's, the sharp metallic ring echoing across the plateau. The force of the strike sent a jolt through her arms, but she gritted her teeth and held her grip.

Verona extended her sword and moved from side to side, sizing up Avalynn like a predator circling its prey. Avalynn, though less experienced, had been trained by the best. "What are you waiting for? Are you too old to—"

"Rah!" Verona charged.

Avalynn barely sidestepped a downward slash. The tip of Verona's sword sliced the edge of her cloak, sparking against the rocky ground. Taking advantage of the miss, Avalynn swung her blade in an upward arc. Verona twisted away, the edge of her blade only grazing the tip of Verona's braid.

"Fine, not too old," Avalynn said between labored breaths, admiring Verona's footwork.

The Sublands steward sliced her sword back and forth through the air. "You've got spirit," Verona said. "But spirit won't save you."

"Save me from what?" Avalynn grunted.

Verona answered with a series of jabs, forcing Avalynn to retreat with quick steps. "From your former home. The Stromms will do anything to end you."

Her breaths came faster now, her heart pounding in her ears. "I suppose you're right." If they were going to attempt to rescue Mateo, it wouldn't be easy. Sweat trickled down her brow as she kept her focus locked on her opponent.

"More!" Verona shifted her stance and swung low, aiming for Avalynn's legs. Avalynn leaped back, but not fast enough. The blade nicked her thigh, a sharp sting of pain blooming where it cut. "Use more than your blade!"

She bit back a cry, gripping her sword tighter. Verona was right. Her blade wasn't enough. She needed to activate herself. "I am the Only One." Avalynn forced out the words as if saying them out loud would awaken her power. As if it was that easy. She feigned to the right, then pivoted, bringing her sword down in a two-handed arc.

Verona raised her weapon to block, but the impact staggered her, forcing her to stumble back a step. It wasn't much, but it was something. "Better," Verona said. "Now more!"

Avalynn pressed her advantage. She unleashed a flurry of swings, leaving Verona on the defensive. Their swords met. Sparks flew. Their strikes grew more intense, and Avalynn felt her strength waning. Her muscles screamed in protest, but she refused to stop. With a yell, she managed a desperate parry. But Verona double swung and pivoted. She disarmed Avalynn with a whisk, sending her sword clanking to the ground. Avalynn fell back, her breath ragged, her vision swimming.

Verona stood over Avalynn, catching her breath. She reached down and held out her hand with a sneer. "You have a lot of work to do."

Refusing the help, Avalynn climbed to her feet. She dusted off her pants. "I wasn't prepared for an attack." Kragar had jump-attacked her several times, but not like this. She walked over to Stormy, who was up and swaying on trembling legs. The wolf shook her head. Her ears flicked as if to rid herself of an invisible haze. "Or for someone to spell my wolf."

Lady Sonia approached. "We want you to be prepared, my princess. That is why you are out here. We have much to do over the next few days before we leave for Summit Range."

Her hand stopped mid-stroke on Stormy's head. "We?" So, Lady Verona and Rhyka were included. She wasn't sure how she felt about that. "All of us?"

"Yes," Rhyka said. She brought out four bedrolls Avalynn hadn't noticed before. "The four of us." She dropped the bedding. "Now..." She clapped her hands together. Her lips twisted into a wicked grin. She rubbed her palms, her eyes glistening like black ice. "My turn."

Sun, Moon, and Stars. Avalynn could handle steel. Magic was another matter altogether. "I'm not ready for that." Her pleading eyes met Lady Sonia's, but her former friend stayed silent.

"You must always be ready." Rhyka stretched her hands outward, her long fingers claw-like. A cold wind spiraled through the camp, scattering dirt and pebbles. "The Only One, hmm?" Rhyka's voice carried a mocking lilt. "Let's see what you are made of."

Avalynn's pulse quickened as a blast of air shot at her like a roaring gale. She stumbled back and fell on her backside with a thud, her hair in her face. Stormshroud growled low, crouched at her side, ready to defend her. "I am not ready!"

Rhyka laughed, the sound sharp and cold. "So you say." She raised her hands, and the red sand all around coiled like living serpents. Stormshroud whined, backing up and pressing against Avalynn's legs. "If you are truly the Only One, you will always be ready."

"You are mad!" Avalynn backed away from the slithering dirt. She held out her hands like a shield as the witch jerked her hands up, sending the sand serpents into the air like arrows. The barrage slammed into the ground in front of Avalynn. The force knocked her off balance, and again, she hit the dirt. Pain shot through her palms as she braced herself.

"Call it forth!" Rhyka demanded, her voice a whip of command. "The power that lies within you. Let me see it!"

Gasping for air, Avalynn struggled to her feet, her hands shaking. She pulled her hair back. "I don't know how!" Frustration and fear clawed at her chest.

Rhyka's smile widened. "Then learn." She sent out another blast of energy, aimed at Avalynn's chest.

She raised her arms, a scream ripping from her throat. A surge of raw, powerful emotion washed over her. The blue light erupted from her palms, brilliant and wild. It blasted forward, meeting Rhyka's attack in a clash. Blue sparks flew into the waning daylight, sending the witch careening backward.

The force left Avalynn breathless. Her hands tingled as the faint blue glow lingered across her skin. She stared at her palms. She did it. She used her power.

"There it is." Rhyka's laughter rang out as she climbed to her feet. "The power of the Only One."

Avalynn's chest heaved as she lowered her arms. The blue light flickered and died, leaving her standing in the aftermath, shaken but alive. Stormshroud pressed against her leg, steadying her. She stroked behind her ears and whispered, "Thanks, girl."

The witch tilted her head. She watched Avalynn like a scholar examining a rare artifact. "You have it," she said, almost in a whisper now. "But it's raw, untamed. Let's see if you survive long enough to master it."

CHAPTER SIX

The four sat around the small fire as the warm day turned into a cold night. Avalynn positioned herself as far away from Lady Verona and Rhyka as possible. She'd had enough of them. Lady Sonia, too, for that matter. But she was at their mercy.

She wrapped her cloak tighter around her shoulders. Manny had said it'd be cold, but she hadn't counted on the temperature plunging so drastically. Avalynn wished for the kind man to be here now. He would've had a thing or two to say to Lady Verona and Rhyka about their techniques. He would've made the fire bigger too and given Avalynn his cloak.

She found a long twig and used it to stoke the crackling fire. The flame's orange glow danced on the rock's weathered edges. Shadows stretched and shifted with the fire, creating fleeting shapes against the landscape. Stars pierced the velvety sky. But their light remained distant compared to the flame's comforting warmth. The crisp air bit at Avalynn's cheeks and fingers despite her cloak. Only the occasional gust of wind stirred the sand, disturbing the desert's silence.

The last time she sat by a fire was in the hunt with Mateo and the others, fighting for their lives. It seemed so long ago. Now, she was in Mateo's homeland, his favorite place, surrounded by two witches and an angry steward.

Stormshroud lay near Avalynn's feet. Her black fur blended with the night, and her ears twitched at the sounds of nocturnal life. She was grateful to have her furry companion. She'd feel so alone without her.

Lady Sonia cleared her throat. "Lady Verona had her turn, as did Rhyka." She got up and moved closer to Avalynn, facing her head-on. "Now it's my turn."

The announcement struck Avalynn like a slap of icy water, stealing the air from her lungs. Her mind churned with Sonia's formidable magic. "Another test?" she asked, her voice cracking despite her best efforts to keep it steady.

"Not a test," Lady Sonia replied. "A lesson."

Avalynn's heart thudded in her chest, but she refused to let it show. Somehow, a lesson sounded worse—deceptive in its simplicity and laden with unspoken threats. She lifted her chin. "Fine. Here by the fire?" Her gaze flicked to the glowing embers before returning to Sonia. "Or should we stand farther away?"

Lady Sonia leaned forward. "Here is fine." The fire seemed to dim as her once friend settled in before her. "Remember how I told you to concentrate on your blue light and your mother and father so that you could go to them in the Passing Place?"

She blinked, relieved. "So this is really a lesson?"

"It is." Lady Sonia nodded and smiled.

Avalynn's shoulders relaxed. *Whew*. A lesson. Thank the Sun, Moon, and Stars. She'd had enough physicality for the evening. "Yes, I remember what you told me."

She leaned forward. "Well, you can use the same technique to visit *anyone*."

The fire crackled, shooting a burst of tiny sparks into the air. Her mind raced to Mateo. Her heart fluttered, and her hopes lifted. She desperately wanted to see him and explain why she did what she did at the finish line. She needed him to understand. "Anyone at all?"

A nod. "Yes, anyone." Sonia glanced at Lady Verona and Rhyka before looking back at Avalynn. "We want you to send your spirit to Stromm Palace, to the king and queen, to see what they are doing. It will help us figure out our next move."

Spy on the king and queen? Her excitement dashed away. Sonia made it sound easy, but she knew her former sires. It would be a deadly endeavor. Her hand found her arm, the spot where the king had left bruises. They were no longer visible, yet the pain lingered deep within.

"What about their witch, Raelor?" she asked. "If he is with them, won't he sense me?"

Lady Sonia sat back. "That, I do not know." She snuck a glance at Lady Verona and Rhyka. "We will have to take our chances. But if we are going for Mateo, we must ensure they are not fortifying their defenses."

She breathed deeply. If she could go to them, she could go to Mateo. Her fingers fidgeted in her lap, and she fought the small, involuntary smile tugging at her lips. But beneath it all, a knot coiled in her stomach. It tightened with every breath. What if she ended up before Raelor? What if he used his magic to send her to the Passing Place? She pushed the notion aside. Mateo was worth the risk. First, she would see what the king and queen were up to, then she'd find him.

"So I just close my eyes and think of my power and the person I want to see?" She needed confirmation. "Same as before?"

"Yes," Lady Sonia nodded. "Same as before."

She swallowed. "Alright then. Let me try."

"Very well," Lady Sonia said. "If I sense anything awry, I will pull you back."

"You can do that?" Avalynn asked with a blink.

"I can," she said.

"Good to know," she said, finding comfort in having Sonia as a safety net. But still, nerves tickled her spine anyway. She folded her hands in her lap and closed her eyes. She steadied her breathing, letting the world around her fade. The fire's crackle softened to a whisper, replaced by her heartbeat's steady hum. She reached deep inside, seeking the energy thread that had burst from her earlier. It responded. A flicker of warmth that surged through her chest, glowing brighter with every inhale.

She visualized the queen first—her coldness and indifference. The way she held her head so high she never even looked in Avalynn's direction. The king zoomed into focus next. His anger, his cruel tongue, his intimidating glares. She shuddered, not wanting to be in their presence but forcing her thoughts to them anyway.

At first, nothing happened. But then, energy rippled through her like a brook expanding into a rushing river. The ground seemed to vanish. A cold wind whisked past her ears. Her spirit lurched forward, drawn like a moth to a flame. Light and shadow blurred together until she could barely tell where she ended and the world began.

When the pull stopped, Avalynn found herself in a dimly lit chamber. A singular orb floated along the simple stone flooring. Brick and mortar walls zoomed into focus. She blinked, not recognizing the space. Where was she?

The High Queen came into view, wearing a long green dress. She sat at a plain wooden table across from Raelor. Avalynn's breath hitched as she backed up. Oh no. The witch. Just as she had feared. Would he sense her? She crept to the other side of the room and hovered near the wall.

"I have discovered that it's the Baffins who are spurring on the Linds and Brunts to challenge us. I have also learned the three houses will travel together. Those fools." She slammed her hands on the table. "But I have a plan for what to do when they arrive."

All three houses were headed to the palace? The Linds and Brunts had each lost hunters in the hunt—Eiric, who deserved the ending he received, and Finnian, who did not. But what were the Baffins up to? And what exactly were they going to challenge? Everyone knew the risks of the hunt.

Raelor sat forward. "What do you have in mind?"

The queen's wicked grin grew. "We will use…"

Raelor shot up from his chair. He silenced the queen with a wave. "We are not alone."

He moved closer to where Avalynn stood, hand outstretched, his bright crystal eyes flicking about. Terror gripped her. With each step he took forward, she took one back. He moved closer and closer, the queen on her feet now.

She turned and darted through the wall, then another, before she slowed to a halt. Her breathing steadied. Her heartbeat returned to normal. She calmed her nerves and looked around. A row of torches lit the brick walls. Across from her, black metal bars divided the space. She gulped. She was in the dungeon.

"Well, lookit. Her Highness, Princess Avalynn Stromm, has graced us with a visit." A man with thick, short red hair dressed in a dingy burlap robe emerged from a dark shadow. A gash stretched across his forehead.

"She is alone too." Another figure followed. This one with long, dark hair and a blood-soaked tunic.

Her stomach dropped, a hollow, sickening plunge that left her unsteady. They were spirits. Dead at the hand of the Stromms when she was one of them. "I-I-I mean you no harm." She gazed about. "I'm not even a Stromm anymore." The dungeon rooms were empty, yet she spotted a thick double-guarded door farther down. Who was in there?

The two dead prisoners burst into laughter as two more joined them. The first one, with the red hair, stepped forward. "Well, we mean you harm." He licked his lips. "Plenty of harm."

She had no idea if the spirit could make good on the threat. And she didn't want to find out. She bolted through the thick walls, out into the night sky, and hurried through the garden. She ran without looking back until she spilled into the palace, finding herself in the library. She hovered next to the bookshelves, waiting for one of the spirits to charge in after her. But none showed.

She gathered her wits. Another spirit could be coming, and she'd been gone for a while. She needed to hurry and find Mateo. She dashed from the library, down the corridor, up the staircase, and to the second floor. A small servant with short brown hair and wearing a white dress carried a tray of water, fruit, and perfume vials. Avalynn held her breath and moved out of the way. The small brownie hurried past and entered Lily's bedchamber. With Lily retiring for the night, and her room undoubtedly empty, that left one option.

She approached the carved door. Would Mateo even listen? She drew in a deep breath. Could he forgive her? Her head spun with all the different ways he might react. But there was only one way to find out. She halted her thoughts, she steadied herself, and she stepped through the wooden door.

The orbs floating along the gilded ceiling were dimmed low. The small fire crackling in the fireplace drew Avalynn's attention. But the chairs facing the hearth were empty. Her gaze swept the large room until she found him.

He stood by the window, his back to her. Her spirit form felt weightless, a stark contrast to the crushing tension that gripped her. Butterflies fluttered in her chest, but the cold reality of her betrayal came rushing back. *Please, let him listen.*

She moved closer, each step a battle against her own rising fear.

"Mateo," she whispered. She hovered next to him, her shoulder so close if she materialized, he'd feel her. She inched forward and turned to face him. His intense stare was fixed on the evening horizon. His brows were tight and his chin set. He had one hand resting on the wall by the window, the other on a necklace around his neck. She moved closer and peered at the chain—a gold pendant with an S for Stromm.

She gasped. Why was he wearing that? She wanted to yank it off and throw it out the window. "Mateo. It's me, Avalynn." She moved in even closer. "Mateo!"

He jolted. His steely gaze searched the space where she stood. She focused her thoughts on him. *Please, let him see.*

His hand dropped from the chain. His eyes widened. "Avalynn?"

"Yes! It's me!" She smiled wide.

His brows knitted together as his mouth parted. "Avalynn? How—" His voice faltered, and a flicker of concern crossed his face. "Are you..." He swallowed hard. "Are you in the Passing Place? Did they—kill you?" His eyes locked on hers, as if searching for answers.

"No! I'm alive!" she said quickly, her voice trembling with urgency. "This isn't death. It's my spirit. I was taught how to do this so I could reach you." She moved closer, her hands hovering near his arm. She wished she could touch him. "I needed to see you. To explain."

His expression hardened, a storm gathering in his eyes. "Explain?" He stepped back. "You betrayed me.

Knocked me to my knees. I would have never done that to you." His fists clenched at his sides, knuckles whitening. "They threw me in the dungeon and kept me there for days. The only reason I survived is..." He faltered, and his hand returned to the necklace. "I am a Stromm. The ones who raised you saved me. You left me for dead."

Her chest ached, guilt rising like a tightening snake. "Mateo, please." She reached for him. But her hand passed through. "I had to. I didn't want to betray you, but I had no choice. If I hadn't..." Her voice broke, and she stopped. She wasn't making any sense. "It was the only way to save you. To save us." Tears welled in her eyes, though they didn't fall in this form. "I thought it was the right choice. I never stopped thinking about you, not for one moment. And as soon as I woke up in the Sublands, I wanted to come for you and rescue you from this place."

A darkness covered his face. "Who did this?" His eyes narrowed. "Who switched us at birth? Who stripped me of my rightful destiny?"

Avalynn froze. Rightful destiny? Shock rippled through her, leaving her thoughts jumbled and raw. How could he ask her this? Mateo despised the Stromms. He loathed everything they stood for. And now, he spoke of a stolen destiny? Like he mourned it? Her sadness deepened, mingling with the unsettling shock of his words. Who was he?

She searched his face, desperate to find the one she had fallen in love with. "Mateo," she whispered. "This isn't you."

"Isn't me?" He cocked his head. "Because I don't deserve it?" He struck his chest with his fist. "Because I was raised a Sublander, I am not worthy?" He flung his arms. "I do not deserve these things?"

"No, no, no." He was twisting her words, making her somehow to blame. She had to explain. "This isn't you because you are better than this!"

His door flung open. Raelor charged in, hands out. A magical force more potent than a tidal wave blasted against her spirit form. She recoiled, her form flung backward in a chaotic tumble. She spun wildly until she slammed face-first into a hard surface, the impact sending shockwaves through her.

Avalynn blinked, disoriented. Her senses sluggishly returned as the gritty feel of red dirt registered against her skin. She pushed herself up slowly, her body trembling.

Lady Sonia knelt beside her, eyes searching Avalynn as if making sure she was unharmed. "My dear." She helped her to her feet and brushed the dirt from her face. "Are you alright?" Lady Sonia's firm voice grounded Avalynn in reality. She was no longer in Mateo's bedchamber.

She nodded, her mind swirling with confusion and the sharp sting of failure. "I...I don't know what happened," she murmured, her voice shaky. She rubbed her forehead. She wanted to tell them she had seen Mateo but stopped herself. They wouldn't understand. And they hadn't even asked her to see him. She needed to focus on the queen and Raelor instead. What chamber were they in? Who was in the dungeon?

"What happened?" Lady Rhyka demanded, her brows raised. "What did you see?"

She swallowed, her mind replaying everything. "I materialized in a chamber I have never been in before. It was dark and near the dungeon. The queen was there with Raelor. They were talking about what to do when the other houses arrived. The Baffins, Linds, and Brunts. Before they could say more, Raelor sensed me and flung his magic at me."

"The other houses are on their way to Stromm Palace?" Lady Verona asked.

"They are. With the Baffins organizing their arrival. They travel together," Avalynn said.

Rhyka leaned forward. "What else?" she prodded. "Try to remember everything."

She took a deep breath, filtering the sequence of events. "I ran from Raelor... and ended up in the dungeon." She hesitated, her gaze flicking toward the others. "The spirits there... they saw me." She shuddered. "And then they charged at me."

Lady Sonia explained to Lady Verona and Rhyka, "Avalynn can see spirit forms. It's part of her human magic."

"From her mother, Princess Gabriela. I remember," Verona said.

Avalynn paced in a tight circle. She pushed Mateo out of her mind as she honed in on the dungeon. "Someone is being held down there," she said, stopping and staring into the distance. "In a place I have never seen before." Her brow furrowed as she turned to Lady Sonia. "The door—it was heavily guarded."

"A secret prisoner?" Lady Verona tilted her head. "Where? Tell me everything you can remember."

"I, uh, don't know." Avalynn closed her eyes, trying to visualize the scene. "It was at the end of a dark hallway."

Lady Verona's head snapped to Lady Sonia. "Did you know about this? Did you go to the dungeon as Maid Nia?"

"No, never," Sonia replied. "But we must focus on the other houses. Forget about the dungeon for now."

Lady Verona crossed her arms, then nodded. "We must take to the road to Stromm Palace then," she said. "We must meet the envoy and find out what they are up to."

"Yes, yes." Rhyka wagged her crooked finger. "They are surely going to challenge the Stromms."

A smile spread across Lady Verona's face. "And the Sublands will join them. That will be our way into the palace."

Avalynn lay on her pallet, staring at the cold and brilliant night sky, her thoughts a tangled mess. Seeing Mateo left her heart heavier than before. She knew he wouldn't forgive her. She knew he wouldn't understand, just as she had feared. But what she couldn't believe was that he *liked* being a Stromm. He enjoyed wearing jewelry the king and queen had given him.

His anger still stung her like a fresh cut. But she pushed it aside, focusing on the plan ahead. She had no other choice. The Baffins, Linds, and Brunts were headed for Summit Range. Together, they would challenge the

Stromms in an unprecedented move. Joining them could get them close to Mateo. Hopefully, her presence wouldn't ruin that.

She closed her eyes and turned to her side, feeling the decision settle in her chest. There was always safety in numbers. With the other houses behind them, she might be able to reach Mateo and get him away from that damned place. And maybe, just maybe, find a way to set things right with him.

CHAPTER SEVEN

"Where is she?" Raelor spat, flinging a second blast of power through the room and nearly knocking Mateo off his feet. "Where?" The mad witch stomped toward Mateo, fingers crooked and curled. As if he had invited Avalynn's appearance.

"Get away from my son!" the queen ordered. She pushed Raelor aside and took Mateo's face in her hands. "Did that vile human witch hurt you?" She patted his chest as if searching for a wound. "Are you all right?"

"Get off me!" He swatted her away. A surge of foreign and unexpected feelings plowed through him. He felt sorrow at seeing Avalynn's spirit form. He'd thought she was no longer alive. But she'd explained her visit, then made a feeble attempt to justify her betrayal. Like he could ever forgive her.

Kragar barreled into the bedchamber. His red tuft of hair flapped, and he raised his axe high. "Where is the trouble?"

Fresh fire flared inside Mateo. His stare narrowed as he thrust out a commanding hand. "Stay back, dwarf."

The madman's mouth fell open before he clamped it shut. His nostrils flared, and he faced the queen. "He will not speak to me like I am nothing!"

Mateo pushed forward, towering over the dwarf, ready to teach him a much needed lesson. He clenched his jaw and gritted out, "You are nothing."

"Please!" The queen clapped her hands. "Enough of this!"

He was the Stromm prince, son of the High King and High Queen. If they were ever to take him seriously, he needed to assert his power. He stood before Kragar, chin raised, and looking down on the lesser being. "I banish you from Stromm Palace and Summit Range, mad dwarf. Banished for disobedience and defiance of my authority as lord prince of House Stromm."

Kragar drew in a ragged breath. He stumbled back as if he'd been attacked. He looked from Mateo to the queen. Raelor clasped his hands behind his back and stepped aside.

If Mateo's mother truly recognized him as her son, she'd support his decree.

"My queen!" Kragar stomped his foot. "This is lunacy! I have faithfully served you and the king for countless years! Done all your dirty deeds!"

"A royal order has been issued by my son." The queen lifted her chin and looked down on the dwarf, matching Mateo's tone. "Your services are no longer needed at Stromm Palace."

Kragar's mouth fell open, gasping. "My queen," he

implored in a low voice. "Please. Let me make this right." His axe clanked to the floor. "I have only served you and the king. I will serve your son, the prince, as well." He turned his pleading eyes to Mateo. "Let me have another chance."

So much for the Master of the Blade. He should have never stood against Mateo. Now he would pay the price. "You may kiss my boots before you leave the palace, dwarf." Mateo smirked. "And only if it pleases me, will I let you walk away with your head."

The dwarf lifted his axe with a grunt, moving it from one hand to the other.

Mateo eyed the blade, itching for a fight. *Come on, dwarf, swing it.* But the queen raised her hand. "Raelor, see Kragar out, at once."

That was right. Kragar was a mere dwarf now, and rightfully so. How did he like Mateo now?

With a flick of his wrist, Raelor summoned a choking grip on Kragar. His magic tightened like an iron collar around the dwarf's thick throat. Kragar grunted, boots scraping the marble floor, axe clanking behind him, as Raelor dragged him from the room. The dwarf's guttural protests echoed, then faded, leaving only a heavy silence.

Mateo stared at the door. His mind flashed to when he had marched past the other hunters. He brushed Avalynn's shoulder to claim his place at the receiving room's head. Raelor had used the exact same tactic on him, dragging him to the end of the line. That's where Sublanders belonged. It felt like a lifetime ago, but it had been mere weeks. Everything had changed since then, and yet here he was—still trying to make sense of it all.

At least he was rid of the dwarf.

A swish of her robe and the queen faced the window. She wiped her eyes. Her shoulders trembled. Mateo froze. Was she crying? The thought unsettled him more than Raelor's raw power. Was it Kragar? Did she care for the dwarf that much?

He stepped closer, swallowing against the knot in his throat. "My queen," his voice softened. "Mother, are you alright?" She didn't answer. "Shall I retrieve Kragar for you?"

The queen's head dipped. Her hand lingered near her cheek, wiping away more tears. When she turned, moisture streaked her face. Her regal eyes glistened. She let out a shaky breath. "Oh, my son," she whispered, her voice heavy. "I'm not crying for Kragar."

"Then why?" His brow furrowed.

"For you." She stepped away from the window, her presence commanding and vulnerable all at once. "Do you not see the danger you are in? That spirit..." She shuddered, gripping his arm with trembling fingers. "That witch. She's a Sublander now. And somehow she used her magic to come like a shadow slipping through the cracks. Avalynn's kind only knows how to hate us, to destroy us. What if she meant you harm? What if she still does?" Her gaze darted about the room. "What if she comes back? With her powers? What if she *is* the Only One?" She placed her hand near her throat. "She will want our heads."

Mateo stiffened, her words sinking in. He hadn't considered that. "Avalynn wouldn't—"

"Avalynn?" she interrupted, scrunching her face.

"She is no longer the girl you once knew. Whatever affection she claimed to have for you has long passed. It's been replaced by resentment, by vengeance. The Sublanders want to destroy us." She wiped at her face. "We gave her everything, and it was never enough. Avalynn always hated us, always hated me."

Avalynn hated them? "I didn't know..." Who was Avalynn really? Sure, they'd spent time together in the forest. But how much of that was an act? How much was actually real? As if it mattered. She had used him. Took everything from him. Had him thrown in the dungeon so easily.

He looked away, his jaw tightening, but his mother's grip on his arm didn't falter. "My son, I..." Her voice cracked, and she touched his cheek with featherlight fingers. "I am terrified of losing you... again. My firstborn. If anything happens to you..." She shook her head, letting the sentence trail off as fresh tears glimmered in her eyes.

He met her gaze, emotions swirling within him. The betrayal he felt from Avalynn, the loyalty he felt to his mother, and beneath it all, the nagging doubts he couldn't shake but also couldn't pinpoint.

"What would you have me do?" he asked, his voice desperate for direction.

"What you must, my son." The queen's expression softened into a fragile smile. "For the good of our house. For Summit Range. For you." She stepped back, regal once more. Her sorrow hardened into resolve. "Cut ties with the past. Trust in your blood. And remember who you are. You are the prince of House Stromm—the future king."

Mateo nodded, the words settling like a heavy rock on his shoulders. His gaze shifted back to the door where Raelor had taken Kragar. The silence beyond that door promised no answers. Yet, somewhere deep within, a part of him still whispered, *Avalynn*.

A timid knock sounded at the door. He opened it and found Lily, the young princess who was always by Avalynn's side. He'd been avoiding her. He had no desire to replace his little sister, Floriana. With terror-filled eyes, she spotted the queen and dashed in. She buried her face in her mother's dress and began sobbing.

"My dear little princess." The queen knelt and hugged her tight. "I suppose you heard the ruckus?"

She nodded. "I did, and it scared me, Mother."

"Oh, my dear." She pulled Lily back and cleaned her face with her sleeve. "We are Stromms. There is nothing to be afraid of."

"B-b-ut Avalynn. She is one of them now." Fresh tears spilled from Lily's eyes. "She will try to hurt us."

"Nonsense. She cannot hurt us. Not now, not ever." She motioned to Mateo. "And we have your brother to ensure our safety."

Lily smiled at him, her tear-soaked lashes fluttering. "Thank you, Mateo."

Maid Penny rushed in and snatched Lily's hand. "My queen, my lord prince." She bowed twice. "My apologies. I will help the princess back to her bedchamber."

"Wait," Mateo said. He bent down to one knee. Eye level with Lily, he said, "The queen, our mother, is right. I will do whatever I can to protect this house and you."

She smiled, her eyes sparkling. She inched closer, her small fingers brushing the pendant hanging from his neck. "I am proud to have you as a brother." She pulled her matching pendant from beneath her robe. She patted it, then she kissed his cheek and left his bedchamber.

As the door closed, Mateo remained kneeling. His gaze caught the carved vines etched into the wooden door. A sense of protectiveness coiled within him, tightening like a fist. It was surprising and unbidden, but undeniable.

Whatever else life had thrown at him, Lily had done nothing to deserve harm.

The thought of an innocent caught in the crossfire gnawed at him. Still, beneath that clarity, lay a whisper of something he refused to name. The fierce loyalty he'd once felt for the Sublands no longer burned as brightly. How could it, when his entire life had been a lie? His heritage—his birthright—had taken root. The truth erased the lie he'd clung to for so long.

He was a Stromm, not a Vela. Manny was not his father.

He had asked Avalynn who had switched them. Who had stolen his life? She had refused to answer. But he had seen it in her eyes, she knew the truth. She protected the wrongdoers. They were all deceivers.

The queen's voice broke through his thoughts as she stepped closer. Her slippers slid quietly against the marble. "We should fortify our defenses," she said, raising her eyebrows. "The Lind and Brunt hunters are dead. Their families desire vengeance. They want your head."

"What should we do?" he asked, rising to meet her gaze.

"Use the dragons." Her words came out calm. Her eyes gleamed. "Use them as a shield, and then nothing can touch this house—not an army, not a Chosen One. With the dragons, nothing can touch Lily or *you*."

He rubbed the back of his neck at the hairline. Suddenly, his loved ones in the Sublands sprang to mind. Despite everything, he didn't want them hurt. "Force should be the last resort."

Her hand settled on his arm. "Of course, my son. We will only act if they force our hand." Her voice softened with reassurance. "That has always been the Stromm way."

Her words lingered in the bedchamber long after she'd gone. They settled over him like a dark cloak. Mateo moved to the hearth. The firelight cast flickering patterns across his face. For all the queen's reassurances, the storm ahead felt inescapable, like a tide he could not control. His mind swam as the flames crackled and hissed. Everything was unraveling, piece by piece, faster than he could respond.

"Everything is on fire," Mateo murmured.

He leaned forward, his hand brushing against the cross stuffed in his pocket. His fingers moved to retrieve the object but stopped and went to the pendant around his neck. He held it tighter. "I'm tired of burning."

THE
MATEO
QUEST

CHAPTER EIGHT

M anny shot to his feet when Avalynn stepped through the door. His chair scraped loudly against the stone floor. His eyes swept over her. He exhaled a shaky breath as if he'd held it the entire time she was gone. Before she could speak, he strode toward her, his arms wrapping around her tightly. She froze, startled by the suddenness, then hugged him back.

"You're okay," he murmured, his voice thick. "*Gracias a Dios.*" His grip tightened, then loosened as he pulled back to search her face. "I'm so relieved." His words almost faltered, and she could see all the fears he hadn't voiced in his expression. He must've known about the plan to test her and thought she wouldn't make it.

Avalynn swallowed hard, guilt twisting inside her. Though his affection touched her deeply, he didn't need to worry about her. "I'm fine," she said, softer than she intended, though she wasn't sure if she was reassuring him or herself. "I'm here."

Floriana entered the room with a hacking cough while Camilla hung back with a raised brow. Manny glanced over Avalynn's shoulder. "Where are the others?"

Avalynn ignored his question as goose bumps lined her skin. "She's coughing."

Lady Sonia entered behind Avalynn. "Sun, Moon, and Stars," she uttered. She rushed in and kneeled before Floriana. She placed the back of her hand on her tiny forehead. "When did it return?"

Manny looked down. "This morning. Little Poppy too. It's the same for others in the village. We're all out of seeds."

After rifling through her bag, Sonia produced a small vial and handed it to Manny. "I am out too but have some liquid from the Green Falls. If you parse it out, it should last until we return with more seeds. Or more liquid."

Avalynn pointed at the vial. "Are you almost out because the Green Falls are drying up?"

"The Green Falls are drying?" Sonia rose to her feet. "How do you know?"

"I was there with Mateo." She forced away the memory of their union on the boulder. "Silverhoof took us there after a shadowblood fox injured me." The healed pain throbbed at her back as she visualized the water. "I'd heard tales of the roaring falls and the vast pool of water. But when we were there, the falls were a mere trickle. The water, a lowly pond. I was lucky to be able to submerge myself in the water."

"All the more reason for us to go to Stromm Palace," Sonia said. "Right away."

Manny's tired eyes perked up. "Yes! My boy!" He pumped his fist. "Bring him back, and bring the healing seeds." He nodded his head furiously. "Quickly."

"That's why we're here," Avalynn said. "To say goodbye before we go." She raised a pleading glance at Camilla. "But also, I will need to borrow some clothes for the journey."

With an eye roll, Camilla turned toward her room, and Avalynn followed. She thought for sure the eldest sister would push back and say she wanted to join them, but the way Floriana coughed and trailed by her side told her Camilla didn't want to leave her little sister. She didn't blame her and would've done the same for Lily.

Camilla pulled a brown bag from her dresser drawer. "You'd better not ruin my things."

"Of course not," Avalynn said. "I will treat your clothing with the utmost care."

Camilla started shoving pants and shirts into the bag, along with a few underthings. "They may not meet your high royal standards, but they're all I've got." A cough from Floriana and Camilla paused with a wince. She shoved in a final garment and then handed over the bag.

"Thank you, Camilla." Avalynn carefully reached for the bag as if receiving precious treasure.

Before the exchange, Camilla grabbed Avalynn's hand. "I love my family more than you will ever know." She held firm. "If there is anything good in you, you will do whatever you can to help us."

The gravity of Camilla's worry and pain struck her like a hammer blow to the chest. This was much bigger than just Mateo. She didn't want to let any of them down. "I promise I will do everything I can." She meant it.

Camilla stepped in close. She leaned in and said in the lowest voice, "I do not trust Lady Verona and Rhyka. And you shouldn't either."

Avalynn blinked, the words chilling her through to the bone. Camilla's tone held no room for doubt, only a stark warning that made her thoughts and suspicions spin. Her mind flashed to the glances between Verona and Rhyka. Their whispers around the fire now seemed far more sinister. A weight settled heavily on her shoulders. For the first time, Avalynn questioned whether she could trust *anyone* in this tangled web. Her heart pounded, and she forced herself to nod, unsure if Camilla could see the doubt now burning behind her eyes.

Another cough from Floriana broke the quiet. Manny entered the room with a cup of water and handed it to the little one. Could he sense the tension hanging heavy in the air? His eyes shifted to the bag still in Camilla's grip. "Thank you, *Mija*, for sharing your things with Avalynn."

"Yes," Avalynn echoed. Her voice wavered as she took the bag. "Thank you, Camilla."

Gratitude felt like a poor response to everything the Sublands had endured. Thanks didn't diminish Camilla's dire warning. But what else could she say? She had no choice but to acknowledge the warning and keep a keen eye on her companions. She would ask Lady Sonia about it later.

After a round of tear-filled goodbyes from Manny and an awkward glance from Camilla, she and Lady Sonia left the tiny home and set out on foot. They hadn't walked far when Lady Verona and Rhyka joined them on horseback, two horses in tow.

Avalynn eyed Stormshroud. She had made it to Summit Range by herself before. Could she do it again? She knelt and rubbed the wolf's head. "We'll be riding fast to Summit Range, so you'll need to meet us there, okay?" Stormy nudged Avalynn with her wet nose and then licked her face. She chuckled. "Good. I'll see you then." Stormshroud let out a series of yips, then bolted, the black-and-white creature racing ahead.

She attached the bag of clothes to the saddle, then Lady Verona's bedroll. After adjusting the sword at her back, she climbed onto the sleek brown steed. She stroked its neck, wishing it was Silverhoof. Manny had said the Enbarr was unpredictable and did whatever she wanted, but it would've been nice to have her for the trip to Summit Range.

With everyone ready, they set out and made their way out of the village. With the last remnant of Sandhaven behind them, they broke into a gallop. Lady Verona and Rhyka took the lead.

The sun beat down on them as they raced across the Sublands' barren expanse. Her bedroll and bag bounced against the saddle. The terrain stretched before her, a patchwork of jagged hills and deep, winding gullies carved by ancient waters.

Ahead, Lady Verona and Rhyka's cloaks billowed behind them like banners of purpose. Beside her, Sonia rode silently, her face unreadable. Did she trust Verona and Rhyka? Or were her witchy skills, as Manny liked to refer to them, detecting suspicion?

The rhythmic thunder of hooves filled the air. The steady drumbeat matched Avalynn's thoughts. Each gallop brought them closer to Summit Range and the houses they hoped to meet along the way. But Avalynn couldn't shake the prickling in her mind. What if they didn't intercept them? What if they did, but they didn't want Sublanders tagging along? She was raised a Stromm, after all.

A thunderclap tore through the sky, startling Avalynn's horse into a frantic whinny. She gripped the reins, her heart racing as the skies shifted from calm to chaos in an instant. The plains, once open and inviting, darkened under a churning storm that materialized out of nowhere. Lightning forked across the sky, striking the earth with terrifying precision. The ground trembled with each impact, sending shockwaves through Avalynn's jittery mount. A torrent of rain gushed down on them as if a dam had been released.

"Ride!" Lady Verona's voice pierced through the storm.

Avalynn dug her heels into her horse's sides, urging it forward, but the beast had other ideas. It reared, its hooves clawing at the air as another bolt of lightning split the ground mere feet away. Red filled her sight as her grip slipped and she was thrown, her body slamming into the wet, muddy earth.

The impact knocked the wind from her lungs. Everything blurred—the rain, the sound of her horse galloping away, the crackle of lightning striking dangerously close. She rolled to her side, gasping, her body screaming in protest.

"Avalynn!" Lady Sonia's voice cut through the storm again, desperate and searching.

She pushed herself to her knees, rain streaming down her face and into her eyes. She squinted, catching glimpses of the others. Verona, Sonia, and Rhyka scrambled to dodge the lightning strikes.

The storm wasn't random. It wasn't natural. She could feel it, the heavy, oppressive magic pressing down on her like a weight in her chest. Raelor. His name whispered through her mind like a curse.

Another bolt struck, so close the heat singed the air, and her teeth rattled. She covered her head with her arms, her heart pounding as the acrid smell of burnt earth filled her nostrils. Her mind raced, panic clawing at the edges of her thoughts. The storm was alive, a weapon, and it wouldn't stop until it obliterated them. Then she remembered. Mateo. The hunt. The shield of blue light she'd summoned to protect them from the dragon. She had to do it again.

"Get together!" she hollered at the others. She plowed against the wind and rain to reach them. She dragged them to the ground. "Together!"

She drew the sword from her back, grasping the hilt and holding it close. She closed her eyes against the mayhem. The memory of that day burned bright in her mind. How the light had come to her, how it had wrapped around her and Mateo like an unbreakable cocoon and saved them.

"Come on," she whispered through clenched teeth, her voice barely audible over the storm's fury. "Do it."

Her fingers trembled as she concentrated, reaching

for the power buried deep within her. The magic was there, just out of reach, like a distant star veiled by clouds. A bolt of lightning arced toward them, blinding and lethal. Her instincts screamed to move, but she stayed rooted, focused. They couldn't outrun the storm anyway; they had to beat it.

"Call it forth!" Rhyka hollered.

My power. The Only One. Ignite. She closed her eyes. She forced her breathing to steady. She slowed her pulse. Warmth gathered at her fingertips. Her hands vibrated. Opening her eyes, her stare landed on her blade. The blue etched into the black onyx glowed like a beacon of hope, pulsing with life as if answering her call. The rhythm matched the beating of her heart. In a flash, power erupted from her hands, brilliant and searing, flooding her senses.

The light expanded outward, unfurling into a shimmering dome of vivid blue that encased her and the others like an impenetrable barrier. An array of lightning crashed into the shield, the impact rattling her very bones. She flinched under the force, but the shield held strong, humming with energy. Avalynn tightened her grip on the blade, her shoulders tight, her jaw clenching. Whatever storm had been sent for them, it wouldn't break her. It couldn't. But the storm fought back. The bolts came faster, slamming against the dome like a battering ram.

"Enough!" she hollered.

And then, as suddenly as it had begun, the storm ceased. As if it had given up. The wind died, the rain stopped, and the clouds parted to reveal a sky streaked in sunlight. She collapsed to her side, the shield dissolving into the air like mist. She looked up, her chest heaving, her body soaked and trembling. The others gathered around her, their faces a mixture of relief and disbelief.

"That was incredible," Verona said with awe.

"It was. And we all know that was no ordinary storm," Lady Sonia said, her voice smooth despite the worried undertone. She glanced upward, her expression grim. "That was magicked. Raelor's doing, without a doubt."

"He is powerful," Rhyka hissed.

Avalynn nodded weakly, her body too drained to respond. She let the heat-filled sunshine warm her, her thoughts on the road ahead. And then she muttered, "I really hate that witch."

A chuckle and Lady Verona let out a piercing whistle. One by one their horses returned, calmer now, as if the storm had never happened. "We continue on," Verona said. "The sun will dry our clothes."

The four women mounted in silence, their shared determination unspoken but understood. As Avalynn took the reins, she cast one last glance at the horizon, her resolve hardening. Raelor had tried to break them, but he had underestimated her.

But she couldn't help wondering... what else did he have planned for them?

CHAPTER NINE

They stopped at a clearing as the horizon faded to deep purples and blues, the stars beginning to pierce the velvety darkness. Avalynn dismounted, her legs stiff and sore. She laid out her damp clothes by the fire, as did the others, and they all put on fresh outfits. *Please, let the night be clear.* The thought of being awoken by a thunderstrike left her anxious. She spread her bedroll out on the cool, packed earth. The others did the same. Their movements were quiet and efficient. The night's silence demanded it. Or was it the secrets Verona and Rhyka might be hiding?

Avalynn tore off a piece of fabric from her sleeve and began braiding her long hair. Above her, the stars glittered in an endless canopy, bright and unyielding. But her thoughts were far away. Mateo's face beamed in her mind's eye—his anger, hurt, and uncertainty. She couldn't push away his voice, the way it cracked under his resentment. Or how his eyes had hardened, unfamiliar and distant. Finished with her hair, she lay on her back, her hands folded across her stomach. She stared up at the sky. Perhaps the answers were written among the stars. But no answers came, only the steady pulse of what had been lost.

"What troubles you, princess?" Lady Sonia asked, her voice taking the same tone and cadence as the friend she had pretended to be, Maid Nia. Her hurt ached for that friendship. She needed Nia now more than ever.

She sat up, eyeing Verona and Rhyka on the other side of their fire. She scooted closer to where Sonia sat. "How about everything?"

"I am troubled by the same." Lady Sonia smiled.

This was her chance to ask about what Camilla had said. Who knew if she would have the opportunity later. She inched over. She flicked her eyes to their companions, then back to Sonia. "Do you trust them?"

Sonia let out a soft sigh as the fire crackled and popped. "I do not know." She moved her head from side to side. "Verona has not been the same since losing her brother, Adrius. They were very close."

Fear struck her like one of those lightning bolts. They were in trouble if a wise witch like Sonia didn't know. "It's terrible that she lost her brother, but are you serious?" She leaned in. "You don't know if we can trust them?"

"Shh," Sonia said.

She gulped, then nodded, trying to act as naturally as possible. "Why are we with them if you don't trust them?"

Sonia tightened the cloak around her shoulders, whispering, "We trust until we cannot."

Now Avalynn was doubly worried. Turning away from Sonia, she stared into the fire, but its warmth did nothing to chase away the cold fear creeping through her. The question had already left her lips, but she wished she could take it back. She shouldn't have asked Sonia anything.

The next day unfolded the same. The steady rhythm of hooves against the earth filled the silence. But as they rode, the landscape shifted. The jagged, dry expanses of the Sublands softened, giving way to rolling meadows.

Grass rippled in the breeze like waves on a green sea, dotted with wildflower bursts swaying in the breeze. The musk of clover and honeysuckle was a balm to Avalynn's nose, reminding her of the place she used to call home. The serene scenery contrasted with the curling tension in her chest.

Lady Verona raised her hand, slowing her pace. She shielded her eyes. "There." She pointed to the horizon. "Dust."

With a squint, Avalynn detected the brown haze rising against the blue sky—travelers ahead. Her heart quickened, figuring it was the other house's carriages.

Lady Sonia's horse trotted in a circle. "Rhyka and I should go back." She studied the horizon where the dust plumed. "I feel it is the best move."

Avalynn's heart sank. Sonia was leaving her? She needed her now more than ever. "Lady Sonia, I trust your judgment. But are you sure? A witch like yourself, even Rhyka, would prove most valuable when encountering the other houses."

"Valuable, but mostly triggering, I fear." Sonia's horse pulled up beside Avalynn. "Rhyka and I will stay close in case you need us. You know how to contact me."

"I do?" she asked. The question sounded dumb against her ears. She knew, but she didn't exactly trust herself with what she had newly learned.

"You do." Lady Sonia nodded.

With a grunt, Rhyka agreed. "We do not know the true intentions of the challenge seekers. Staying out of the way, for now, will only help you."

"Very well," Lady Verona said, cutting the conversation short. "Avalynn and I will continue on our way." She spurred on her horse. "Ride!"

Avalynn tightened her grip on the reins. She gave her horse a nudge. The sword strapped to her back shifted with the sudden motion. The meadow blurred as she rode into a full gallop. The wind whipped against her face as hooves thundered, shaking the calm.

As they closed the distance, three carriages came into full view, their ornate wooden frames jostling over the uneven terrain. The crest-laden banners of the Brunt, Lind, and Baffin houses flapped in the wind—the Brunt's with its sprawling oak tree and white-painted B, the Lind's with the elk antlers and red-painted L, and the Baffin's with its bluebonnet flower and black-painted B. Of course, there was no Stromm mountain peak and tree-lined forest with a gold painted S. She had once held so much pride for that banner. Now, it all meant something else to her. Something dark and cunning.

She glanced at Verona. Did the Sublands even have a banner? She didn't think so.

The travelers within the carriages must've noticed their approach. The convoy slowed to a halt, the horses stamping and braying nervously.

Avalynn drew her horse to a stop alongside Lady Verona. Her pulse pounded in her ears as she scanned the scene. They knew her only as a Stromm. What would they think when they saw her? What would they do to the newly discovered remaining heir to Strong Haven and ally to the Sublanders?

Lady Verona dismounted and approached. "I am Lady Verona, Steward of the Sublands," she called out with caution in her tone. "I seek an audience with the leaders of the convoy."

The middle carriage's door swung open. A tall figure with cherry-red hair stepped out. Avalynn did a double take. Selene Baffin of Sand Bluff? She was the leader of the group? Impossible.

Selene's green eyes narrowed on Avalynn. She snapped her fingers. A servant from the carriage behind stepped out. He scurried over, running to her with a small fabric stool. He placed it on the dirt, and Selene fluffed her purple dress. Then she sat, clearing her throat. "I am Selene Baffin, of Sand Bluff, representative of House Lind and House Brunt, and my own house, of course. I carry the necessary seals in my satchel."

"What's the meaning of this?" Avalynn hopped from her horse and stomped over.

With a syrupy smile, Selene answered, "When my beloved Eiric met his untimely passing, I became betrothed to his younger sibling, Heiric, who is unwell and unable to travel. So, I am here in his stead with his house's full backing and authority."

"Heiric?" Avalynn burst out. "He's half your age!"

Selene ignored Avalynn, keeping her attention on Verona. "As for the Brunts, they were scrambling for a representative to replace Finnian. Graciously, I volunteered to step in during the interim." She looked Avalynn up and then down. "Not that it is any of your concern. You have no house. You have no place on the council." She shooed Avalynn away, turning toward Lady Verona.

"Dearest lady, what audience do you seek with me?" Selene asked.

Lady Verona clasped her hands behind her back. Her nostrils flared as she glanced at Avalynn. "My companion and I have it on good authority that House Lind, House Brunt, and House Baffin are challenging the Summit Range hunt results."

Selene raised her fingers, inspecting her nails. "Yes, of course we are. Our forces are gathering as we speak. We will attack, should my talks with the Stromms fail, which I expect." She rolled her eyes. "That horrid Mateo Stromm came in dead last."

"And you"—she pointed at Avalynn—"whatever your surname is, you deceived him and came in first." She waved off Avalynn. "We don't really care about you. We care about Mateo's head and Stromm Palace. And we will have it. Three houses against one. Strength in numbers and all that. We will not fail."

"Is that so?" Avalynn muttered. Selene breathed her own stink. Or she was way more clever than Avalynn thought? Or maybe someone pulled Selene's puppet strings?

"One more thing..." Selene's eyes widened, staring at the hilt poking from Avalynn's cloak. "I want that sword."

"I think not." Avalynn stepped back, her hand itching to run the blade straight through Selene's smug face.

"We are not negotiating for weapons," Lady Verona answered with a curt tone. "But if the Stromms fail to recognize the Sublands as the hunt victor, we stand ready to join the quest for Mateo's head."

Avalynn glared at Verona. What in thunderation was she talking about? They were on a mission to *rescue* Mateo, not destroy him. She shut down that idea in her mind yet kept her silence. Surely, Verona had a plan. Right? Or was this part of Verona and Rhyka's traitorous agenda?

"Ooh, so tempting." Selene's smile widened. "But why would you do that to someone who used to be one of your own? A Sublander?"

That's exactly what Avalynn wanted to know.

"To save the Sublands from banishment and gain a rightful seat at the table of whoever takes control of Faevenly after the Stromms are ousted." Verona frowned. "My people are dying, and we need healing seeds." She glanced at Avalynn. "If I have to sacrifice a former Sublander like Mateo to save them, then I will."

Avalynn conceded in her mind that Camilla was right. Lady Verona didn't care for Mateo in the slightest.

"Hmm." Selene crossed her legs, bouncing her top foot. "It would behoove us to have the great Lady Verona's sword on our side. But I want something."

"What is it?" Lady Verona asked.

Selene's smile deepened as her gaze settled on Avalynn. "When the Stromms bend, you will give me that sword. In return, I will give you Mateo to do with as you will."

Avalynn's breath caught. Her mind raced. The nerve. She narrowed her stare on the horrid harpy. The sword at her back contained more than steel and power—it was part of Avalynn. It carried the weight of her father's bravery and her mother's sacrifice. It possessed a power that could change everything. She couldn't give it up. Not to sniveling Selene or anyone.

The blade was hers by blood and by right, a symbol of power. She couldn't risk it falling into the wrong hands. Yet the idea of Mateo—his life hanging by a thread— twisted her insides like a cruel vice. She couldn't lose him again. But she also couldn't part with the sword. She'd have to find another path to saving Mateo.

She straightened her shoulders. Heat burned in her chest. "You will never touch this sword." She'd strike Selene down on that plush stool if she could. "Not in this life, and not in the next."

A cackle burst from the harpy. "I'll get it from you one way or another... Sublander." She drew out the word *Sublander* like a slur. Avalynn fought to resist the urge to slap Selene's annoying face.

The harpy turned her eyes back on Verona and nodded. "On behalf of my house, the Brunts, and the Linds, I accept your offer. You prove your worth by helping us take down the Stromms and Mateo. They'll change the hunt results, or we'll force them to do it. When we succeed, the Sublands will have a seat at the table. And your precious seeds too."

Dusting herself off, Selene got up and climbed into her carriage. And, the caravan continued.

Avalynn stomped over to Lady Verona. "There is zero chance anyone will touch my sword. And there's no way I'm helping anyone take down Mateo."

"I expected no less." Verona kept her stone-cold expression, her horse snorting. "We play our parts. We'll come out of this in one piece, including Mateo."

CHAPTER TEN

The library doors opened, and Lily, the young princess, skipped in. She wore a ruffled purple dress with a sparkling skirt. Her long silver hair stretched back in a trio of braids. She halted when she spotted Mateo. Her eyes widened, and her mouth opened. "Dawn's blessings to you, Brother." A rosy pink flushed her cheeks. She batted her eyelashes like butterfly wings.

Mateo paused his reading, tipping his head at the princess. "You may call me Mateo." He wasn't ready for anyone else to call him brother. That title belonged to Floriana and Camilla. He wasn't ready to abandon them.

"Okay, Mateo," she said, smiling with a curtsy.

The princess moved to the far end of the room and sat at one of the long tables. She opened her book but held it low. Her eyes flicked between him and the pages. But he didn't want an audience.

He returned to the shelf filled with Faevenly's history books, removing a few. He returned to his seat, with his back facing her. The queen had charged him with learning about the dragons in the North. She feared for his life now that the other houses were moving on the palace. He feared for his life too.

The pages of a book closed, rustling filled the air, followed by light footsteps. Lily approached the shelves again, stayed there a few seconds, and then slid into the seat across from him. "What are you reading?" she asked, tilting her head.

He hesitated, not wanting to scare her. "I'm researching dragons. The queen asked me to protect the palace and everyone in it."

"Everyone?" She batted her long lashes. "Even me?"

"Yes, even you." A most precocious one. If only she would leave.

She tapped her chin. "You know, I remember a book about dragons." She dashed to the shelves, climbed on a stool, and plucked out a book. She brought it to him with her chest puffed out and her smile wide. "This might contain something useful to you."

He took the large book, running a hand over the crinkled cover. "Thank you, Lily."

"You are most welcome, Broth—I mean, Mateo." She left the library with haste, leaving Mateo alone with the tome.

He eyed the gold-embossed title, *Mysteries of the North: Relics, Creatures, and Magic*. He opened the book, sending the scent of stale parchment and dried herbs into the air. He studied the uneven hand-cut pages. How old was this? Inside, the ink was a faded black. Intricate illustrations adorned the margins—dragons of all sizes, spindly runes, and detailed maps of icy, desolate landscapes. This was not a book for casual reading, but rather a guide for ancient kings, queens, and their witches.

Flipping through the pages, Mateo stopped at an elaborate sketch of an orange-and-red-petaled flower with a black stem. It had jagged, silver-edged leaves with curling tips, resembling flames. Beneath it, bold letters spelled "pyrosia."

He read the text out loud. "Pyrosia: a flower associated with dragons. Acts as lure and sedative. The leaves emit a scent that drives dragons into a euphoric state, lowering their aggression and focusing their attention on the source of the aroma. Older dragons are more unpredictable under its influence, but for younger ones, the effect is almost hypnotic. Those who come across the plant must proceed with caution as the effect on other animals is not fully known."

Excitement buzzed in his stomach like a beehive. If they could find pyrosia, they could control the dragons. He closed the book. His fingers drummed on the table. This provided the answer they needed.

Scooping up the book, he left the library and headed for the garden, where the queen took her tea. As he walked, Maid Penny trailed behind, as usual. At first, he had resisted her assistance. But over time, he found her surprisingly helpful.

Instead of sitting with her drink, he found the queen pacing the garden. Her hands fidgeted in front of her. Her distant gaze and her stiff posture looked as if she were waiting for something—or someone.

"My queen," he called as he neared.

She stopped, turned, and smiled. "Ah, my son," she said. Her eyes darted to the book in his hands. "Have you found something of interest?"

"I believe I have." He held out the book, happy to have the answer she sought. "It's a flower called pyrosia. It's used on dragons as both a lure and a sedative. If we locate it, we should be able to influence the dragons and bend them to our will." He leaned forward, overcome with the possibilities. "This will keep all Stromms safe."

The queen paused. Her fingers halted their restless wringing. Her expression flickered, turning unreadable as her gaze shifted away. "Pyrosia..." The word left her lips in a whisper as though she tested its sound. Then she nodded, her focus returning to him. "Keep researching it, then. The dragons are only part of the picture."

A strand of her long dark hair shifted with the wind. She tucked it behind her sharp, pointed ear. "There's something else."

"What is it?" Mateo asked, moving the book from one hand to the other.

"Our lookout reports that the Linds, Brunts, and Baffins will arrive this evening. We must be ready." Her firm voice betrayed a hint of fear. "Your father and I will have a feast prepared for them. It will be a celebratory gathering before the formal assembly in the morning. We need to appear welcoming yet remain cautious."

His brows furrowed. "A feast?" His blood boiled. "If they want my head, why not let them ask for it right away? Then we can shut them down!"

"Why not?" She wrapped her hands around his arm. "Because you must be introduced as the heir. They must see us standing beside you." She touched the pendant around his neck. "It's time they know who you are." She pulled out her pendant. "Who we are."

A heavy silence settled between them. The garden's peaceful surroundings seemed distant compared to the thickening air. He moved his hand on top of hers with a nod. Her wisdom and planning made sense. The welcome feast would be more than a formal introduction —it would be a turning point. And no matter what, he would be ready.

Mateo stood in front of the full-length mirror, not recognizing himself. His hands hovered over the royal tunic the queen had sent him. The luxurious crimson fabric shimmered under the light, the gold thread embroidered across the chest in intricate, sweeping patterns. His fingers brushed over the material. The fine silk slipped beneath his touch. He had never been one for opulence. As a Sublander, he had been raised to value utility over luxury. The stark simplicity of his homeland had always suited him fine. But now, as he prepared for the official meeting with the Brunts, Linds, and Baffins in his new role, he understood the importance of appearances.

They were here to judge him, to measure him. He couldn't afford to show weakness.

He slipped on matching dark pants and then threaded the belt through the loops. The layers of clothing felt foreign at first, the weight of the fine materials unfamiliar. But as the garments settled around him, he began to feel the shift. He wasn't simply Mateo anymore. He was a prince. He was heir to the Stromm throne, and this attire symbolized power and status.

Maid Penny entered after a knock. "My lord, you look quite the part."

"The part?" He didn't even know what 'the part' really was. "Do I?" His voice sounded unsure even to his own ears.

She paused, meeting his eyes in the mirror. "You do," she said firmly. "The king and queen will be pleased."

"Right." His gaze fell to the gold-tipped boots that completed the outfit. By any standards, they seemed too much. But the other houses weren't only coming for a feast—they were coming to decide his fate. The queen thought this outfit would help his cause. Who was he to argue?

Maid Penny followed his line of sight. "The boots are a nice touch."

With a deep breath, Mateo straightened his back and adjusted the layers one last time. The tunic felt heavy, but not as he expected. It wasn't a burden—more like a reminder of the stakes. He looked at Penny, who stood patiently beside him. "I guess there's no going back now."

"No, my lord prince. There isn't," she said.

Mateo took a steadying breath. He walked down the corridor, descended the staircase, and approached the receiving room. Inside, the queen and king were dressed in crimson and gold too. Dramatic crowns of gold mixed with crystals and gems adorned their heads. They sat upon formal evening thrones carved from rich, ebony-hued wood. The intricate detailing along the armrests and high backs depicted vines and leaves. The dark, polished finish gleamed in the candlelight, exuding an air of foreboding and authority, as if the thrones bore the weight of the Stromm legacy.

Lily stood beside the queen. Her eyes lit up at his presence. She, too, wore the same crimson. Ignoring her, Mateo took his place beside the king. His posture remained stiff yet composed. To the side, Raelor lingered in the shadows. His crystal eyes watched with quiet intensity. The room felt heavy. For the first time, Mateo understood how much was riding on this evening—and on him.

He prayed to the Sun, Moon, and Stars he wouldn't botch it. But he knew he would somehow.

CHAPTER ELEVEN

Avalynn rode in silence, gripping the reins so tightly her hands ached. The rhythmic clopping of hooves on the gravel path did little to soothe her frenetic nerves.

Ahead, Selene's carriage rolled steadily forward. Its finish gleamed, catching the occasional ray of sunlight. Beside her, Lady Verona rode. Like a blank slate, her face betrayed nothing. Avalynn envied that composure, wondering if her expression matched. Probably not.

Her thoughts tangled, and her heart beat faster with every step closer to her former home. The spires of Stromm Palace grew larger, jutting into the sky like jagged blades. The sight brought back a flood of memories she wished she could bury. Practicing her hunting skills in the training circle, exploring the gardens, reading until dawn in the library. With their frosty glares and clipped words, the king and queen had treated her like an intruder rather than family. They had tolerated her presence, nothing more. Finally, she knew why.

She didn't belong to them, and somewhere deep inside, they had sensed it. The idea of walking into their court made her stomach turn. What would they do when they saw her? The one they used to call daughter? But that wasn't her worst fear.

Mateo. His name played in her mind like a haunting refrain. How would he react to seeing her in the flesh? Avalynn the betrayer. Would his face twist with anger like it had when she saw him in her spirit form? Would he turn away and refuse to even acknowledge her? Or do something worse? He was the Stromm prince now.

The uncertainty gnawed at her. Each possibility more agonizing than the last. How could she face him after betraying him? That thought clawed at her more than anything else, a sharp, unbearable weight. She wasn't sure which terrified her more—him hating her or not caring at all.

"Remember, Avalynn, we will enter last," Lady Verona said. "Let Selene and her entourage take the room's attention."

She knew the plan. But now, with the palace looming and the gate a stone's throw away, things were getting real.

She lifted the cloak's hood over her head, as did Verona, and they followed the circular path to the entrance. Guards and maids rushed out to tend to the carriages. Avalynn led Verona to the hitching post. Staying toward the back, they secured their horses.

A voice she didn't recognize called out. She craned

her neck and saw a tall, thin fae. She had lavender hair pulled up in a tight ball on the top of her head. A replacement for Maid Nia, no doubt.

"Welcome, distinguished guests," the fae said. "I am Maid Elizabeth. House Stromm welcomes each of you. Please follow me to the receiving room for the royal family's formal presentation. The celebratory feast will follow. The assembly addressing your concerns will take place after sunrise."

Murmuring broke out, and everyone started shuffling forward. A string of violins started playing inside. Selene's maddening voice rose above all others. She ordered her escorts and attendants to remain behind her.

Avalynn kept her gaze down, tugging her hood snug. Her heart beat like a war drum. She needed to make it inside.

She stepped inside the palace entry. The sweet floral fragrances consumed her senses. So that's what Mateo had meant when he called the scents suffocating. Did he still think they were too much? Or was he used to it? Mateo Stromm probably enjoyed it now.

They sorted into a long line, inching forward. Finally, they reached the receiving room. The marble floor's gold flecks were dazzling beneath her dirty boots. The music played louder. She heard the voices of the king and queen greeting Selene. But Avalynn couldn't hear a word they were saying. One glance upward, and her eyes found him instantly. He stood tall beside the king. Mateo.

Her lips parted. The sight of him stole her breath, sending butterflies alight inside of her stomach. His high cheekbones and strong jaw framed his face. Devastatingly handsome. Slightly vicious. His long, dark hair shimmered like silk under the chandeliers' glow. His steely-gray eyes pierced the room's stillness.

He wore the finest crimson and gold threads. The rich fabrics were perfectly tailored to his broad shoulders and lean yet muscular frame. Every detail—from the intricate embroidery on his tunic to the polished boots—spoke of a prince ready to claim his place.

His piercing eyes stopped scanning the crowd. He fixed on Selene like a hunter finding his kill. His eyes cut sharp as if decimating her where she stood. Good. He hadn't forgotten what she was like. Maybe, just maybe, he wasn't entirely lost to her after all.

The line ahead dwindled, one by one, until only she and Lady Verona remained. This was it. Time for the big reveal. The steward stepped forward, her movements smooth and deliberate. She pulled back the hood of her cloak, revealing herself to the room. A ripple of tension followed as Avalynn lowered hers too.

Lily gasped, her hands flying to her mouth. So, she hadn't missed her. The music stopped. The king and queen sat frozen. Their regal composure masked the tempest clearly brewing. Raelor, ever watchful, emerged from the shadows at the back of the room. Silently, he glided behind the queen like an ominous cloud.

And then there was Mateo. For a moment, the world seemed to hold its breath as his gaze locked on to hers. It was as if no one else existed. The weight of his stare pressed on her—the heat, the fury, the questions, and the unspoken words. Time slowed, and the room blurred. All she could see was him—burning her with a look that made her heart thunder and her breath catch.

"Why are *you* here?" the queen asked in a low, menacing tone.

"My queen." Lady Verona bowed. "The Sublands are here—"

"Not you!" The queen sprang to her feet like a viper poised to strike. She pointed at Avalynn. "You!"

Sun, Moon, and Stars. Her. The queen was talking to her. It was the most words her once-mother had spoken to her at one time. She stepped forward. She held her head high and pulled her shoulders back. She was House Strong's last surviving member. The Only One. She needed to remember that. "I am here as a champion of the hunt and the Sublands' representative. Avalynn Strong, of the noble House Strong."

A rush of whispers rippled throughout the grand room. A chuckle came from Selene. The king raised his hand, and the crowd fell silent. She swallowed her fear. What was he up to?

Stepping forward, the king's expression hardened. His eyes moved from her face to the sword on her back, poking through the cloak's opening. "That name does not exist, lowborn." He growled like a feral beast. "Neither does that title. You are a deceiver and a charlatan. You are hereby labeled an enemy of House Stromm and traitor to all of Faevenly."

A shiver of dread crawled down Avalynn's spine. Her thoughts scattered like leaves on a breeze. Was she going to be struck down? Tossed out? Should she reach for her weapon?

She scanned the room for the red-haired madman but didn't see Kragar. Instead, a stocky dwarf stepped forward with thick bushy eyebrows and long blond hair tied back in a thick braid. His axe was strapped to one side, and he rested a hand on the dagger strapped to the other. She had never seen him before. Kragar's replacement?

"What is your order, my king?" the dwarf asked with a wicked smile. His fingers tapped on his dagger.

The king raised his chin, pointing in Avalynn's direction. "To the dungeon!"

Her stomach dropped. No, no, no. Not there. She tried swallowing, but the lump wouldn't go down. If the spirits threatened her in spirit form, what would they do to her in physical form? What would the Stromm guards do to her?

"No," Mateo said. His smooth and powerful voice halted the new Master of the Blade. "Let her stay for the feast. Send her to the dungeon after."

Lily's eyes nearly exploded from her head. "She cannot stay!" Anger and fear were plastered over her tiny face. Just like she thought, dazzled by Mateo and replacing her so easily. She wanted to shake Lily.

The queen hushed Lily with an aggressive pat on the shoulder, then tipped her head in Mateo's direction. "The prince has spoken. The Sublander can stay through the feast and will be sent to the dungeon after." She snapped her fingers two times. "Under the watch of Master Keeth."

A string of violins began playing, and everyone started milling about awkwardly. Of course Selene rushed to Mateo, gushing all over him like the little harpy she was. So much for her wanting his head.

Lady Verona tugged at her sleeve and pulled her aside, Master Keeth staying close.

"We survived our announcement unscathed," Verona whispered, gripping the sword's hilt on her side.

"Survived?" The fear nearly strangled her, the word coming out scratchy and forced. "You call me being branded an enemy and a traitor and ordered to the dungeon, surviving?"

"You will not be going to the dungeon," Verona said as servants filtered through the room. They carried silver trays of lavish foods and drinks aplenty. Verona grabbed a tall glass of wine from a passing tray and downed it. "We will leave here before that happens."

Avalynn turned her nose up at a tray of fresh fruit, her stomach tied in double knots. "Okay, so what do we do?"

"Get information." Verona jerked her chin toward a group of Selene's attendants. Most were young servants, though one wore a longer cape and had a shrewd look on his face. "That taller one. I'm going to talk to him." She kept her hand on her hilt. "You talk to Mateo. Let him know the rescue plan. We make our move when he is ready."

Taking her cue from Verona, Avalynn snatched a goblet of wine from a passing tray and gulped it in two chugs. The rescue plan was simple, in theory. Tell Mateo they had come for him and then bust out of Stromm Palace. But would he want to go with them? He appeared wrapped up in his birthright, clothed in full royal

Stromm regalia. How much of him was still the Mateo she knew? How much was a carefully constructed facade? And did he need rescuing after all?

Bells chiming cut through her thoughts. An attendant weaved through the room. All eyes shifted as the king and queen rose from their thrones. Their hands joined in a clasp as they glided toward the adjoining dining hall.

Avalynn followed in their wake, her heart heavy with what was to come. Sun, Moon, and Stars. Please, let her break through to the real Mateo.

CHAPTER TWELVE

T he dining hall shimmered with candlelight. The golden glow glinted off silver goblets and polished crystal. Selene followed Mateo's every move like a wolf bitch in heat, sitting beside him at the long table. All she wanted were his riches and title. He'd make sure she never saw neither. Lady Verona and Avalynn were fools to join Selene. Or were they playing at a different game?

Selene leaned closer, her words a constant thrum of noise that grated on his last nerve. "Houses ... the hunt ... Faevenly ... alliances ..." She raised her voice slightly. "Are you even listening to me, Mateo?"

Her shrill tone pierced his hazy mind. Still, he didn't turn to her. He couldn't. His focus was locked on Avalynn, seated at the far end of the hall, her hood cast back and her face unhidden and defiant. He couldn't think straight. His mind had tumbled into a frenzied mix of wanting to toss her behind metal bars and wanting to wrap her in his arms and kiss her. She wouldn't look at him, but that didn't matter. Her mere presence swirled the tempest in his chest, a whirlwind he couldn't yet navigate.

Here she was, after everything. She had betrayed him. But Mateo battled with something far more dangerous. Longing. Though she had a new name and a new title, she hadn't truly changed. Her hair a shade lighter and streaked with silver, and her ears were not quite as pointed, but her posture remained poised with the same strength that had drawn him to her.

His jaw clenched as he stole another glance at her. She had no right to appear so calm and composed when his damned world had been turned upside down. Did she even care that she would be sent to the dungeon after dinner?

Selene cleared her throat. Her perfectly manicured nails tapped against her goblet. "You're ignoring me."

"I'm thinking," he replied curtly, dragging his gaze away from Avalynn and forcing himself to look at her overly painted face.

"Oh? About what?" Her lips curved into a knowing smirk, but it only irritated him further.

"Things that do not concern you," he said. "Now, leave me."

She stood with a huff, her chair scraping across the floor. She threw her balled napkin on the table. "You have insulted the wrong person, Mateo Stromm."

He paid her no heed, shifting his attention back to the far end of the table. He wasn't sure what burned hotter—Avalynn's presence, defying him and his birth family in their own palace, or the ache of wanting to be near her and touch her.

She finally raised her eyes. Those blue eyes made him forget who he was and who she had been. He only saw her heart. In that precise moment, he realized the most unsettling truth of all... she would be his undoing.

She rose from her seat, then walked to the other side of the room, Master Keeth trailing her every move. She approached the double door that led to the gardens and stepped outside.

This was his chance. Mateo left his place, his boots striking the marble floor as he crossed the room. He yanked the new Master of the Blade aside. "You are relieved."

The dwarf blinked. "But my lord prince, the queen has tasked me with keeping watch over the Sublander."

"*I* am tasking you now." Mateo inched closer. "You will leave the Sublander to me."

Master Keeth hesitated, eyes shifting, and then bowed. "Yes, my lord."

The hum from the dining hall faded with each step into the garden. The air shifted, cooler and fresher, carrying the sweet aroma of night-blooming flowers. Overhead, the sky stretched out like a tapestry. Stars scattered across its surface, sparkling like shards of broken glass. A soft breeze stirred the branches of towering trees. The leaves rustled like whispers in the dark wind.

Mateo slowed his steps. The palace gardens did not compare to the Summit Range Forest. But the spicy scent of damp earth and fresh blossoms took him there. Every moment with Avalynn in the hunt rushed forth. Sitting with her by the fire, opening up to her like he'd never done with anyone. Fighting side by side. Her injury, riding the Enbarr together while holding her for his life's sake. And then, their time at the Green Falls. Her kiss, smell, and taste. It all came rushing back.

The anger, the resentment, and betrayal that consumed him slipped away. Now, those feelings were replaced by an ache so deep it might swallow him. He needed her like the sun needed the moon. Forever connected, they could lie together, again, under the stars.

Avalynn paused near a spraying fountain. The moonlight illuminated her perfect profile. He tightened his fists at his sides, steadying himself. Too many truths had been revealed after the hunt. Too much trust shattered between them. Still, everything that happened at the hunt spoke to him. The pull to confront her—to ask her everything—became unbearable.

"Avalynn," he whispered.

She tipped her head. "Hello, Mateo." The breeze stirred her braided hair, sending loose strands across her face. He reached out and brushed them back, tucking them behind her ear. His fingers lingered for just a moment as he remembered every intimate touch between them.

"Ears not as pointed, and now you have a white streak." He clasped his hands behind his back, hiding his trembling fingers. "What else has changed?"

"My name and my title, like you heard inside. Everything else is still the same. And you?" Her eyes landed on his necklace. "I see you've embraced your Stromm heritage and wear their emblem." She reached out to touch the pendant, but his hand blocked her.

She stepped back, the corners of her mouth downturned and her brows stitched together. "You want to be one of them? Is that what this is?"

Deflecting, as usual. As if this whole mess wasn't about her. Wasn't her fault. "Why did you do it?" he demanded, heat rising through his chest. "Why did you betray me and leave me for dead?"

"Mateo..." She gulped, wringing her hands in front of her. "I promise, I thought I was saving you."

"Saving me?" He laughed and folded his arms. "By sending me to my death?"

"Listen to me." She placed her hands on his forearms. "If we had crossed the finish line together, the king would've found a way to kill us both. I thought that if I won, then I'd be in a position of power to help you and the Sublanders." She squeezed, locking eyes with him. "I have spent time with them. I know how wonderful they are. Manny, Camilla, and Floriana. And Mateo, they don't care about your name. They love you and want you back home. You are their son. That's why I'm here... for you."

Her words swirled in his mind, each one striking like a stone cast into an already rippling pond. Her urgent plea tangled with his anger, his love, and the gnawing question of who he truly was. Stromm? Vela? Royalty? Sublander scum?

He brushed her hands off and turned his back to her. He touched the pendant around his neck. Did he want to be a Stromm? It felt as natural as stepping into a role he'd been rehearsing for his entire life, even if he hadn't known it. Even if he initially hated it.

Still, he couldn't deny the ones who raised him. Manny. His mother, Faeryn. He couldn't deny his sisters, Camilla and Floriana. Could he?

He faced her. He needed to know more. "Who switched us at birth? Who robbed me of my upbringing?"

She glanced down, holding her gaze on the ground before looking back up at him. "The other houses are here to challenge the hunt results. If they win, the Sublands become the victor. But you, the Stromms, will be declared the loser. They want your head, Mateo. Selene confirmed the other houses are readying their forces. But if you side with us, we can get out of here right now. Together."

The raw storm unleashed inside him. Mateo readied himself to cut down whoever had taken his birthright. Through clenched teeth, he said, "Who robbed me of my name?"

A growl tore through the night, and Stormshroud bounded from the garden's darkness. The wolf's black-and-white fur gleamed in the moonlight as she planted herself firmly in front of Avalynn. Her teeth bared and eyes blazing.

Mateo froze, his rage colliding with a searing ache. That used to be *his* wolf. The bond they had shared was unshakable—until it was severed by Avalynn. Now Stormy guarded her as though *he* was a threat. It gutted him more than any blade ever could.

"Stormy," Avalynn said. "It's Mateo." She moved in front of the wolf. "He won't hurt me."

Wouldn't he? His hands shook at the thought. No. He didn't want to hurt her. But the fiery pain inside of him still burned. So he did the only thing that made sense.

He closed the gap between them, took her face in his hands, and kissed her in an unrestrained clash of rage and longing. His lips crushed against hers, demanding and desperate, as though trying to pour into her all the words he couldn't say. Raw heat flared between them. Her hands wrapped around his neck and gripped him like an anchor. The world around them vanished. No court, no kingdom, no hunt, no betrayal—just passion igniting between them, burning away the newfound destinies that had separated them.

Hollering broke out from the palace. Boots pounded the crushed gravel garden path. "Remove her!" the queen screeched.

Mateo pulled back, chest heaving. He stared into her beautiful blue eyes. His fingers traced her face. "Go and promise me you will never come back."

She yanked him closer. "No, Mateo. We don't have to do that. I have power. I have the sword. I'm the Only One; they can't hurt me," she rushed out. "Please, come with me now. I'm begging you."

Mateo's jaw tightened. She didn't understand. The belief in her voice wasn't bravery. It was recklessness. If she stayed, it wouldn't be the king and queen that broke her. It would be him. His fury, his confusion, the darkness that clawed at his mind every time he looked at her. His name ruled him now—Mateo Stromm. It belonged to him whether he wanted it or not.

"It's not them hurting you that worries me." His words came out low. The unbridled truth cut through the chaos within him. "Don't you see? It's me who will be your end."

Her lips parted with a gasp. "No, Mateo." Her eyes welled with tears. "No. I refuse to believe that."

The rhythmic clatter of boots striking the garden path reverberated through the air. Each heavy step struck the jarring chord of impending danger. The guards broke into the clearing, fanning out like a tightening snare. Master Keeth stood at the forefront, his axe steady and ready to strike.

"Take her!" the queen ordered.

A sharp whinny split the tension. Silverhoof burst into the garden like a streak of radiant moonlight. The Enbarr reared, pawing the air as Avalynn reached for the mane. Without hesitation, she swung herself up onto Silverhoof's back.

"Go!" Mateo hollered, smacking the horse's flank to spur her into motion.

The horse leaped forward, hooves thundering against the crushed gravel as she carried Avalynn into the night's shadows, away from the encroaching guards and the queen's dangerous screams. Stormshroud bounded away next, but not before a quick glance back at Mateo. Did Stormy want him to go with them? It was too late for that now.

Mateo stood motionless, watching until they disappeared. A hand latched on to his arm, dug in, and pulled him around.

"You let her go!" the king yelled.

"I told you not to lay hands on me." He gripped the king's fingers and pried them off with a growl.

The queen barked orders for the guards to give chase. She separated Mateo and the king. "We have guests inside the palace. Stop this nonsense." She smoothed her long dark hair and raised her chin high, leveling Mateo with a stare. Her lips trembled as if she held back whatever she wanted to say. "We will return to our guests as if nothing has happened." She took a deep breath, held it, and then blew out the excess. "And we'll discuss our next steps after the feast."

Mateo ignored everyone when he returned to the dining hall. Foolish chatter, looks from Selene, and the penetrating gaze from Raelor were of no concern to him. Fiddling with his pendant, he kept to himself. His mind replayed every moment with Avalynn in the garden. She claimed she wanted to save him and escape the palace with him. But she also knew who switched them and wouldn't tell him. She protected someone, but who? And why?

The night dragged on until, finally, the last guest left. They were escorted to the guest houses at the far end of the palace grounds. And when the dining hall was empty, he found himself alone with the king, the queen, and Raelor.

The queen tapped her fingers on the table. "Raelor,

please see if Master Keeth has returned with our prisoner."

"Yes, my queen." He bowed low.

A chuckle came from Mateo. "He will not return with her."

"And why not?" she asked, slapping her hand on the table.

He rose from his seat, circling the room. "That was an Enbarr she was riding." Standing near the glass doors, he looked out at the garden. "She's probably back in the Sublands by now."

Mateo hoped Avalynn rode far away to the Sublands, to tell his former family he was lost to them. The sooner they forgot about him, the better. The blood in his veins could not be ignored.

The queen sighed. "She will be found. If not now, then later." She rubbed her forehead. "Now, about tomorrow. That fool Selene will demand your head on behalf of the other houses. She wants my throne. She and her family always have. I fear you are at grave risk, my son."

He'd grown tired of always being at risk. Tired of struggling. He pressed his forehead against the window's cool glass. He'd never possessed power before but now had plenty. As a Stromm, he had riches and forces. He even had Raelor. But it wasn't enough. The challengers stood three houses strong. The odds were stacked against them. He had already researched the dragons. Now, he needed to act.

He turned around to face them. "Dragons. I will set out for them tonight. No one will stand against House Stromm with dragons on our side."

The queen glanced at the king and Raelor before bringing her gaze back to Mateo. "It's the only way, I fear. Especially with Avalynn on the loose. She is especially dangerous."

Raelor rubbed his chin. "She won't matter with dragons in our arsenal. We would be invincible."

After a long exhale, the queen rose from her seat. "It will be a perilous endeavor. But attending the assembly tomorrow would be worse."

Mateo resumed circling the room. If the other houses were gathering their forces like Avalynn had said, then the queen was right—attending the assembly would be foolhardy. He needed to leave at once. Who knew how long it'd take to find the pyrosia, locate the dragons, and train them to do his bidding. Assuming they could even be trained. "I will leave tonight, straight away."

"We support you, my son." The king folded his arms across his chest, nodding.

With renewed purpose, Mateo made his way out of the dining hall. He barked orders to Maid Penny, who'd been standing with her back toward the wall. "I'll need the fastest horse, a pack of food and water, and a traveling cloak. Meet me outside with my things."

Mateo strode through the palace corridors. His pendant rested heavily against his chest. It reminded him of his responsibility to his new family and his role as the lord prince of House Stromm. But, for the first time since he'd been at the palace, a surge of fresh energy roiled through him. It wasn't anger or confusion but excitement. A hunt for the pyrosia and the dragons—this was familiar territory, where survival depended on instinct and skill, not politics and deceit.

Alone in his bedchamber, he stripped out of the ridiculous royal attire. He flung the clothes in the corner. He put on his outfit from the hunt and stuffed a change of clothes in a bag. He hung a pouch at his belt for the pyrosia, tugging it to make sure it was secure.

He'd never been to the Wild North and longed to see it. He imagined the crisp and biting air, the warming scent of pine and moss, and the quiet hum of nature's rhythm. The adventure of the Wild North called to him like an old friend. Tracking something deadly and untamed thrilled Mateo. He smiled, thinking of who he used to be before bloodlines and betrayal overshadowed his view.

He scanned his bedchamber, making sure he had everything. His eyes landed on the carved wooden cross by his bedside. A chill shook him. How long had it been there? His hand moved to his empty pocket. His stare remained on the religious symbol of the human who'd raised him. Manny. Those beliefs were foreign, and didn't belong to him. Not anymore.

Faith is a warrior. *Pfft.* That concept had never helped the Sublands. Or him for that matter. Faith had seen him lose the hunt and get thrown in the dungeon. It saw loved ones get sick and die. He touched the pendant at his chest. Power is a warrior.

He strode across the room, snatched the wooden cross, and tossed it in the fireplace's dying embers. He left his bedchamber without a second glance, hurrying down the stairs where the king and queen waited.

The queen took his hand. "My son. Your horse and your things are ready in the wild area of the garden, away from our guests so that you are not seen." She and the king started walking him through the palace toward the rear exit through the cookroom.

"Your steed will have your weapons too," the king added. "The finest sword, a shield, a spear, and a bow and arrows. Master Keeth will join you. He returned, without Avalynn, as you suspected. And no sign of Lady Verona either. Keeth will protect you, my son."

Mateo turned and faced the king. "I need no protection."

"Of course you do." The king pounded his hand in his palm. "You are heir to the throne. We are not sending you without a protector by your side."

He didn't like it. But maybe the blond-haired dwarf could be useful. "Fine." Outside with the fresh air invigorating him, he nodded. "I will return as soon as possible."

The king stepped back while the queen moved forward. She placed her fingertips on his pendant and then hugged him. "May the Sun, Moon, and Stars be with you." She kissed his cheek. "My brave son."

He hugged her back and held her for a few seconds. Everyone had the queen wrong. Beneath the ruthless exterior was a lady who cared deeply, especially for him. He could feel it in the way she held him—firm yet protective, as if shielding him from his doubts. She wasn't only a ruler. She was his mother, and she cared in a way no one else could. "Thank you, Mother."

He picked his way through the grounds, staying in the shadows. When he got to the garden's edge. The manicured landscape gave way to untamed brush, and he found a jet-black steed—a beauty with a long, braided mane. He extended his hand, letting the horse sniff him before stroking its muzzle. "Well, hello, boy. Nice to meet you. I'm Mateo." He looked over the bags fastened to the saddle, pulling each one to make sure they were secure.

"Everything is in order, my lord prince." Master Keeth emerged with his own steed, brown colored. Too bad he showed up. Mateo preferred to take the journey alone.

Placing his boot in the stirrup, Mateo swung up onto the saddle. "The king and queen insisted I needed your protection, though I do not."

"May I speak openly?" the dwarf asked.

An interesting question he welcomed. He was tired of all the niceties in the palace. He placed his hands on the pommel of his saddle. "You may."

"I didn't want to be here either, but here we are." He grunted. "So let's make the best of it."

Mateo sat back. He could see the anger brewing in the dwarf's eyes, his bushy eyebrows so close together they looked like a living creature ready to pounce. "Please, do not hold back on my account, dwarf. If you have more to say, then say it."

With a growl, the stocky Master of the Blade pointed his thumb at him. "You are trouble! Butting heads with Kragar and having him cast out! He was my friend!" He leaned over and spat. "I want nothing of that sort from you, you hear me!" he grunted. "You will not call me dwarf either. I have a name!" He pounded his stocky chest. "It's Keeth Graddor. You will call me Keeth, or you will call me Master Keeth. But you will not call me anything else!" He growled. "If you want my help to get you to the North and back in one piece, you won't forget that!"

Mateo raised a brow and nodded. "Of course, Keeth." At least the dwarf had spirit.

"Arrr!" Keeth yelled, pulling on his reins and spurring his horse into a trot.

Mateo followed, and the pair rode out of the garden and into the night, heading north. As the Summit Range mountains loomed, Mateo's thoughts turned from the dragons to Avalynn. The queen's rage had been palpable, and Mateo couldn't shake the fear that even with her powers, Avalynn might underestimate the danger she was in. Sure, she had her plan. And, he had his. Nothing would get in his way. Not even her.

CHAPTER THIRTEEN

The wind whipped through Avalynn's hair as she raced away from Stromm Palace and into the forest. She gripped the Enbarr's silver mane, holding on for dear life. The palace guards' shouts quickly faded, no match for the Enbarr's tremendous speed as Avalynn clung tightly to the mane. Her heart rested in her throat, the weight of what she had left behind pressing against her chest like an anvil.

Mateo had rejected her rescue plan. He said no to *her*. But why would he do that? Her lips still tingled from his unexpected kiss, fierce and desperate, as though he'd poured every word, thought, and feeling he couldn't voice into that fleeting moment. It had stunned her, sparking hope for the briefest second that he would come with her. That he would let her save him. But Mateo slapped the Enbarr, sending her away.

She clutched the mane tighter, the chill of the night air stinging her bare hands. The weight of her sword pressed against her back, steady but cold, offering no comfort. What was she going to do now?

She slowed Silverhoof to a trot. She guided the Enbarr into a wooded grove. She dismounted, her boots sinking into the soft ground. She leaned against Silverhoof, burying her face in the mare's warm neck.

"I'm sorry," she whispered, though she wasn't sure to whom she apologized. Mateo? Herself? For the way everything had unraveled so painfully fast? She seemed to be doing a lot of apologizing lately.

Silverhoof nickered, and Avalynn ran a hand across the Enbarr's sleek neck. "Thank you for showing up when you did."

The solitary grove stilled, save for the rustling leaves and the chirping nightingales. Tall, darkened trees encircled her. The branches intertwined, forming a canopy that let faint moonlight dapple the mossy ground. The cool air remained still; the earthy scent of bark and damp leaves filled her nose. So much like the hunt, but so different.

This time she braved it alone.

She lowered herself to her knees, her cloak pooling around her like a shadow. The ache in her chest swelled as she thought of Mateo. She pressed her hand to her mouth, as if she could hold on to the kiss a little longer, but it was already slipping away, like water through cupped hands.

Tears pricked her eyes, but she refused to let them fall. She had to be strong, even if the world crumbled beneath her. She had to figure out her next move.

Stepping out of the tree cover, her eyes fixed on the

brilliant night sky and half moon. She'd go west to the Sublands. Lady Sonia and Rhyka would be there. Together they'd figure out their next move. Surely Verona would have taken off after learning Avalynn had fled.

She wiped her hands on her cloak and adjusted the sword at her back. She stroked Silverhoof's nose as she steadied herself. "Off to the Sublands, girl."

Silverhoof snorted, her warm breath reassuring. Avalynn took the mane, then climbed back aboard the steed. She nudged the Enbarr forward.

The grove faded behind them. The forest stretched endlessly ahead, vast and uncertain. She took every precaution, avoiding Faevenly's common roads. The Stromm guards wouldn't come this far for her, especially with the Brunts, Linds, and Baffins on the property. But if they did, she must remain hidden.

Silverhoof slowed, coming to a small brook for a drink. Avalynn slid off the steed to quench her thirst too. But she found only a shallow puddle in the streambed. Strange. Had the Mother of Rivers turned away from this land? Avalynn crouched, scooping up what moisture she could. Her brow furrowed. Why had the water stopped flowing here?

"Do you know what happened to the water?" she asked Silverhoof as if she might answer.

"No matter," she mumbled. She'd ask Lady Sonia later.

Back on Silverhoof, she leaned forward, resting her back as fatigue set in. An hour into the trek, Silverhoof's ears twitched. Then her head jerked to the side. Her muscles tensing and nostrils flaring, the Enbarr pawed at the forest floor.

Avalynn straightened. Before she could make sense of the mare's changed demeanor, Silverhoof reared as a pair of horses burst by. She tumbled to the ground with a thud.

"Don't attack!" a voice hollered. It sounded familiar, but she couldn't place it. Someone from Stromm Palace? Or Selene's entourage?

Silverhoof neighed, her warning call slicing through the air, her hooves stomping the earth.

"My horse will end you if you get near!" Avalynn hopped to her feet, removing her sword with a sharp hiss.

The pair of horses circled back, their riders silhouetted by the moonlight. Avalynn blinked, her vision sharpening as they drew closer. What in the Stars? She recognized the familiar lines of Lirien's broad shoulders. His long cloak billowed behind him. She knew Gareth's watchful gaze, even as his steed snorted and pawed.

Her heart clenched at the sight of them, but the sting of anger quickly overtook it. Her blood boiled seeing their faces. "You charged at me!" she snapped, her grip tightening on the sword's hilt.

"We were only trying to catch up with you!" Lirien yelled, his eyes flicking to Silverhoof. The steed's ears remained pinned down, her nostrils flared.

Gareth swung down from his brown horse. His boots struck the ground without sound despite his towering frame. Facing Avalynn, he raised a fist to his chest, moving it in a slow circular motion before dropping it. His expression remained earnest, his mouth downturned.

The gesture was unmistakable—an apology. But she still didn't care for them.

Lirien dismounted and edged in. He wore his silver hair loose down his back. His sharp, angular features were drawn in, brows furrowed, and violet eyes narrowed. "None of us like you. Okay? You are the reason why Mateo is with the Stromms." He huffed and then lowered his voice. "But Camilla sent us."

"Camilla?" She stepped back. Now that was a surprise. Mateo's eldest sister despised Avalynn more than any other.

Nodding, Lirien's jaw tightened. "Camilla doesn't trust Lady Verona or Rhyka. So she sent us to back you up."

Avalynn's mouth parted. "She did?" Camilla had mentioned her distrust of the pair, but to send Mateo's best friends? It might have been a good idea if she hadn't been branded a Stromm traitor and Mateo hadn't chosen to claim his birthright over her and the Sublands. "Well, the two of you can go. Things have changed."

The friends moved in closer. "What do you mean, things have changed?" Lirien asked, looking around. "Why are you alone?"

The faint glow of dawn began stretching across the horizon, softening the night's hard edges. The dark sky lightened to a pale gray. Hints of pink brushed the clouds like delicate strokes from a master painter's hand. The trees around them stood like watchers; their leaves whispered secrets in the cool morning breeze.

Avalynn glanced at the shifting sky while organizing

her thoughts. She exhaled a long, weary sigh. "I escaped from the Stromm Palace," she said, her voice steady but edged with pain. "I tried to get Mateo to come with me, but..." Her gaze dropped to the ground. Her fingers clenched around the sword's hilt. "He didn't want to be rescued. He chose to stay. He chose the Stromms over the Sublands."

Lirien froze, and Gareth shook his head. "No way," Lirien finally said. "Mateo may have their name, but he's a Sublander. A lowborn." He tapped his chest. "He's proud of it. We all are."

Gareth and Lirien turned to each other, their hands moving quickly. She couldn't make out any of the gestures. "What are you saying?"

Lirien faced her again. "We are going to the palace and rescuing Mateo by force." He nodded to Gareth before adding. "Without you."

Her blood boiled. "No. You are not," she snapped.

"Yes, we are," Lirien said.

Then an idea blossomed in her mind. The friends could get through to him despite whatever ridiculous loyalty he had to his birthright. Surely he'd listen to them. But they would need her palace knowledge.

She stepped in front of Lirien, blocking his path to his horse. "You need me. The palace is heavily fortified. Guards are posted everywhere the eye can see. The visiting houses plan conflict. But with my knowledge of the palace, we can pull it off."

"How?" He rolled his eyes. "We can do everything you just said."

"Because." She stepped closer, raising her chin. "I know the hidden passage onto the palace grounds." It was the underground tunnel she and her cousin secretly accessed when they were little. The last time Avalynn tried to find it, she couldn't. But that was a long time ago. With Mateo's friends, she was sure she could find it again.

Lirien turned to Gareth, motioning something more, and then turned back to her. "Fine. We'll go together. But we still don't care for you."

"The feeling is mutual," she said. But then a hovering cloud of doubt doused her lifting spirits. "There's still a chance Mateo won't want to come with us."

"Oh, he'll come with us. Even if we have to knock him unconscious, we'll drag him from that horrid place." Lirien slapped Gareth's arm. "Right?"

Gareth nodded. He used a close fist, moving it up and down.

She looked between the two of them, her pulse quickening. With their help, she could get Mateo out of the palace. But another doubt plagued her. What if he wasn't alone? With her dramatic garden escape, he might have a guard with him at all times. If she knew anything about palace protocol, she knew the Master of the Blade would be clinging to him like a shadow at dusk. "Before we go, I should use my magic to make sure he's not surrounded."

Lirien's brow raised. "So, you *can* wield magic," he said in a hushed tone. He glanced at her sword. "So the stories about the Only One are true?"

She shrugged. "I'm still figuring it out." With the sky

continuing to lighten, the palace would be awakening. "We need to hurry."

Avalynn found a low, moss-covered boulder nestled beneath a towering oak. She strode over, brushing away the dew before sitting. She settled her sword in the sheath at her back and drew her cloak tighter around her shoulders. She eyed Lirien. "Do not harm or leave me," she warned.

"Harm you?" Lirien's eyes bugged. "Look, ice princess, we're not like the Stromms or the highborns you're used to." He nudged Gareth, as if rallying support. "If we say we're going together, then we're going together."

Good to know they possessed honor. Even if they didn't like her.

With a steadying breath, she closed her eyes. She focused. She allowed her mind to reach outward like a thread weaving through the waking world. *Mateo. Go to him.*

She pictured his full lips, chiseled high cheekbones, and perfectly pointed nose. Those steely-gray eyes. A prickly sensation tickled the base of her neck. Her weightless spirit rose, light and shadow blurring. She soared beyond herself, floating and drifting. Then, as if someone had sparked a light in a dark room, the world came into focus. She was getting good at this.

Beneath the sprawling canopy of a forest, she found him. He stood beside the stocky, broad-shouldered dwarf she'd seen at the palace. They had called him Keeth. The dwarf's axe reflected the morning light. They walked beside their horses along a narrow path, their conversation muted but clear.

"You are a fool for attempting this," Keeth grumbled. "They'll end you like they did Engrendorn."

"Perhaps," Mateo replied, his voice firm. "But the North holds what we need. The Strong Haven ruins will be our next stop."

Avalynn's heart sank. Her spirit yanked back, and the vision dissolved. She opened her eyes, goose bumps covering her forearms. Mateo wasn't at the palace grounds. He chased something far more dangerous.

"What is it?" Lirien asked.

She climbed to her feet and dusted herself off. "He's heading north, to the dragons."

"Dragons?" Lirien asked, his voice tinged with horror and surprise. "But they don't exist anymore."

"They didn't, but somehow they're back. One came to the hunt and took out two of the hunters," she explained.

Lirien blinked, exchanging glances with Gareth. "Is that fool trying to get himself fried?"

"I have no idea what he's up to. But we need to stop him." She let out a whistle, and Silverhoof trotted over. She swung herself onto her back. "He and a dwarf from Stromm Palace are heading north. Their next stop is the Strong Haven ruins. If we hurry, we can catch them."

Lirien and Gareth quickly mounted their horses, the animals shifting eagerly beneath them as they, too, felt the urgency in the air. "To the ruins!" Lirien shouted.

Silverhoof jetted forward, snorting and tossing her head as she matched the pace of the other horses. What in the Sun, Moon, and Stars was Mateo up to now? They had barely survived a dragon attack during the hunt, and now he set out looking for them on purpose? It didn't make sense. She only hoped she'd find him before the dragons scorched him from Faevenly for good.

CHAPTER FOURTEEN

he winds grew colder as they rode north. Avalynn's mind refused to settle despite Silverhoof's steady rhythm. Would Mateo want to see her again? His kiss still lingered on her lips, but his rejection had cut deeper than any sharp blade. But with each gallop closer to their destination, thoughts of Strong Haven began eclipsing her worries about Mateo.

The ruins lay to the north of Summit Range, before the great crossing into the Wild North—a remnant of a once proud legacy. Now that birthright rested on her shoulders. Avalynn Strong. She was the last of them, the final thread of a lineage severed by House Kane's cruelty. And she knew nothing about the Strongs.

What would it feel like to walk the land her ancestors had fled? Would she sense their presence? Their strength? The echo of their despair?

Her grip on Silverhoof tightened. Her stomach plunged. Sun, Moon, and Stars... would their spirits litter the grounds? She gulped. Would they rush her like those in the dungeon? She was, after all, the Strong heir who used to be a Stromm. Would she need to explain herself to them? Would they already know her history? Her mind spun like a cruel gale. But she pushed all that aside. She had to be brave. She had no other choice.

She eyed Lirien and Gareth riding beside her. They had stopped twice already, and in that short amount of time, she had learned much about them. Lirien possessed keen hunting skills and boasted of his talents with his daggers. He carried a confidence laced with arrogance. Gareth, on the other hand, preferred the axe he wore strapped to his back. But he was gentle and caring, and he often looked after the horses or studied the skies. They were a study in contrasts—one loud and eager, the other quiet and watchful. But both possessed unwavering loyalty to Mateo. Would they be loyal to her too? Probably not.

Silverhoof snorted, tossing her head. Avalynn followed the mare's gaze to the horizon, where a silhouette rose against the bright blue sky. At first, it looked like nothing more than jagged rocks jutting from the earth. But as her eyes adjusted, she realized it was the Strong Haven ruins.

She tugged at Silverhoof's mane, slowing her to a trot. She pointed ahead. Lirien and Gareth eyed the horizon too.

"That it?" Lirien asked, shielding his eyes against the glare of the sun.

Avalynn nodded. "It has to be."

They picked up their pace, galloping in earnest. They

slowed when they came to a rusted and broken gate that was swung open and covered in moss and vine. Avalynn scanned the perimeter for signs of life, but she saw none. Though she wasn't exactly sure what she'd see. Just... something.

"Maybe they're not here yet," she said.

Gareth crossed his hands at the wrists. He moved them downward, his brow furrowing.

Lirien interpreted. "He's saying it's quiet, too quiet."

"Agreed," Avalynn replied, sensing the ominous stillness too. "Let's get closer."

They nudged their horses forward, closing the distance at a cautious pace. The ivy-clad ruins of Strong Haven grew clearer as they got closer. Broken spires once tipped with gold and ivory were now jagged and blackened. Decorative walls buckled and crumbled under the weight of time. Massive gates leaned, the ironwork marred with rusted inactivity.

They reached the ruins' edge, and Avalynn raised a hand, stopping the group. What if danger lurked inside? Like Shadowblood Foxes or Ruin Rats? "Let's prepare our weapons. We'll go on foot from here."

The pair nodded. They dismounted, tying the horses to a cluster of scraggly trees. Silverhoof pawed the ground again, as if protesting. "Sorry, girl," Avalynn murmured, patting her neck. "We'll be back soon."

She unsheathed her sword from her back and kept it in front of her. Lirien pulled a pair of daggers from his belt. Their silver edges gleamed in the light. Gareth drew this axe. Its weighty head rested in his grip.

The trio crept forward, stepping lightly on the overgrown path. It led into the heart of the ruins. The thick smell of dirt and musty leaves clung to the air like a second skin. Avalynn gripped her sword tighter, the scent of decay assaulting her senses.

Every shadow seemed to hold a threat, every rustle of wind a warning. A flicker of movement caught her eye. She whipped her head around, heart pounding. A young boy drifted about. His translucent form glowed, his facial expression stiff. He didn't notice Avalynn or the others as his spirit disappeared through a broken column.

She blinked, her pulse quickening. More figures emerged. A group of maidservants, their spectral forms moving with purpose. Blood-stained skirts swaying as though caught in an invisible breeze. Missing limbs. Gashed heads. She froze, her breath catching in her throat. Their vacant eyes bore into her. One of the servants pointed, her mouth wide open in a silent scream. The group retreated, vanishing into the ruins.

Avalynn staggered back a step, her hand tightening on her sword.

"What is it?" Lirien hissed, his daggers raised, eyes darting around. "Did you hear something?"

"I probably should've mentioned that I can see spirits," she whispered, her voice trembling.

"You can what?" Lirien lowered his daggers.

A deep, guttural growl echoed through the ruins, sending a chill down her spine. "Thunderation, what could that be?" Avalynn asked.

Lirien and Gareth swung their heads. "What do you hear?" Lirien asked. "We don't hear anything."

A hulking figure appeared, dragging a jagged axe in

one hand and a chipped sword in the other. A deep gash ripped across his face, and half of his mouth was missing.

"Daughter of Strong Haven!" the hulking figure bellowed, the sound like a grinding stone. "Here to collect your dead?"

"Sun, Moon, and Stars," she gasped. "It's a spirit troll. A big one."

Lirien and Gareth tensed, their weapons ready, but their wide eyes betrayed their unease. "Where?" Lirien asked.

"S-s-straight ahead." Avalynn's voice wavered. "But it's a spirit... It can't hurt us."

Lirien stayed sharp. "You sure about that?"

Was she?

The hulking spirit roared, raising his axe above his head. The weapon beamed with an eerie light. Its edge looked impossibly sharp despite its spectral form. With a furious yell, he brought it down on Avalynn with a brutal arc.

"Aaah!" She raised her arms. The axe disappeared through her upper body. A searing sensation like molten lava tore through her. She gasped, stumbling backward. Her legs gave way, sending her crashing onto her backside. She clutched at her chest. Pain smoldered like embers in her ribcage. She glanced down—no wound, no blood. Her gaze hung on the blow's phantom ache.

"Avalynn!" Lirien shouted, his daggers raised while Gareth loomed over her like a shield. "Are you okay?"

"I'm fine," she rasped, pain throbbing all over. She scrambled to her feet, her sword trembling in her grip.

The spirit's hollow eyes narrowed as he gripped his

axe, his voice thundering through the ruins like a death knell. "Strong Haven's Daughter must pay for the sins of her ancestors!"

"Where is it?" Lirien hollered, slashing his daggers in the air. He and Gareth planted in front of her.

She saw the spirits everywhere now. The boy from before peeked out from behind a crumbled pillar. The maidservants hovered in the shadows. The ruins sprang to life with more spirits too, each one's pointed stare heavy with judgment. "They're everywhere," she said, shaking her head. "And they know me."

"What do we do?" Lirien's gaze darted around.

A faint, creeping hiss started in the shadows. It slithered through the ruins like a serpent. "Sssss."

Avalynn's breath hitched. The hiss wrapped itself around her. The spirits scattered, even the troll. Their faces twisted with fear, eyes darting around like wounded elks. "Something's happening," she said. One by one, they flickered and vanished, retreating into nothingness.

Gareth grunted while he and Lirien moved even closer. "What?" Lirien asked.

"I don't know." Avalynn paused as silence reigned. Her chest heaved, but she steadied herself. "They're gone. But there's something else."

The hiss deepened, growing louder, more insistent, like a serpent curling closer. A shadow emerged from the far end of the ruins. A figure cloaked in a long, dark robe with a garnet-red sheen. The red illuminated the demolished walls and overgrown vines, casting the ruins of Strong Haven in burning firelight.

"Thunderation. It's another spirit." She narrowed her eyes. "A demon witch, I think."

"Great, a demon witch," Lirien muttered.

The figure moved closer. The hood obscured its face until it halted a few paces away. Slowly, deliberately, the spirit pulled back its hood, revealing pale and luminous skin and hair like liquid onyx cascading over his shoulders.

His diamond-like eyes glittered with malevolence. But even as she stared, the spirit's beautiful face flickered, twisting into something gaunt and skeletal, the smooth features replaced by sunken hollows and jagged teeth. Just as suddenly, he snapped back to his pristine beauty, the transition seamless.

"Daughter of Strong Haven," the spirit hissed, his voice a silken thread laced with venom. A cruel smile curved his lips. "Daughter of House Kane."

What? Shivers raced up her spine. Daughter of House Kane? She swallowed, her voice trembling. "Who are you?"

The witch tilted his head, amusement dancing in his unnatural eyes. "Draven the Witch," he purred, savoring every word.

Her gut clenched. Draven, the feared and murderous witch. Terror and dread swirled within her. "Get away from me," she said, backing up against a half wall.

Draven vanished from sight and then reappeared inches before her, their noses almost touching. "I am honored to meet you," he said, studying her face for the longest pause. "I am honored to end you as well."

He plunged his hand into her chest. His cold touch

burned like a frostbitten blade. She gasped, the sensation stealing life from her lungs. His fingers wrapped around her heart and squeezed. Tears seeped from her eyes, and her knees buckled. How was he doing this?

She flicked her gaze to Lirien and Gareth who were holding her, hollering, desperate to help. Every beat of her heart felt like fire, her vision dimming as she struggled for air.

"Your power," a voice urged from behind Draven. Another figure emerged from the ruins. A tall, thin fae with long silver hair and piercing violet eyes. "Use your human witch power!"

Yes. Her power. She needed it now. She closed her eyes, envisioning the blue light all around her, like radiant sunlight. Rhyka's words rang in her mind. *Call it forth.* A tingle, then a surge of energy stirred deep within her. A faint pulse grew stronger with each beat of her failing heart. *Call it forth.*

Her trembling hand found its strength and gripped her sword. Her chest radiated with warmth, building into a firestorm. *Call it forth!* She reached out, touching Draven's face as a sudden rush of blue light erupted from her, engulfing her in a blazing aura.

Draven reared back. His ghostly form writhed in the radiant brilliance. She gasped as his grip on her heart released. His hand dropped from her chest. A sinister laugh exploded from his mouth, then he flickered like a dying flame. *Poof.* He vanished.

The ruins fell silent, the air stilled, and she fell to her knees. She grabbed the tunic at her chest and held on as the blue light faded.

Lirien and Gareth crowded around her, their faces etched with worry. Lirien asked, "Are you okay?"

"I think so." She swallowed and nodded, rubbing her chest. Her eyes fixed on the spot where Draven had stood. He was gone now, but the silver-haired fae who came to her aid lingered. He watched from a distance before turning and disappearing into the ruins.

She scrambled to her feet. "Stay here. I need to talk to that fae."

He knew her, or at least, her family. He knew about her powers. And he had answers.

"Wait!" Avalynn hollered, rushing around chunks of debris and overgrown brush. "I need to talk to you!"

He stopped, then slowly turned to face her. He bowed. "Princess."

She waited while she caught her breath. "How do you know me?"

He smiled, studying her. "The streaked hair of your mother. The facial features of your father. You are Gabriela and Leaf's daughter, Celyse and Julio's grand-daughter."

She was right. He did know them. "Yes, I am." She swallowed. "My name is Avalynn." She hesitated, then added, "Strong. Avalynn Strong. And you are?"

"I am Traeliorn Letormis, friend and ally to the Strongs. You may call me Leto." He glanced around the ruins. "I was once the steward of Strong Haven. I fought and died here."

Avalynn blinked. Her fingernails dug into her palms, grounding herself against the surge of emotions. "You knew my mother and father? And died for them?" she murmured.

The family she didn't know and had only met at the Passing Place tied her closer to Strong Haven than she expected. His sacrifice for her lineage humbled her and sent a tear rolling down her cheek.

"They were my dearest friends," Leto said, his gaze softening.

"I am just now learning who I am, and I have so many questions." She glanced around for the ominous witch, Draven, but he was still gone. "Why is Draven here? And why are you here?"

Leto's brows lowered, his form flickering as though touched by a breeze that didn't exist. "Walk with me, and I will share what I know," he said. He worked his way through the ruins and began explaining. "Draven lived for one purpose—revenge on the Strong bloodline. He is tied to this place, his oath binding him even in death. As for me, I protect that same bloodline. My vow was made to Prince Julio before his end."

Draven was bound by vengeance, Leto by duty, and Avalynn was caught in the middle of a misunderstood legacy. Now a mistrusted prophecy? "But I'm more than a Strong." She gulped, replaying what Draven had said. "I'm also of House Kane?"

"You are." Leto nodded as if admitting a truth best kept buried. "Your father carried that bloodline."

Avalynn's steps faltered. Her heart hammered as if the ruins had shaken beneath her feet. She knew nothing about herself. Nothing. And now this? House Kane?

"But why didn't Lady Sonia tell me? Or the human,

Manny?" she asked, shaking her head and grappling with the hidden truth. "Why keep me in the dark?"

"Ah, Manny still lives. Such news brings me great joy." He smiled. "Manny is the greatest person I know. As for keeping you in the dark, perhaps they thought they were protecting you," Leto said, quirking an eyebrow. "Or perhaps they feared how you'd take it. The Kanes were devious, but your father was not. He was noble and brave and as close to me as my own blood."

The ruins seemed to press in around Avalynn, the weight of her history closing in. "So I'm part of the family that destroyed the other part?" She let out a sigh. "How messed up is that?" She gripped her trembling hands. And she was in love with a Stromm prince. And his family wanted her head. History repeated itself.

Leaving the ruins behind, they entered the garden. Vines covered the dilapidated fountains and benches. Wild and overgrown vegetation overtook the once manicured landscape. Leto exhaled, and the sound carried a sorrowful note that drifted through the ruins.

"Yes, your path is complicated. But it is your path." Leto gestured back to the sprawling ruins. "Look at Strong Haven. Once, it was the heart of strength and unity. Now it is broken. Yet here you stand—alive, whole, and unbroken. You are a bright light in an otherwise bleak place. You are proof that even from ruin, something strong and enduring can rise."

She squared her shoulders, meeting Leto's gaze. The smallest thread of hope pulled at her chest. "You're right. My past doesn't define me. I can choose who I will become. I am more than the legacy of those who came before. I am Avalynn Strong, the beginning of something new."

A flicker of pride crossed Leto's face. "And this makes you more than your bloodline, princess. This makes you powerful." He nodded at her sword. "The Only One."

They stopped walking, his words lingering like a distant bell. More than her bloodline. Powerful. She wasn't sure if she believed him, but the conviction in his voice gave her pause. Her past was a storm she could not change. But the future she would forge in her favor. She inhaled deeply as something like resolve settled over her. She wasn't defined by the shadows of her lineage. She was ready to step into the light.

But then her breath caught. Before them stretched a barren expanse where a lake should have been. In the sunlight, the cracked earth twinkled. It mocked the memory of water that once filled it. "What happened here?" she asked.

Leto followed her gaze. "This was Torch Lake. Long ago, the shimmer portals to the human realm were stored and guarded here. But the portals were destroyed, keeping the realms separate. As for the water, no one knows for certain why it has dried."

"Why are you showing me this?" Avalynn stepped closer, her boots crunching against the dry ground.

Leto's gaze sharpened as he turned to her. "Something is wrong with the Mother of Rivers."

"Wrong..." She swallowed, her gaze sweeping over the barren sight, her mind taking her to the trickling Green Falls and the shallow riverbed she had passed not long ago. "I have seen it like this in other areas. What do you think it is?"

"That is for you to find out," he replied.

The hiss of the wind whispered around them. It carried the earthy scent of moss and brush. Her gaze dropped to her dirty boots. She was tangled with questions, doubts, and fears. Now, there was one more thing to add to her list of worries.

She raised her gaze, ready to ask Leto more questions, only to find the spot where he'd stood empty. "For me to find out," she said to herself.

Lirien and Gareth approached with cautious steps. "So," Lirien said. "That was, um, some conversation you were having." He glanced at Gareth. "Do youuu... want to talk about it?"

He handed over her sword, which she sheathed behind her back. "No. Not now."

For the first time, she wasn't running from her legacy but embracing it and transforming it as her own. The Only One. Mateo needed her, but so did Faevenly. She eyed the skies again. The sun hung high, warming but not overbearing. A gentle breeze stirred, carrying sweet hints of dormant wildflowers. A good sign.

She faced Mateo's friends with renewed purpose. "We wait for Mateo, not in the ruins, but where the horses graze. If he doesn't show soon, we'll continue north to the dragons and try catching up to him on the way."

The dragons, the waters, and her sword... it was all connected. And she needed to piece it all together before it was too late.

CHAPTER FIFTEEN

Mateo kept his head down, racing to the Strong Haven ruins. Everything he'd read about the dragons in the palace library slow-played in his mind. Dragons once soared the skies. Some were massive, with gold scales bigger than castles. Others were long and thin with green and yellow scales, and they lived in the seas. There were also tiny purple and pink ones, no bigger than a finger.

Dragons disappeared ten thousand years before the Great Shimmer War. Some said they migrated to another realm. Others claimed they had killed each other into extinction. Still others theorized that the great beasts simply stopped reproducing. But none of those theories were true. He'd seen one at the hunt. And barely lived to tell the tale.

Through the dense forest and across the craggy mountains, he and Keeth galloped. Mateo's hunger for the dragons grew with each stride. With the wind in his face and the temperature chilling, he felt as though he could achieve anything. He'd find pyrosia, then the dragons, and take one as his own. He'd save Stromm Palace from the likes of Selene Baffin and anyone else who dared threaten it. With a dragon, he would be unstoppable. His name and his birthright would be carved into Faevenly legend.

"Fweeeet!" Keeth's whistle broke his focus. Mateo turned to the dwarf, who gestured wildly to the left. "That way, you!" he shouted, his voice nearly drowned out by the wind's rush. Then he muttered something Mateo couldn't catch, likely far from complimentary.

Keeth was a two-sided coin. On the one side, he was gruff, blunt, and an exhausting thorn in Mateo's thumb. On the other, he was a welcome companion with sharp eyes and a steady hand with a blade. His skills had proved invaluable so far. Still, if the dwarf wasn't careful, he'd end up crispy from a dragon's breath.

The terrain flattened out. The dense forest gave way to a grassy green expanse. The horizon came into view, and there it loomed—Strong Haven. The ruins jutted skyward, imposing against the muted blue sky. Mateo jerked his reins to the left, guiding his horse toward the ancient stronghold.

He leaned forward, patting the animal's neck. "Almost there."

They needed a break, maybe a nap, before crossing into the Wild North. Their stay at Strong Haven wouldn't be long. Although eager to see the ruins, it was what lay ahead that sent a thrill through him. But then his horse slowed. His ears pinned back, flat against his head. Mateo exchanged a curious look with Keeth.

He tightened the reins. "What is it, boy?"

The steed halted, then reared back with a shrill whinny. Keeth's horse followed suit, tossing the dwarf to the ground like a sack of potatoes. "What in the—" Mateo clenched his thighs as his mount bucked, sending him flying. He smacked to the ground, hurting his back.

A low rumble like distant thunder rolled from the clouds. Birds took flight from the treetops, frantically scattering. Small animals darted from the underbrush. They fled as though the ground might swallow them whole.

His pulse quickened. A cold shiver raced down his spine. That sound from the hunt. He knew it well. Dragons.

Mateo scrambled to his feet, his heart pounding. Keeth bounced upright, brushing dirt from his trousers and cursing under his breath. "Well, lad. I think we found your dragons," the dwarf said.

Mateo's gaze snapped upward. A pair of dragons sliced through the sky. The sunlight caught their iridescent scales, casting a dazzling array of colors that shimmered like a liquid kaleidoscope. Their wings beat in unison, sending gusts of wind rippling across the landscape. His breath caught as they spiraled lower. Then the dragons dove with suddenness, his stomach lurching as the dragons plummeted.

They free-fell toward the ruins, their sleek bodies slicing through the air like arrows. Mateo's eyes widened as they opened their massive jaws. Twin torrents of fire erupted and engulfed the crumbling stone. His skin felt the heat from his distance, their fiery growls filling his ears.

Mateo stood firm. His terror mixed with a fierce, undeniable excitement. This was what he had come for. But even as his exhilaration swelled, a new question clawed at him. What were they attacking? He motioned to Keeth. "Let's go!"

He headed toward a cluster of trees near the outer wall. Too many things kept nagging at him. They hadn't yet found pyrosia, the dragons wanted something or someone in those ruins, and his shield was on his horse's back. He unsheathed his sword. They were doomed.

Pressing his back to the trees, he watched Keeth chugging after him. The dwarf pumped his stiff arms, slamming his back against the trunk beside him. "Now what?" he coughed out with a spit, still clutching his axe.

Mateo raised a brow. "Not much of a runner, are you?"

"Well, I oughta—" He raised his axe.

A searing spray of fire hissed above their heads, forcing them to dive for cover. Mateo hit the ground, the smell of scorched earth clogging his nose. He dared a glance upward, catching the dragons. They thundered overhead, their immense wings carving their wind-driven path. Dipping low and skimming the grass, they surged skyward, climbing.

Scrambling to his feet, Mateo tracked their ascent. They spiraled into the clouds and veered north. Their colossal silhouettes shrunk with each mighty flap of their wings.

"By the hammer's edge!" Keeth wiped his brow, following the sight. "What do ya make of that?"

A rumble of hooves reached his ears. He turned toward the ruins. His eyes narrowed against the smoky haze. Out of Strong Haven's crumbling heart, three riders charged forth, their outlines born by the setting sun's golden light. With horses galloping toward them, Mateo squinted, his heart skipping a beat. He recognized the figures. Lirien. Gareth. And—he froze for a breathless moment—Avalynn.

"They've seen us!" Keeth barked.

"So what?" Mateo said as the approaching riders pulled their horses to a sharp halt. The labored breaths of their mounts gave way to recognition. Lirien and Gareth leaped from their saddles, their faces lit up with joy.

"Mateo!" Lirien cried, his voice bursting with relief. He reached him first, throwing his arms around his neck in a fierce hug. Gareth followed, gripping Mateo's shoulder, enveloping the pair in an embrace. Mateo clung to his old friends, a rare laugh escaping as the tension melted into something warm and familiar.

His gaze flicked to Avalynn, who was dismounting and taking her time. She stayed close to the Enbarr. *Their Enbarr.* Mateo's joy wavered, giving way to a jumbled surge of emotions. Surprise that she was here. And a thorn of suspicion. What was she doing with his friends?

"Avalynn," he said, her name heavy on his tongue. He left his friends to face her.

She met his eyes, her face unreadable. "Mateo."

The air between them crackled with unspoken words, the weight of their shared history pressing down like an imminent storm cloud. The taste of her lips still lingered on his own.

"What brings you all here?" Mateo asked.

Lirien stepped into Mateo's line of sight. "We were headed to rescue you from the dreaded Stromms. Then Avalynn saw where you were going, so we came here."

Dreaded Stromms? His jaw tightened. "You shouldn't call my family such names."

"What? The Stromms?" Lirien gave him a playful shove. "Why not? They don't even deserve to breathe. You know that."

Lirien's words stoked the fire in his chest. Mateo pushed Lirien and clapped back. "You don't know them like I do." He'd spent time with the king and queen. Lily too. He'd seen their world and understood them like his friends never could.

"Don't know them?" Lirien frowned, then shoved Mateo again. "They've kept us down for all our years. Or have you forgotten?"

He hadn't forgotten, but everything was different now. The Stromms were misunderstood. But he didn't have time to explain all of that to Lirien or Gareth. Would they even listen? "I'm one of them." Mateo closed the gap between them, threatening to unleash. "So be careful with your next words, old friend."

"Or what?" Lirien practically pressed his nose against Mateo's.

"Stop!" Avalynn cut in. "Both of you!"

"No, keep going." Keeth laughed. "I'd like to see how this scrap plays out."

A hand grabbed Mateo's tunic, yanking him back. He

spun around and faced Gareth. His friend's eyes bore a hole through him. He brought the fingers of one hand together at the tips, then angrily opened his fingers toward Mateo. He completed the thought by jerking his hand up and lifting his chin.

"Yeah," Lirien echoed. "What's wrong with you? Our people are still sick!"

What? Mateo took a step back. Sick? He'd sent healing seeds, twice. He glanced between Gareth and Lirien. "Did you not get the healing seeds?"

"The Stromms sent healing seeds?" Avalynn asked with a tilt of her head.

"We got nothing from the gracious Stromm kingdom," Lirien mocked. "Like always."

"Nonsense. The king and queen sent them," Keeth replied. "I saw them loaded up on the carriages with my own eyes, along with plenty of food."

"Well, they never arrived." Lirien crossed his arms.

"Then there's trickery at play," Keeth seethed, jerking his axe toward Lirien and then Gareth. "By your kind, not ours!"

"What do you mean, 'your kind,' Dwarf?" Lirien challenged.

"Lowborns!" Keeth yelled.

A Keeth versus Lirien shouting match ensued. But Mateo's mind narrowed to the queen. She said the Sublands had been offered a position on the council, but Lady Verona had refused. Now the seeds and food never arrived. The dwarf was right. Trickery was at play. Her trickery. "Then it must be Lady Verona who bears responsibility because I assure you, I sent the supplies!"

"Aye," Keeth added with a growl and a spit. "Verona, the wicked!"

Mateo's and Keeth's horses trotted over, pausing the tension for a moment. They joined the other horses, tails swishing without a care. Avalynn kept her focus on him. "Why are you heading north, Mateo?"

"Why do you want to know?" he asked, like she could ever be forgiven for what she had done to him. But then another thought took shape in his mind. Did she miss being a Stromm? Did she somehow want back into his family? Who wouldn't?

She kept her head tilted, her brow furrowed. "I don't know what's gotten into you, but this doesn't make sense."

Typical Avalynn, always making it about him. Now, she had really stooped low, turning his friends against him. Her treachery knew no bounds. Why not tell her the destination? She couldn't stop him anyway. "I go north for the dragons. And my quest does not concern you."

"You're hunting dragons?" Avalynn's lips parted.

"Tracking," he explained. "I have my reasons."

"Have you gone mad?" Lirien pointed at the smoke drifting from the ruins. "You will end up like that pile of rubble if you continue with your plan."

Gareth pointed to his temple, then brought his fore-fingers together side by side, fists closed and pointer finger facing out. Of course he would agree with Lirien.

Mateo rubbed the back of his neck and turned away. His friends had a point. The dragons had torched the ruins without effort. During the hunt, he'd seen one of

164

them snatch up Finnian like a mere twig. He had Keeth, but maybe he needed his friends for backup.

He faced them again. "I need a dragon to protect Stromm Palace from Selene Baffin and the other provinces. Will you help me?"

Lirien and Gareth exchanged glances. "But why?" Lirien asked. "Why help *them*? They've done nothing for us! Our people are still sick. Manny, Floriana, and even Poppy. Others too. Or have you forgotten the Sublands while playing prince in the palace?"

Those last words cut deep. *Had* he forgotten his home? His hand itched for the cross, no longer in his pocket. Instead his fingers found comfort in touching the Stromm pendant around his neck. The mention of Manny, Floriana, and Poppy twisted in his gut, sharp and unforgiving. Their faces flashed in his mind. Manny's warm smile, Floriana's and Poppy's curious eyes. They were his true family, weren't they? And yet, here he was, wearing the emblem of the palace who kept the lowborns down.

What was becoming of him?

A knot swirled in his chest. He couldn't let it show. Not here, not now. His gaze hardened as he looked at Lirien. "I have not forgotten," he said. The words felt hollow in his throat, and deep down, he wondered if he really believed them.

"I think you have," Lirien murmured.

Mateo needed to press on. Pushing away Lirien's words, he offered a plea that would make sense to them. "I can finally help the Sublands, and others, but only if the Stromms succeed." The bond that had grown for his mother plucked at his heartstrings. "And I can allow nothing to happen to my mother now that I have finally found her."

Lirien winced. "*She* is your mother now? That cold-hearted ice queen?" He jabbed his finger at the pendant. "And now you wear their emblem?"

Mateo snatched his hand and twisted. Through clenched teeth, he gritted out, "Don't ever touch that again."

Lirien slammed his hand against Mateo's chest, sending him stumbling. Mateo's boots scraped the dirt, fighting for balance. But the uneven ground tripped him, and his back slammed into the mossy ground with a dull thud, knocking the air from his lungs.

"Stay down," Lirien warned.

Dust rose around Mateo, swirling like a taunt. No way was he staying down. "You asked for it." Mateo sprang to his feet with a snarl. He lunged forward, but just before landing a blow, Gareth stepped in.

He grabbed Mateo's shoulder and jerked him back with a grunt. He slapped the top of Lirien's head with a thwack and let out a throaty guttural, "nho."

"Enough!" Keeth barked, stopping the action like a dungeon's closed door. "Nobody harms the prince!"

Lirien spat, still bristling. He glared at Mateo but didn't advance further.

Keeth shook his axe. "Save it, you lowborn," he growled at Lirien. "We've got bigger enemies than each other. Or have you forgotten the dragons?"

Mateo pulled away from Gareth. His jaw tightened, and his chest heaved. He shot one last glare at Lirien before turning away. The dwarf was right to remember the mission. He'd have a much better chance with the dragons with his friends, but he wasn't going to beg them.

"I don't need you," he said to Lirien. He looked at Gareth and then Avalynn. "I'm better off by myself."

Silence settled over them like snow-laden branches, threatening to break regardless of who stood below. The setting sun painted the ruins of Strong Haven with hues of amber and crimson. The ruins' edges glowed as they burned. The cold air nipped at Mateo's skin, a reminder of the coming night. Above, streaks of gold and violet bled into a deepening indigo sky. The stars began winking as if awake.

Avalynn stepped forward. "I will go north and help you," she said, cutting through the tension. "But only if you promise me one thing."

Mateo's eyes narrowed. "What is this one thing?"

"When you find the dragons, you don't hurt them or use them to wreak havoc. No wars and no destruction. Use them to protect and nothing more."

Mateo's jaw clenched. "What if protecting the realm means fighting?"

Avalynn kept her gaze razor sharp. "Fight only in defense. Swear it to me, here and now."

"Yeah. Swear it, and Gareth and I are in too," Lirien replied.

Mateo hesitated. Avalynn had no right to make such demands of him. She had no business turning his friends against him. But he needed them.

He glanced toward Lirien and Gareth, then back at Avalynn. He nodded. "I swear."

Avalynn studied him, extending her hand. "Then I'll help you."

Mateo reached out. His hand clasped hers. For a fleeting moment, his grip lingered. Unforgotten memories flooded his mind. Her hands intertwined with his at the Green Falls and the intimacy they shared there. A pang shot through him. He pulled away, masking the moment by turning to Lirien. He clasped his friend's forearm, then Gareth's, who gave a nod of solidarity in return.

Mateo straightened and cleared his throat. He nodded to Keeth, but Keeth's eyes still narrowed.

"Whatever is happening here," Keeth said, "as a Stromm guard, I must remind everyone that Avalynn Strong is wanted by the palace."

Mateo hadn't forgotten, but he was hoping Keeth would let it slide. "We can deal with that when this is over," he said. "By my order."

Without another word, they mounted their horses. Mateo's gaze flicked to Avalynn once more before he turned his focus northward.

"To the north," he said, his voice steady. But his mind churned like a restless sea. With a snap of the reins, their journey began. The cold wind whipped his cheeks. The ruins of Strong Haven faded behind them. He needed a way to stay true to his word while breaking his promise.

Now that he was a Stromm, it shouldn't be that hard.

THE DRAGON QUEST

CHAPTER SIXTEEN

Avalynn stood back and watched Mateo reunite with his friends. Their joy at seeing one another lifted her heart like an autumn leaf on a cool breeze. The three of them locked in a real, honest, and heartfelt embrace. But as the laughter settled and the hugs ended, something shifted inside Mateo. The light in his eyes dimmed. His smile faltered, turning tight. It was like an invisible weight settled on his shoulders, one that hadn't been there moments before. Her heart twisted at the sudden change in him. A nibbling worry took root at the reunion now shadowed by his changed demeanor.

She studied him quietly, her stare following the hints of conflict across his face. The easy camaraderie with his friends slipped away like sand in the wind. His posture grew stiff, his movements less fluid, as if his insides waged a war. His carefree spirit, once so effortless, was now veiled, hiding behind a guarded, distant gaze. The strain radiating from him was blatant. Did he recognize it? Not a chance. Did his friends? She was sure they did.

She took a step closer, a wave of worry washing over her. Her fingers ached to touch him. Had she done this to him? Her throat tightened at the thought.

Earlier he'd spoken of his mother and the pendant. His words now smacked her like a thunderclap on a sunny day—sudden, deafening, and impossible to ignore. Mateo was a Stromm. And now he was acting like it. He even liked it. Hidden before, that fact now sprouted. No upbringing could replace his bloodline. But she wasn't willing to give up on him.

She had offered to help with the dragons in exchange for his promise not to harm them or use them for destruction. But really, she wanted to stay close to him and break through to him somehow. His friends had joined in, and Mateo agreed. But she had seen that hesitant look in his eye. His lineage pulled him in an uncontrollable and dastardly direction.

Knowing the Stromm way, she remained ready for that pull.

By the half moon's light, they rode for hours before finding shelter. The group stopped in a thick grove of cone-bearing fir trees. Everyone gathered wood, and soon a comfortable fire blazed. They sat in silence, passing around fruit flats and water.

After his last bite, Keeth stood with a stretch. "We'll take shifts through the night. The prince and I will take the first watch." He pointed his stubby thumb at Lirien and Gareth. "You'll take the second. Avalynn is off duty."

The dwarf was no fool for not wanting her alone with Mateo. But she didn't need Keeth's approval for anything. "I will join the first watch then."

Mateo's gaze shifted to her.

Keeth raised an eyebrow. "Suit yourself."

Gareth and Lirien settled on the far side of the fire. They rested their packs under their heads and flung blankets over their bodies that the dwarf had brought. Keeth sat across from Mateo, axe by his side and the fire between them. Avalynn rose to her feet, stretched her legs, and shifted her sword, and then she plopped next to Mateo.

The secluded grove provided a calm pocket. They were surrounded by sentinels of trees, the dark boughs whispering faintly in the night breeze. The fire crackled and popped, casting luminous sparks like fireflies. The trail of rising smoke released a cozy pine aroma. The horses clustered nearby, their breaths visible in the crisp night air. Their ears twitched while grazing on sparse patches of grass. Above them, the sky stretched vast and unbroken, a tapestry of countless stars glittering like tiny diamonds. A half moon hung high, its silver light bathing the scene in an ethereal glow.

The firelight flooded Mateo's face, and Avalynn ignored everything else. What was he thinking behind those distant eyes? She wanted to tell him about the drying brook and Torch Lake, but now wasn't the time. Her fingers toyed with a loose thread at her knees. Her mind wrestled with the words she wanted to say. She had finished apologizing for what she had done. He'd never understand or accept it anyway. Now, all she wanted from Mateo was answers.

The fire popped again, breaking the silence. Still, she hesitated. Everything about this moment—the glow of the fire and the distant night calls—appeared fragile. It was like a dream she didn't want to disturb.

She recalled her shared moments by a fire like this with Mateo. It was during the hunt, a different time when he held her like they wouldn't survive the morning. Glancing at this new him, her heart beat a little faster. Whatever she needed to say or do, it had to be now.

She picked up a long stick and stoked the wood. "It's so strange sitting together again by a fire." Her words came out low and calm, masking the turmoil churning within. "Don't you think?"

"It is." His short answer matched her tone. A good sign. She hoped it signaled his willingness to continue the conversation.

She shifted the embers with the stick. "I don't know anyone who's crossed into the Wild North, except Engrendorn, and he perished." She faced him. "But you're convinced we can do it?"

"I am." He nodded.

Cool and confident, as always. Traits she had once admired in Mateo, but which now roused her suspicions. "I hope you're right. I'd rather not face Engrendorn's ending. There's still much to do with my young life."

He nodded again, but kept silent.

She tossed the stick in the flame, then snatched another. "Assuming we make it across, how do you plan to capture a dragon?"

Mateo's eyes blinked as he pursed his lips. Was he really going to hold back? Or would he tell her his designs? Eventually, he'd have to since they had now banded together. It might as well be now. "We need to know the plan."

His head swung in her direction. "There's a flower called pyrosia that is said to control the beasts. I aim to find it and use it to bend a dragon to my will."

"Pyrosia." She repeated the name as if saying it would jar a memory. But she had no knowledge of it. "Never heard of it. I suppose I should've paid closer attention to my palace lessons." She smiled, hoping her sad attempt at humor might soften his tough exterior. But he kept his demeanor stoic.

"It exists, trust me." His gaze stayed locked on the flames.

She cleared her throat, eyeing Keeth. The dwarf crammed a sharp stick between his teeth, searching for a leftover morsel.

"You think the dragons will help the Stromms keep their position then?" She angled slightly toward him. "You really think the Stromms are at risk?"

He turned and faced her, eyes narrowing. "I don't think, I know. You saw Selene at the palace representing her province and the others." He leaned closer. "But it's not only them. I can liberate the Sublands from Lady Verona and her meddling ways. And from that witch, Rhyka, too. I will make sure they never go without food and healing seeds again. But I cannot do that if Selene and the others are successful." He added a stick to the fire.

Good. He hadn't forgotten the family that raised him, or the others in the Sublands. And he was right about Selene and the other provinces. She inched her knee closer to his until they touched. Her eyes fixed on the pocket of his pants where he kept his cross. She reached under her tunic, pulling out hers, letting it shine in the firelight.

"I have a cross like yours now," she said with a smile. "It was passed down to me from my part-human mother, Gabriela of Strong Haven." She held it for him to see before tucking it away under her tunic. She patted the place where it rested near her heart. His eyes followed, carrying a quiet ache. Perhaps he mourned the life he'd been so determined to free himself from. Mateo Vela, Sublander. She would break through to him. "Faith is a warrior. Right?"

His jaw clenched, and his facial muscles tightened. His eyes darkened, erasing any trace of vulnerability. "Faith is not a warrior," he snapped while tapping the pendant on his chest. "Power is the only warrior." Lowering his hand, he gripped his knees, his knuckles turning white. "You should know, having been raised with unlimited power. You've never gone without, Avalynn."

The air between them turned brittle. Her heart stumbled, and a response failed her. His cross, whittled by Manny, carried enduring and profound lessons. It'd been Mateo's lifeline to the values that had once defined him. How could he have lost that part of himself? She narrowed her focus to the flat pocket. Was his cross even in there?

"Where is your cross?" she asked.

"I don't need it anymore." He stood, towering over her. His words sounded final, like the door slamming, never to be opened again.

Her breath caught as he turned on his heels, heading toward the horses, moving with purpose as though nothing had happened, as though he hadn't just severed a huge part of himself. Her pulse pounded in her ears. *I don't need it anymore.* His words replayed in her mind, each repetition hacking deeper. The cross wasn't only a faith symbol. It connected Mateo to Manny, the man who raised him. It bound Mateo to the sisters he grew up with, Camilla and Floriana. It even kept him close to his mother Faeryn, who was no longer alive. What would they think if they knew what Mateo had said?

Avalynn's hands balled into fists. A surge of emotion rose within her. She wanted to shake him, remind him of who had carved that cross and why. But when she looked at him now, the moonlight traced his harsher features. He had become a stranger.

"Mateo," she whispered, the name tasting like a prayer he couldn't hear anymore. She said it again, firmer this time. "Mateo." She refused to let him slip away.

She strode over to him and snatched his arm. She pulled him to the other side of the horses and out of sight. "I understand that you're mad at me. I get that you hate me for what I did. But I will not stay quiet as you throw the Vela name away, favoring a name like Stromm."

He pulled his arm free. "You think you know me, but you don't. So please, leave me before I hurt you further." His gaze dropped. "I couldn't bear it if that happened."

She watched him, her chest aching from the weight of his words. They'd already damaged each other so deeply; no further damage could be done. So, she pressed on. "Your bloodline does not define you." She placed her hand on his thudding heartbeat. "It's what's inside you that matters." Her fingers curled against his chest. "What we shared at the Green Falls matters."

He placed his hand on hers. But this time, he didn't pull away. He held on. "I would not trade Green Falls for all the stars."

The cool night air wrapped around their heated bodies. The vapor of their breaths blended in the space between. His steely-gray eyes brimmed as they locked on to hers. His free hand moved to the curve of her jaw. His thumb brushed her skin with a tenderness that made her knees weaken.

She leaned in as if pulled by an invisible thread. Neither of them could hold back any longer. Their lips met in a kiss filled with all the passion and longing they had kept bottled inside. Their kiss deepened, growing more urgent, and her fingers gripped his tunic. His hand slid behind her neck, pulling her closer.

Their breathing mingled, ragged and warm. The kiss took on a rhythm, singing of a desperate hope for another night together. Mateo's hand settled at her waist, holding her and protecting her against anything that might shatter the fragile moment.

Time stretched, the world around them dissolving into the star-dappled night. They finally broke apart, not for lack of wanting but needing air. His eyes searched hers, exposed yet filled with an intensity she couldn't decipher.

"What are you thinking?" she asked. She was afraid to hear his answer but needed to know.

He stepped away with a heavy breath. "I'm thinking everything will change when we cross into the Wild North. And I think you need to let me go."

CHAPTER SEVENTEEN

Mateo rode alongside Keeth. Lirien and Gareth followed behind with Avalynn. With each passing moment, the company grew quieter, and Mateo found himself drawing further into his thoughts. Avalynn's words and kiss clung to him like a stubborn thorn, increasingly intolerable. Her claims served herself, not him.

He touched the pendant and tucked it inside his tunic. His mother had given it to him. Avalynn would never understand the bond to his true bloodline, the true pull of the Stromm legacy. None of them would.

They would see, though, once he had a dragon at his beck and call.

The winds blew cooler, a simple breeze launching an army of shivers. The thin blanket wrapped around him and tied at the neck provided little insulation. Mateo and the others needed warmer clothing but had passed no villages along the way. He would look for something with thicker threads when they crossed into the North.

Peering ahead, a sparkle in the path met his eye. Then another, and more. Magic? He was getting tired of magic. He raised his hand, and everyone stopped. Squinting, he studied the air.

"What is it?" Keeth asked.

Lirien's and Gareth's horses trotted alongside Mateo. "Did you see something?" Lirien asked.

"I thought I did." Mateo kept his gaze steady. "A sparkle. Though I don't see it anymore."

Avalynn's Enbarr moved forward, its hooves clomping against the dirt and grass. "I see it," she uttered as if speaking any louder might awaken something lurking beyond. "It looks like some sort of magical boundary, like at the hunt."

Mateo's brow furrowed. "More magical trickery." He tilted his head and scanned the area. He swung down from his horse. His boots scraped the rocky ground. The sparkle shone again. "I see it now. Right there." He pointed.

The others dismounted. Gareth knelt down and scooped up a handful of dirt. With a flick of his wrist, he tossed the pebbles into the air. They soared before disappearing as if swallowed mid-flight.

Lirien's eyes widened. Gareth's usual calm faltered as he looked over his shoulder at the others.

"That... that wasn't right," Lirien said.

"Makes sense." Keeth's stubby hands clenched around his axe; he stood frozen, staring at where the pebbles had vanished. "It's the Wild North." A dark look settled on his face.

Mateo faced him. "What do you mean?"

"When I was a lad, my elders told stories of those who dared to venture this far north," the dwarf said, his eyes widening. "Eaten by goblins and trolls, they used to say. They even spoke of an icy curse plaguing the region." He spit over his shoulder. "Scared us youngins from ever traveling these parts." His eyes narrowed, the weight of his words heavy. "As I grew older, I began to think those stories were nothing but fiddle-faddle. But now, seeing that dirt disappear, maybe they were all true." He stepped back, motioning with his hand. "Maybe this magical border here is telling us something. To stay away, lest we face horrors on the other side."

Mateo's gaze stayed on the empty space, his brows furrowing tighter. He didn't believe in childish horror stories from history. Still, the change in Keeth made him pause. "If there's a magical border, why does no one speak of it?"

"Because any who enter rarely come out," said a melodic, flute-like voice.

The group leaped back as a creature emerged from the shimmery boundary. A creature Mateo had never seen before. He had goat-like legs covered in sleek, tawny fur, ending in small, cloven hooves that thudded softly against the mossy dirt. A simple green tunic hung loosely over his slender frame. A leather cord knotted around his waist and pouch, which dangled below.

The faun smiled, flashing dimpled cheeks. Large, almond-shaped eyes the color of forest leaves peered at them. Curiosity or caution? His pointed ears protruded through a mop of chestnut-brown hair and twitched as if sensing every shift in the air.

"Who are you?" Mateo's hand hovered near the hilt of his sword.

The faun studied him with a gleam in his eyes. Then the creature bowed, one arm sweeping across his chest. "I am Bramble." His smooth and lilting voice carried in the wind like a young robin's song. "Keeper of the Boundary and guide to those who dare tread the edges of Faevenly and the Wild North."

A guide? Mateo raised his brow. Maybe their luck had changed. This Bramble could help them find the dragons, and pyrosia too. He tipped his head. "I am Mateo."

He pointed as he introduced the others. "This is Keeth, Lirien, Gareth, and Avalynn. We are traveling to the Wild North in search of dragons and pyrosia."

"Dragons *and* pyrosia, you say?" Bramble huffed and piped a musical laugh, ending in a high-pitched snort. "Good luck with that," the faun said, the words dripping with disbelief. "You are far braver—or perhaps far more foolish—than I thought. But then again, how would I know anything about your party?"

"You watch your tongue, calling us foolish, ya hear?" Keeth pointed his weapon at the faun. "Or you'll end up meeting the sharp edge of my axe."

"Sliced, diced, and roasting over a fire too," Lirien added, brandishing his knives.

"Testy, testy." Bramble rolled his eyes. His legs shifted, turning in a circle. His tail flicked playfully. "The

Wild North doesn't abide wanderers, let alone dragon seekers. But who am I to stop you? Just don't blame me when your bold quest ends in..." He trailed off, covering his mouth with three fingers and chuckling. "Let your imaginations fill in the blank."

Mateo had a good mind to let Keeth and Lirien have their way with Bramble. But they needed help. They'd been gone long enough. He needed to get back to the palace. Who knew the havoc Selene and the other provinces were wreaking. "What will you provide as our guide?"

"Many things!" The faun's grin widened, showing small, nubbed teeth. He held his arms out wide, then brought his hands together in front of him. "But first, you must decide. Turn around and remember nothing of this conversation or enter the Wild North and forget who you are."

Mateo glanced at the others, receiving no help. "What kind of choice is that?" he asked.

"Oh, you Faevenly fae. Always asking the same questions." Bramble chuckled, clearing his throat. "Let me explain it to you like you are a newborn." He pointed to the left and then the right. "This is no ordinary border. It does not merely separate lands; it severs ties to where you came from. When you cross, you lose everything—memories, identity, and any connection to Faevenly. Who you love." He placed his hands over his heart, batting his long lashes. "Who you hate." He grabbed his neck in a chokehold, sticking out his tongue. "The Wild North becomes your only truth."

"Thunderation, we can't do that," Lirien mumbled, edging in close to Mateo. "No way."

"I agree with Lirien," Avalynn said in a low tone. "Everything we have been through will be for naught if we lose our memories."

Her words hit harder than they should have, cutting through the chilly air. His jaw tightened, and for a fleeting moment, he let himself imagine what it would mean to forget the pain and the betrayal. Forget *her*. His life would be easier without Avalynn Strong's face etched into every corner of his mind.

The lingering ache after their kiss and the hollowness he carried after her betrayal would all be gone. But memories could not be picked apart. If he let them go, he would lose it all—triumphs, lessons, his newfound birthright. Yet keeping them meant keeping her. Given no choice but to carry her with him, he'd bury her deep. Mateo would shove his feelings for her into the farthest corner of his mind and lock it away where it couldn't reach him and couldn't hurt him anymore. He'd hold her in the same regard as when they had first met.

It was the only way.

"That will not work. We cannot lose our memories," Mateo said to Bramble, finally.

Bramble's lips curled into a knowing smile. The faun reached into the leather pouch at his side, producing a handful of small orange seeds. "You don't have to, Mateo. These seeds come from the Wild North's first tree, blessed by the ancient dragons who created the boundary long ago. Eat one, and you will keep your memories for three sunsets. You will remember who you are and why you came."

"And after three sunsets?" Mateo's gut churned.

Bramble's gaze held steady, his tone growing solemn. "If you are still in the Wild North after the third sunset, the seed's magic fades. The North will claim you. Faevenly will become a mere twinkle in your eye."

Mateo turned and faced the group, ready for the challenge. "We can do it. Three sunsets is plenty of time."

"I don't know," Avalynn cautioned. "Three sunsets can pass quickly. What if we don't make it out in time?"

He knew it. She had said she'd help him, but something deep inside had warned him she might not follow through. Like at the hunt, all she cared about was protecting herself. And now, that sword on her back.

"I'm with you. We can do it." Lirien stepped closer, resting a steady hand on Mateo's shoulder. Gareth gave a silent but resolute nod.

Mateo recognized his friends' loyalty. Despite bickering from time to time, the three of them had weathered many storms. This would be no different.

"It is a fool's errand." Keeth's gaze remained on the unseen border as if in a trance. He raised his bushy brows and turned to Mateo. "But I am charged with your protection." He spit twice. "Where you go, I go."

"I need a yes from one more?" Bramble said with a smile. His ears twitched. "What say you, Avalynn?"

She crossed her arms. "I say I'm in."

The faun hopped with delight, then held out the seeds, his tail swishing. "Well then, my brave little dragon seekers, shall I guide you to the brink of your doom? Or would you prefer to scurry back where you came from?"

He hadn't traveled this far to stop here. He needed to go all the way. Mateo stepped forward, plucking a seed from Bramble's hand. His gaze fell on the others. "If this is what it takes to keep our memories and accomplish our mission, then so be it."

He popped the seed into his mouth and bit down. A burst of tangy bitterness spread across his tongue, followed by an electric jolt that tickled his spine.

Avalynn reached out, taking the next seed. She held it up, inspecting its strange glow, then put it in her mouth and chewed. "Not bad," she muttered.

One by one, the others followed. Lirien and Gareth took theirs, crunching down without hesitation. Keeth glared at his seed as though it were made of troll dung. "I've eaten worse, I'll bet." He shoved it into his mouth. A second later, his face twisted. "Ugh. On second thought, maybe I haven't."

Bramble clapped his hands and hopped on his hooves. "Wonderful fools! The magic is now bound to all of you for three sunsets. No going back now!"

Fools? Mateo raised a brow. *No going back?* He didn't like the sound of either. But the faun was half right. They'd made their choice.

"Do you think we'll regret this?" Lirien asked.

"Undoubtedly," Keeth replied.

Bramble chuckled. "There are two other matters to address before entry. First, your horses must stay. Second, you are allowed only one weapon each."

"You should have told us that." Mateo stiffened, irritation sparking inside him. At himself, for not asking about the details earlier, and at the faun, for not being forthcoming.

Bramble's smile widened, a mischievous gleam in his eyes as he shrugged. "You should have asked."

"Fine," Mateo grumbled, eyeing the others. It wasn't as if they had a choice. And maybe they were all fools. "We will do as instructed."

"I don't like it. Not one bit," Keeth muttered, gripping the handle of his axe and setting down his dagger.

"Neither do I," Lirien said, slipping one of his daggers from its sheath. He tucked it into his horse's saddlebag. He patted the remaining blade at his hip with a sigh.

Gareth shook his head as he ran a hand along his horse's neck in a silent farewell. His axe remained strapped to his back.

Mateo didn't have to look at Avalynn to know what weapon she'd choose. The sword of so-called power. The sword of the Only One. So far, it had been of no use on their journey.

He turned to his horse, surveying the weapons secured there. His choice was simple. He slid his sword into its sheath. He clutched his bow and quiver of arrows. A far-range weapon would be essential when facing dragons.

"Very good." Bramble clapped. "Please, follow me." He waved, then disappeared through the boundary with a twitch of his tail.

With a deep breath, Mateo stepped through. A sensation consumed him, like walking through a freezing waterfall. Needles of ice pricked his skin, and for a heart-beat, his lungs refused to draw air. But as abruptly as it came, the feeling dissipated, leaving him gasping and disoriented. Blinking, he found himself in a world pulled from the pages of a frost dream.

The meadow before him sparkled with frost-kissed grass. The blades shone like crystal shards. Snow-dappled trees with silver bark towered over them. Their branches hung heavy with thick cones and wintry blossoms of silver and gold. Small sprites, or some other ethereal beings, floated through the air. They left shimmering dust trails in their wake. A brook meandered throughout the landscape. Its clear water reflected the vibrant hues of an otherworldly sky, streaked with ribbons of lavender and cerulean. The sharp, cool air carried sweet hints of blooming flowers hidden beneath the snow.

What lay beyond held Mateo's eyes. A towering, snow-capped mountain. The vivid sky outlined its jagged peaks. Its steadfast ridges and ancient shadows formed a profile that faced the Sun, Moon, and Stars. No doubt the dragons dwelled there.

Mateo's heart pounded, taking in the brilliance surrounding them. "Our new journey begins," he said as everyone stepped through the boundary and joined him. "We're no longer in Faevenly. Welcome to the Wild North."

CHAPTER EIGHTEEN

Nothing could have prepared Avalynn for the sight before her. The winter wonderland stretched as far as her eyes could see—brilliant, dazzling, and fresh, as though the Sun, Moon, and Stars had newly created the land. Despite the snow-dappled trees and the snowy mountain, the air was only cool, not the biting cold she had expected.

"Well, my foolish little Faevenly fae, here we are," Bramble announced, clapping his hands. "The Wild North. Isn't she lovely?"

"Where are the dragons and the pyrosia?" Mateo asked, his voice edgy.

"My, my, so eager!" Bramble replied, wagging a finger at him. "As Keeper of the Boundary and your guide, I shall give you the knowledge you need before I take my leave and return to my duties." The faun cleared his throat. "Please pay attention." He clasped his hands together as though preparing for a grand performance.

"The sun has newly risen," Bramble said, gesturing toward the dawning sky. "So today is day one. Do not lose track." He pointed at the region beyond the meadow. "You will find the dragons at the top of Skywatcher Mountain." He turned his head to the side and looked up, tracing his own profile. "Get it? Skywatcher?"

For the love of all the Stars. "Yes," Mateo said with a warning tone. "We get it. Please continue."

"Very good." Bramble smiled. "Pyrosia grows over there too, although I have never seen it. Now, beware as you approach. The dragons are dangerous, sure, but the Valians? Doubly so."

"Valians?" Avalynn asked.

"Dragonfolk. They live in Frost Vale over there." The faun pointed toward the mountain.

Avalynn hadn't imagined fae tied to the dragons. What were these Valians like? Tall, deadly, fire-breathing? If they were anything like the dragons, she feared the worst.

Bramble tapped his chin as if recalling a forgotten detail. "Ah, yes. The Wild North is freezing cold, but the magic keeps it..." He held up two fingers close together but not touching. "This cold. So those flimsy blankets tied around your necks? Not needed. Unless you desire them, of course. It will get warmer the closer you come to the dragons. You know, with dragon breath and all."

The faun paced in a small circle. "One final thing. The boundary protects the Wild North from the withering touch of Faevenly's decay. That magic must remain unbroken, or both realms will suffer." With a flourish, the faun turned and bowed low. "And now, I bid you farewell. Until we meet again, you adventurous fools!"

"Wait!" Avalynn called out, taking a step forward. She had questions. About the dragons and the dragon-folk, but especially Faevenly's decay. But Bramble was gone.

"Why that good-for-nothing faun!" Keeth shouted, slamming his axe into the frozen ground with a spit. "Bramble's the foolish one, not us!"

Avalynn felt certain the faun was right. "What did he mean when he said Faevenly's decay?" She figured it meant the Mother of Rivers. But something in Mateo's grim features and the way he kept touching his pendant told her to keep that tidbit to herself.

"It means the provinces threatening the Stromms," Mateo snapped. "They are the decay. They must be sawed off like rotten limbs."

She didn't think so. But she let him keep his theory as he walked to the head of the group and headed toward Skywatcher Mountain. His shoulders were pulled together, the bow and quiver at his back bouncing with each movement. Without a word, everyone followed, and Avalynn's mind grappled with how she would handle this new Mateo.

The snow crunched underfoot as they moved across the meadow. Keeth trudged behind Mateo. He muttered about snow being the most useless weather. Lirien and Gareth stayed behind, their sharp eyes scanning the horizon. Should she tell Mateo's friends her theory on Faevenly's decay? Should she share her worries about Mateo? Would their loyalty to him blind them?

"This meadow rolls on forever," Keeth grumbled, kicking at a clump of snow.

"Sure does," Lirien muttered, adjusting the dagger at his side.

Avalynn paused mid-step. Her gaze swept across the landscape. Keeth was right. The meadow stretched endlessly, unbroken except for the occasional snow-dappled tree or frozen bush. They were walking in place, it seemed.

Her eyes fell to the ground where Keeth had kicked at the snow. Her breath hitched. That same clump of snow—with Keeth's wide, unmistakable bootprint—lay in her path again. Her tracks, which should have been behind her, remained beneath her boots. Thunderation. She raised her hand and called out, "Wait!"

The group stopped, exchanging puzzled looks. Mateo turned his head, his features unreadable.

"What is it now?" Keeth asked, huffing and rolling his eyes.

"We haven't moved," Avalynn replied, pointing to the snow at their feet. "Look. That's the same bootprint you made earlier. We're walking in circles." She studied the path. "Not circles. We're stuck in place. Some sort of magic toys with us."

Lirien knelt, inspecting the ground. "She's right. These tracks don't make sense."

Gareth crouched beside him, his brow furrowed. He traced the imprints with a finger while shaking his head.

"That's great," Keeth groaned, flinging his arms. "Magic snow. Just what we needed. We are the fools!"

"Calm down, Keeth." Avalynn stepped around,

examining the ground. "We only need to figure out what it is and then how to break it."

Mateo narrowed his stare on her. "Are you calling the shots now, Ice Princess?"

She blinked. *Ice Princess?* So he was reverting to the Mateo she first met? Fine. Two could play at that game. "Maybe I am, Lord Prince Stromm because you sure didn't notice us going around in circles."

"Come on," Lirien said. "Can we just focus on getting out of this forsaken meadow?"

Gareth clapped to get everyone's attention. He made an L shape with both hands, his right hand in the front. He hooked the forefinger of his left hand over his right thumb, and then pulled his free forefinger and thumb up and down.

"Run?" Lirien asked with a laugh. "Across the meadow?"

"Won't work," Mateo said, shaking his head. "We're not all fast runners."

"Hey, now!" Keeth burst out. "I can run fast enough!"

"Let's try and see what happens." Avalynn didn't think it would work, but they had to do something.

With everyone's agreement, the group formed a line. Suddenly Avalynn's memory harkened back to the hunt with Mateo, when they had taken off after the Shadow-blood Foxes together. Did he feel it too?

"On my count," Lirien said. "Three... two... one!"

They broke into a sprint. Arms pumped, snow crunched, and snow clumps sprayed the air. Avalynn's breaths came in vapor-filled bursts. Her legs strained keeping up with Mateo and Lirien, who surged ahead.

Hulking Gareth stayed by her side, while Keeth gasped and grunted behind them.

With each stride, the far edge of the meadow loomed closer. The frost-kissed grass beckoning in the distance like a promise. A sliver of belief gathered inside her. Gareth's idea was working! They were almost there! But then the horizon shifted. The meadow ahead stretched further like a cruel trick of the eye. Avalynn's feet slowed, dread gripping her. No matter how hard they ran, the meadow pulled away from them.

"Stop!" Avalynn called out, gasping for air. She bent over, hands on her knees as her chest heaved.

One by one, the others stumbled to a halt, their breaths coming in ragged gasps. Keeth collapsed into the snow, red-faced and panting. "That... was not... my fault," he grunted between gulps of air.

"It's the dragons," Mateo said, his jaw tight and his brow furrowing. He looked toward the looming mountain. "They don't want us going there."

The boundary and now the meadow. She was beginning to think Mateo had a point.

Lirien cursed under his breath, throwing a snowball at nothing. "What now? We can't just sit here."

Avalynn straightened her back. Her gaze narrowed, studying the meadow's unnatural stillness. Her lesson with Rhyka in the Sublands and Leto's words at Strong Haven repeated in her mind. She had the power and needed to call it forth.

She reached for the sword sheathed at her back. With a steady motion, she drew it free. The blade slid from its sheath with a soft metallic hiss. The sword settled in her hand, the vibration of its energy tickling her palm. She smiled. The sword was getting used to her, and she to it.

"You think that can help us?" Mateo neared with a raised brow.

She nodded. "Only magic can beat magic." She wasn't sure, but it made sense.

"Then by all means." Mateo stepped back with a sweep of his arm.

She wanted to smack the smug look off his face but took a deep breath instead. *Concentrate on the sword, not Mateo.* She faced the mountain. Somehow the dragons were responsible for the meadow's magic. She wrapped her hands around the hilt. *Feel the power.* She held the sword close. *Call it forth.* She closed her eyes. With the shape of the mountain fixed in her mind, she recalled the two dragons cutting through the air over the Strong Haven ruins. Beautiful, deadly, fire breathing. She even thought of the dragon that had snatched Finnian. *Release us*, she said in her head.

A tingle of heat collected at her palms. Warmth crawled up her arms. *Release us. Now.* The words echoed in her mind. The warmth swept through her chest, filling her up like sunshine. The sword vibrated, humming with energy. The tip of the blade moved downward, guided by an unseen force, until its point faced the endless meadow before them.

She opened her eyes to a sea of blue light. It radiated from the blade, its glow growing stronger with every heartbeat. Her hands tightened around the hilt. The sword tugged forward. She peered down, then thrust it into the ground. The blade punctured the snow-dusted grass, slicing deep into the earth.

A blinding haze of light poured from the impact. It spread outward like ripples in a still pond. The glow intensified, gathering and swirling until it formed a shimmering path that cut through the endless meadow's illusion.

"Great Stars above," Keeth whispered. "She did it." His eyes widened. He took a shaky step back, then jerked his thumb toward the glowing trail. "Go, go! Before it closes!"

The group paused, looking at each other, and then broke into a run. But Mateo stayed behind. He tugged at Avalynn's waist. "Come on!"

Avalynn pulled the sword free and followed.

They ran, darting forward like their lives depended on it, then spilled onto a rocky surface, the meadow now far behind. She eyed Mateo, then stood and sheathed her sword. "I honestly do not understand you."

"Stop trying so hard." He adjusted his bow and arrow.

Gareth pushed Mateo and pointed at the mountaintop.

Avalynn looked up, then gulped. Dragons. They soared in an erratic crisscross pattern. Five of them. Four the size of the ones she and Mateo had encountered at the hunt and a much larger one. Their iridescent scales glinted in the sky. "We've angered them."

"Ya think?" Lirien asked.

"Let's not wait for them to introduce themselves!" Keeth hollered.

"Run for cover!" Mateo called. "To the base of the mountain!"

They sprinted, the icy crunch of boots mingling with their frantic breathing. The frosty meadow became a snow-dusted grove. A piercing shriek, followed by a thunderous roar, shook her insides. Heart pounding, she weaved between the towering trunks. Their gnarly branches clawed at her as if trying to hold her back.

The closer she came to the mountain's base, the thinner the forest grew. Its cover peeled away, revealing a barren stretch of rocky ground. A fierce gust surged around her, scattering leaves and broken branches. Her braid unraveled and her hair whipped into her face. She clawed at the strands, her stomach plummeting. They had lost the safety of the trees. They were exposed now. Sun, Moon, and Stars. Just like Finnian before his demise.

"Keep running!" Mateo shouted, his voice cutting through the chaos and matching her stride.

She glanced at him, his face set with ferocity. Still, her terror swelled. They weren't going to make it.

A shadow fell over them, blotting out the sun. It plunged them into a suffocating darkness. She heard hollering from Lirien and Keeth. She felt the chill before a deafening, guttural roar exploded over her.

Her fingers reached toward Mateo. Their fingertips brushed for the briefest moment. Then something massive and unyielding clamped around her. The pressure almost crushed her, pulling her upward and squeezing the air from her lungs. Wind howled in her ears. The ground fell away. Mateo's wide-eyed face shrunk below. The dragon's wings battered the air, each beat a thunderous crack.

"Mateo!" she screamed, her voice swallowed by the roaring wind. The dragon carried her higher, and the air grew thinner. Each breath became a desperate gasp, barely filling her lungs. Her vision blurred. Stars danced at the edges of her sight. A crushing weight settled over her chest, the icy air clawing at her skin. Her breathing faltered.

Everything went black.

CHAPTER NINETEEN

Mateo lunged for Avalynn. Their fingers touched as the dragon's talons slammed around her waist and jerked her away. "Nooo!"

He snatched his bow and arrow. His eye locked on the dragon's neck, and he let loose. A miss. He reached for another arrow when rumbling roars erupted from the skies. Mateo crouched low as a swarm of dragons plunged down from every direction. Their wings tightened, diving like iridescent lightning bolts. Talons snatched Keeth, Lirien, and Gareth in a flurry of scales and claws. Their desperate cries were lost in the whooshing wings and booming shrieks. The deadly beasts spiraled upward into the sky with his friends and Avalynn.

Mateo lined his arrow, the string taut. He nocked it with precision. He held steady. His arms swung back and forth, his focus darting after the streaking dragons. But the creatures moved too quickly. Their erratic paths became impossible to follow. *Come on, come on.*

He fired, then reloaded. Aiming again, the air shifted. A shadow darkened the skies. He froze, his gaze lifting skyward. A dark dragon eclipsed the others as if they were mere hummingbirds. Its wings spread wide, hammering the air with a roaring rhythm. Its massive form blotted out the sun. The scales gleamed like polished steel, refracting light. Its eyes—searing red like molten lava—locked onto Mateo. Not merely a predatory beast, the dragon was a tempest given flesh. And the wave came toward him.

Mateo got a sinking feeling in his gut. He stood zero chance against a beast like that. His hopes of saving Stromm Palace, and even the Sublands, were obliterated. His friends were probably dead. Avalynn too. He had nothing left to lose.

"You coming for me?" he snarled, blood boiling. He reached for another arrow, lined it up, and aimed for the dragon's eye. "I'm not going down without a fight."

Mateo stilled, waiting for the dragon to get closer. His heart pounded. His breathing quickened.

"Yes, I'm coming for you, Stromm prince."

The voice crashed through him like thunder ripping apart his mind. Each word vibrated with an ancient power, a primal growl, from the depths of the earth. It shook him to his core.

His mind reeled. How did it know him?

His rage ignited, flaring brighter. This wasn't how it would end for him. Not while he could still fight.

His jaw clenched. His focus narrowed. He drew back the string. With a defiant cry, he let the arrow fly, then bolted. He drew another arrow, his boots skidding over loose gravel. He sprinted toward the mountain's base. He needed cover for the next shot.

A gust slammed into his back, sending him sprawling face-first. A deafening roar shook the ground. It rattled every bone in his body, and darkness fell over him.

He scrambled as thick talons clamped around his torso. It wrenched him into the sky. Thrashing against the crushing grip, he punched and kicked. The icy wind slapped his face. The ground disappeared beneath him. His breath came in gasps. The Wild North's chill blasted his lungs. His vision narrowed when the talons released him in a freefall. He plummeted, then crashed in a heap onto the hard ground.

He couldn't move. Could barely think. Was he still alive? A set of hands gripped his shoulders, sending shooting pain all over. He coughed, spitting out blood. His eyes focused on Gareth, Lirien, and then Keeth. His heart surged. "You're okay!"

"Up, Up," Lirien urged. "Before they come back."

Dragons. Mateo climbed to his feet, looking skyward. His breath caught seeing the trio of smaller dragons. They darted around the larger one like angry hornets. Their cries pierced the air, sharp and shrill, contrasting the guttural roars of the colossal beast.

"What's happening?" Lirien asked.

"They're fighting," Mateo muttered, his eyes glued on the dragons.

"Over us?" Lirien asked with raised brows.

"I don't know," Mateo answered. Though Lirien's question rang true. Why else would they fight?

One of the smaller dragons flew high, then dove

toward the larger one. Nearly parallel, the smaller snapped its wings open and soared over the larger dragon's back, raking its claws across the steely-gray scales. Sparks flew, and dark blood sprayed. It shimmered like liquid obsidian raining down.

"The smaller one got him!" Keeth shouted.

The large dragon roared, twisting and whipping its spiked tail in a wide arc. The smaller one dodged, but the tail clipped it. It tumbled, shrieking as it fell. The massive foe's deafening roar drowned out its helpless cries.

The remaining smaller dragons circled. Their cries blended into a unified roar. They swooped in from opposite directions and attacked. Their claws tore and jaws ripped, taking turns with their assault. The larger dragon faltered. Its movements became labored and sluggish under the dual onslaught.

"They're taking him down," Lirien said.

"I don't think so," Mateo replied.

With an earth-shaking roar, the larger dragon unleashed a furious burst of flame. It swept it around, flapping its colossal wings. The shockwave sent the smaller dragons scattering, unable to match the raw power.

Mateo was right. They couldn't take him. His hopes rose, realizing the larger dragon was the one for him. With that beast by his side, no one could or would challenge him.

A triumphant roar blasted from the beast as if announcing its victory. It turned and flew toward the horizon, growing smaller with each flap of its wings.

"What was that?" Lirien let out a shaky breath.

"I don't think we want to find out." Keeth spat over his shoulder. "Dragon business doesn't involve us." He faced Mateo. "We should leave this instant. Flee this forsaken place!"

Mateo had no intention of leaving without that dragon. But then he realized something else. She wasn't there. "Where is Avalynn?" He scanned the area.

Lirien's eyes cast downward. "The dragon that took her hasn't returned."

Gareth held his hand in front of his face with fingers slightly closed, then brought his fingertips together and pulled his hand out.

"Gone?" Emptiness cut through him like a dull knife. He wiped his bloodied mouth. Avalynn was gone, and he had no clue if she would return. Mixed feelings overtook him. He hated warring emotions, but he couldn't help himself. He had fallen in love with Avalynn. He would have done anything for her. But her betrayal changed all that. Still, he didn't want her mauled to death by a dragon.

Did he?

"I still can't believe we're alive," Lirien whispered with wide eyes.

Gareth squeezed Lirien's shoulder.

They were alive, but for how long?

Mateo patted his body, searching for wounds from the encounter. Besides cuts and bruises, he was okay. His hand shot to his tunic, patting for the pendant his mother had given him. He found it and exhaled. He kept his fingers pressed against it. He needed its power now more than ever, especially since that colossal dragon knew him.

203

He turned to his friends. "The big dragon spoke to me in my mind. He called me the Stromm prince and said he was coming for me." Their eyes widened. "Did any of the dragons speak to you?" he asked.

"No," Lirien replied with a shake of his head. "But that can't be good."

"No, it can't," Keeth echoed, fright still settling in his eyes. "This frosty land is not meant for us, I'm telling ya."

Leaves rustled, branches snapped, and Mateo's senses kicked into high gear. He reached for his bow and arrows, but they were gone. Gareth and Lirien came up empty-handed too. But Keeth still had his axe.

"You'll have to pry this from my cold, dead fingers," he said, rising and shaking it wildly. He was ready for whatever was coming their way. The dwarf was definitely growing on him.

Mateo climbed to his feet, bracing himself. He was in no shape for a fight.

A group of fae emerged from the woods. They wore simple green attire with long, iridescent, dragon-scaled cloaks. Their cloak's scales glinted with each movement. Dragon scales marked their faces and hands. No doubt these were the dragonfolk. The Valians.

A tall, muscular one walked ahead of the others. With sharply pointed ears, half the fae's long, dark hair was twisted in a tight bun. The other half flowed down his back. He was the only one with dark hair and eyes.

"Sun, Moon, and Stars. Engrendorn!" Keeth lowered his axe, laughing. He rushed forward.

Engrendorn held out a long, dark spear, halting him

in his tracks. "Stay back, dwarf. There is no Engrendorn here."

Keeth's mouth fell open. "Engrendorn, it's me. Keeth Graddor of Stromm Palace."

"The seeds. He doesn't remember," Mateo uttered. Just like Bramble had said.

"Remember what?" Engrendorn swung his spear toward Mateo.

The tales of Engrendorn's athleticism were known far and wide. Mateo had expected him in the hunt but got Avalynn instead. "Lower that thing, and I will tell you."

"I prefer to keep it pointed," he replied.

"Fine." Mateo would do things Engrendorn's way, for now. "Magic surrounds this place," he explained. "Those who enter from Faevenly and remain have their memory taken. That is what has happened to you." He eyed the other Valians. Their silver hair and chrome eyes placed them in the cold region. Did Engrendorn notice that he was different?

"You were investigating the dragon sightings," Keeth went on. "It was said that you perished. But you must've crossed the boundary and stayed."

"Or he didn't make it out in three sunsets," Lirien added.

The Valians moved closer to Engrendorn. Their faces tightened, and their eyes narrowed. "This has always been our home," the one standing closest to Engrendorn said. She must have been a leader with Engrendorn, maybe even a mate. "And you have provoked our dragons with your magic."

Lirien stepped forward. "They're the ones who attacked us. They took our friend."

"And they took your memory, Engrendorn!" Keeth jerked his axe. "Don't you remember anything?"

"Is that even your name?" Mateo asked.

He lowered his staff. "I am Dorn. I have always lived here." He motioned to the lady by his side. "She is Zalarae, my mate."

Dorn, as in Engrendorn. The warrior must've held his name until the last second, reducing his identity to the last syllable. A chill raced down Mateo's spine. Would that happen to him? He tipped his head. "I am Mateo. My companions are Keeth, Lirien, and Gareth. Our missing friend is Avalynn."

Dorn tapped his staff against the ground. "You may stay and see if the dragons return your friend. One day only. After that, with or without her, you must leave and return to your land." He pointed back the way he and his people had come. "Our village is called Frost Vale. You are welcome to stay while you wait. We have food, water, and healing salves for your injuries."

Keeth's stomach growled like a bear waking from a winter's sleep. "I guess we can stay until tomorrow," he mumbled with a shrug.

They followed the mysterious Valians to their home. Mateo's eyes scanned the forest floor, searching for pyrosia. Reddish orange petals and black stems. He didn't think the Valians would offer it. So he needed to find it. The first day dimmed. And they were running out of time.

CHAPTER TWENTY

"*Come forth, Only One.*"

C A hum filled Avalynn's head. A tickle met her ears. Her eyes fluttered open. All she saw was endless white. The cold crept in, chilling her straight through to her bones. Where was she? She blinked again when the humming repeated. Finally, it registered as a voice. Its rich and melodic timbre resonated like a song coming from a canyon wind. It carried an ancient wisdom. Each word wrapped around her like a warm blanket on a frigid chill.

Her dreamlike haze faded. Everything rushed back. She was taken, plucked by a dragon. She sat up, shivering.

"*There you are.*" The terrifying beast that had taken her now spoke in her mind. Her heart raced, but as she turned, her fear ebbed away, making way for awe.

The dragon sat still, watching her, in a serene-like state. Lustrous scales gleamed under the sun's rays, shifting from purple to silver and then blue. She took in her surroundings. They were perched at the highest point of Skywatcher Mountain. Just the two of them.

She inhaled sharply, heart thundering, as the beast opened its mouth. This was it. Her days had ended. She flinched and raised both hands, expecting the flames. But a gentle trail of heat flowed out against her face. It felt like the morning sun's first rays. The coziness swirled around her, steadying her. Comforting her like an old friend.

Avalynn rose, swallowing. She had no idea how long she had been out or what the dragon wanted with her. And yet, there it sat. Watching. Patient. Silent. Waiting.

"Hello, my name is Avalynn Strong," she said.

"The Only One. I know who you are." The dragon tipped its head. The words swirled in Avalynn's mind like a magical melody.

"How do you know me?" she asked in a near whisper.

"Daughter of House Strong. Daughter of House Kane. Daughter of the human realm." The dragon looked at her with knowing eyes. *"I am Izel. Mother of Frost Vale."*

"Nice to meet you," Avalynn said. Mother of the entire vale? She wasn't sure what that meant, but she didn't ask. She had other burning questions. "Why did you and the other dragons attack us?" She glanced around. "And where are my companions?" Avalynn's hand itched for her sword that had stayed snug against her back. The dragon might still turn on her.

"Not attacking, Princess. Protecting."

"Protecting us? From whom?" she asked.

Izel leaned forward. *"Your magic in the meadow*

208

alerted us, my brood and me, to your presence. The largest one who lives in the furthest regions of the North heard you as well. His name is Teyocel. He is a destruction bringer. He felt your magic and the magic of the other."

Magic of the other? Her brows stitched together. "You must be mistaken. We have no other magic, just my sword..." Her words trailed off, her thoughts taking her to Mateo. In his bedchamber, he had worn the necklace and raged when she questioned the pendant. He said it was a gift from the High King and High Queen. They must have done something to it, and Raelor helped them.

"Sun, Moon, and Stars," she whispered, touching her lips. "Mateo's necklace must be magicked."

The beautiful *Izel* leaned forward, bringing her head down. Her long silver eyelashes curled up and back. "*The other's magic is sourced of dark shadows. It cannot stay here in this place.*"

She saw Mateo touching that cursed pendant. Each contact must have been changing him into someone he wasn't. And he had no idea. He didn't even have his cross anymore, and he had valued it more than anything. Her hand found the cross lying beneath her tunic. "I saw all the signs." She shook her head, stomach plunging. "I should have known."

"*You know now.*"

The dragon's face presented a chilling masterpiece of nature's power. The elongated snout tapered into sharp edges. Each shimmering scale caught the light and show-cased a cool rainbow's subtle shades. Her molten golden eyes burned with something that looked like wisdom, like two suns setting into shadows. Sharp ridges framed her head, accentuated by a crown of jagged horns. They jutted out with a regal air. Her maw, lined with rows of razor-sharp teeth, hinted at destruction. The faint lifting of her lips suggested to Avalynn an otherworldly wisdom.

She needed that wisdom and advice now. Everything inside of her said to trust the dragon. "What do I do?"

Izel breathed in, and tufts of smoke came from her nostrils with an exhale. "*I cannot tell you what to do. You must rely on yourself. Consider everything you have learned during your life. Your choices, the pain you have endured, and the strength you have found. Each lesson is a piece of the puzzle.*"

Avalynn frowned, her mind racing with everything that had happened since the hunt. "You make it sound so easy."

Izel's long lashes fluttered. "*There is no such thing as easy or hard. There are only choices and actions that follow. It is that simple and that difficult.*"

Avalynn's breath hitched. She whispered, "Choices and actions."

Izel nodded, the glow of her iridescent scales catching the light. "*Trust what you know. Trust the pieces you have been given. They will come together and light the way. And when that happens, you must have the courage to act.*" She paused, her nostrils flaring. "*But I tell you this: I also have choices and actions. The shadow magic cannot stay here.*"

Cold needles skittered down Avalynn's spine. The necklace. She needed to get rid of it above all else. But there was also the matter of Mateo and why they had come here. He wanted to find pyrosia to lure a dragon.

Should she tell *Izel?* Not yet. She would get through to Mateo on her own.

"I think I know what to do," she said.

"Very well, then." Izel shifted, her towering body moving elegantly. *"I will take you to the vale now."* She unfurled her wing with a whispering whoosh. The leathery membrane caught the sun, scattering a rainbow across the snow. The sharp spines along the edges glinted like a row of polished blades. *"Climb my wing,"* she instructed. *"Sit at the base of my neck and hold on tightly. The descent into Frost Vale is not gentle."*

Excitement mixed with nervousness swirled within Avalynn. She hesitated, but only for a moment before stepping forward. She climbed, her boots finding their footing on the sturdy surface. Reaching the base of *Izel's* neck, she settled herself, positioning her body as if mounting a horse, a really big one. Her fingers latched on for support, brushing against the cool, iridescent scales. Leaning forward, she tightened her legs and grasped the smooth ridge just below the curve of *Izel's* neck.

"I'm ready," Avalynn said, her shaky voice giving away her nervousness.

"Here we go."

Avalynn tightened her grip, bracing herself as *Izel's* body shifted beneath her, the ripple of muscles rolling like waves under her legs. With a mighty push, *Izel* rose to her feet, her wings unfurling in a sharp snap before whisking down in a thunderous beat. The force sent them surging upward from the mountaintop. Avalynn's stomach tumbled, a small scream escaping her lips before she could stop it.

A low, rumbling laugh vibrated through *Izel*'s chest, the sound resonating like rolling thunder in Avalynn's ears.

"That was scary," she said with a chuckle.

"You will get used to it." Izel soared higher and then flew in a wide circle. *"While we are flying, you can communicate with me through your mind."*

"I can?" Avalynn's long hair whipped in her face, the strands catching in her mouth. Spitting them out, she thought, *"Like this?"*

"Yes, like that." Izel flew a little faster now. *"Before I take you to the vale, I want to show you something."*

"Okay."

The cool wind caressed Avalynn's face and body. Her stomach tumbled every which way, then steadied as her body adjusted to the soaring heights and the beast's rhythm. She relaxed her hold, improving her view. Flying up high, they soared south. From her vantage point, she easily spotted the magical boundary, the soft haze extending like a light fog as far as the eye could see.

"Why did the dragons establish the magic boundary?" she asked.

Something like a sigh came from *Izel*. *"Initially, to protect us from the Faevenly fae. Too many of you crave power and resources. It is why we are rarely seen outside of the boundary. Though, from time to time, some of us cross over looking for adventure."*

"What do you mean, initially?" Avalynn's mind processed the implication of craving power and resources. What hand did the Stromms play in that? But the Stromms didn't hold power until recently. Before

that, it was the Strongs who ruled. Her family. What did they crave? What role did they play?

"*Look closely at Faevenly.*" The dragon soared to her right now, heading east. "*You will see.*"

She rested her head against the dragon's neck and peered down. The world stretched out wide, like a patchwork of wild beauty. From the height of *Izel's* flight, the frosty Wild North gave way to rolling forests. The dark-green canopy sprawled like an unbroken ocean of trees. Rivers snaked through the land, glinting silver in the sunlight.

As they moved further southwest, the forests thinned, giving way to vast prairies painted in shades of golden wheat and yellow and orange wildflowers that danced in the breeze. Occasionally, she spotted a lone dwelling or a village, their chimneys releasing smoke tendrils that faded quickly into the air.

"*This is all so beautiful, Izel. But am I supposed to see something?*"

"*Keep looking, dear one.*"

Her breath caught as they neared the edge of the Sublands. The fertile plains dissolved into a cracked, arid expanse of rust-colored earth and sharp ridges. Shadows pooled in the crevices of towering buttes and jagged spires, their stark forms jutting out like brave sentinels of a forgotten age. Dust storms rose in the distance, swirling and dancing like lovers, painting the horizon with stunning hues of amber and gray. It was beautiful. At first, she had dismissed the Sublands as barren and unremarkable. But now, seeing its raw and quiet beauty, a pang of guilt struck her for ever thinking it so.

Izel took a wide turn, circling the region. Was there something she wanted her to see here? She squinted, peering closer. She narrowed her gaze. Red rock, dirt, Spirit Butte. What else was there? She craned her neck. A river slicing through the terrain drew her attention, and that's when she saw it. A scar instead of gleaming waters. A light-green haze hovered over the stream. The land around the edges appeared dirty and gray.

"*Oh my Stars, the water.*" She swallowed. Bramble's words finished her thought as her heart sank. "*Faevenly's decay.*"

A soft, low whine rumbled in *Izel's* chest. "*The Mother of Rivers is being poisoned in the Sublands.*"

Avalynn's eyes teared up, not from the wind but from heartache. Someone was deliberately doing this? She wiped her face. "*I don't understand.*"

Izel's flight followed the river. "*Greed. Hate. Power. Destruction.*" The dragon sighed. "*It is hard to know why some Faevenly fae do what they do. Why some hate so much.*"

Avalynn kept her eye on the river, the haze following like a phantom tethered to its path. Terror struck her. She thought of what she had seen at the creek, Torch Lake, and even the Green Falls. "*Whoever is doing this is also destroying Faevenly,*" Avalynn said.

"*Yes. It is true.*"

The conversation with the spirit girl on Spirit Butte flashed back. She had warned Avalynn about the realm, but she had disappeared when Camilla showed up. She hadn't finished what she had been saying, but this had to have been what she meant. Poison was killing the realm.

Izel's path veered north. Avalynn hugged the great beast's neck. She pressed her hot cheek against the cool scales and cried. *"My heart hurts."* She was a Faevenly fae, and one of their own was doing this.

The air grew cooler and the day darker. Avalynn didn't even know how long she and *Izel* had flown when the dragon touched down in a frosty meadow. She slid off, slowly stretching her legs and back. She steadied herself on the earth, her body swaying despite standing still.

She pushed her hair back and tucked the loose strands behind her ears. "Thank you, *Izel*," she said out loud. Her somber tone gave away her mood. "Thank you for showing me."

"Do not despair, Only One," Izel said. She let out a soft puff of heat that flowed over Avalynn like a mother's embrace. *"You are here. And I have great faith in you."*

Izel spread her wings, then soared up and away.

Faith... She held on tight to Manny's words, even if Mateo had forgotten them. Faith was a warrior. She touched the sword slung at her back. And so was she.

She had to be.

CHAPTER TWENTY-ONE

The group followed Dorn and the Valians along a narrow, well-worn path winding through towering pine trees. The crisp air carried the scents of sweet maple sap and smoky bark, sending Mateo's stomach rumbling.

"Ahhh..." Keeth inhaled deeply. "I smell meat cooking." He took another whiff. "And potatoes."

"I could eat a herd of elk," Lirien added. He jabbed Gareth in the ribs. "So could he."

Gareth smiled and jabbed him back. He made a C shape with his hand and moved it down from his throat to his stomach.

After a short trek, the forest thinned. They emerged into a clearing and found lighted orbs like the ones in Stromm Palace. They floated in the air, casting a soft, golden glow over the snow-dusted thatched huts. Some orbs hung low, near doorways and pathways, while others drifted higher, their light reflecting off the frost-laden branches above. They had stumbled onto a magical village.

Dorn gestured toward the orbs. "Vale magic," he said, his voice tinged with pride. "A gift from our bond with the land and the dragons."

"We have those at Stromm Palace," Mateo said. "Provided by garden gnome magic."

"At the Sublands, we have oil lamps," Lirien said with a sneer. "We're not good enough for magic." Under his breath, he added, "Remember?"

The sting landed on Mateo like a snake's fang. He hadn't forgotten about the Sublands, but he couldn't help anyone without a dragon. If Lirien didn't understand, then that was his problem. He'd grown tired of holding Lirien's hand.

Mateo's gaze traveled beyond the village to Skywatcher Mountain. A rolling mist curled into the vale like a living thing. Warmth radiated from it, contrasting the cold air that clung to his skin from the long walk.

"That is dragon breath," Dorn said. "It keeps the valley from entirely freezing over. Without it, this place would be as lifeless as the glacier fields."

Villagers milled about, dressed in the same all-green attire as their escorts. Like Dorn and Zalarae, they wore dragon-scale facial markings. They moved with purpose, tending to daily tasks as they flashed curious glances at Mateo and his companions.

At the heart of the village, a robust fire roared. The flames crackled as they licked at the carcass of an animal roasting on a spit. Beside it, a massive pot bubbled, its contents hoisting savory aromas into the air.

"That's what I'm talking about," Keeth mumbled as he licked his lips.

The group stopped, and Zalarae faced them. Her facial markings caught the light of the fire as if she were a dragon herself. She inclined her head, her pale eyes studying the group. "Welcome to Frost Vale. Soon, the meat and stew will be ready. Sit. Rest. You have traveled far."

They gathered around the fire, and Mateo sank onto one of the logs. But his mind churned. The stew and the fire's warmth would have to wait. He needed to find pyrosia before nightfall. He wouldn't be able to search in the dark.

"I need some time to myself," Mateo murmured to his companions, rising to his feet. "I will return shortly." His friends exchanged questioning looks but nodded.

Keeth rose to his feet with a grunt. He cast a forlorn look toward the feast. "You won't be going anywhere without me."

"Come on, now." Mateo waved for him to sit. The last thing he wanted was the dwarf trailing him. He'd only get in the way. "There is no need for all that. I won't be far."

Keeth gazed at the fire pit like it was his first lover. "Well... Do not be gone long, then."

"I won't." Mateo left the group and walked into the shadows. With limited daylight left, he needed to hurry. His pulse quickened as he moved toward the vale's edge where pyrosia might grow and where he could remain unseen.

He found something else instead.

Avalynn stood at the far end of the clearing, her figure framed by the soft glow of the setting sun as she walked toward the vale. For a moment, Mateo froze, unable to believe his eyes. Relief surged through him, washing away every ounce of resentment he'd carried for her and all the conflict she had stirred within him. His heart hammered as his legs propelled him forward.

She spotted him, her stride faltering for the briefest second before she broke into a run. They raced toward each other, the distance between them vanishing in seconds. When they collided, Mateo wrapped her in his arms, lifting her off the ground as if he would never let her go.

"Avalynn!" His voice cracked with raw emotion. "You're alive!"

She clung to him as though the world might tear them apart again. Her arms tightened around his neck, and her breath came in soft, shuddering gasps. "I am," she whispered, her voice trembling. "Thanks to the Sun, Moon, and Stars."

Pulling back just enough to see her face, he cupped her cheeks, his thumbs brushing away smudges of dirt and tears. Her blue eyes, impossibly bright even against the fading light, searched his face as though she, too, couldn't believe this moment was real.

Without thinking, without hesitating, he kissed her.

Their lips met, and the world seemed to fall away. The chaos of dragons, the weight of the pendant, the battles they had fought—it all dissolved in the heat of their reunion. The kiss was desperate and tender, filled with everything he couldn't say, everything he'd longed for since the hunt. She kissed him back with equal fervor, her hands clutching him as if afraid to let him go.

But then she pulled away, her breathing ragged. He blinked, stunned by the abrupt end to their kiss, his heart still pounding. "What is it?"

Her fingers lingered on his chest, brushing against the pendant underneath his tunic before falling to her sides. "Mateo..." Her voice was soft but heavy with meaning. She stepped back slightly, the space between them like a physical wound.

"Talk to me," he prodded.

She exhaled, her breath mingling with the cold air between them. "You've changed since the hunt."

"You mean because you betrayed me?" He took a step back, his hurt and anger triggered, his defenses raised. "Is that what you're talking about?"

"No. I mean... Yes, I betrayed you. And I'm sorry! But I'm talking about something else." Her eyes shimmered with unshed tears as her voice wavered. "There is something dark within you. I can feel it, and I'm trying to understand what it is."

Mateo raked his fingers through his hair, his jaw tightening. "You don't get to do this, Avalynn. You don't get to tear me apart and then demand answers."

"I'm not demanding anything. And I'm not trying to tear you apart," she said, her voice rising. "I'm trying to reach you!"

"You can't," he snapped, stepping back, the words spilling out before he could stop them. "You are a Sublander now. A betrayer. You did this to yourself." He paused, his throat tightening as he added bitterly, "You can't stand what I have now, what I've become."

Avalynn flinched as if he'd struck her, but she didn't retreat. Her expression hardened, and for the first time, he saw something in her gaze that mirrored his own pain —an unyielding determination.

"What you've become?" she echoed softly, her words holding a thread of steel. "What is that exactly? Can you tell me?"

He shook his head. "A prince, someone with power, Avalynn. Someone better than you."

She moved in closer. "I'm not afraid of you, Mateo. I'm afraid *for* you. That pendant around your neck. It's poisoning you. Warping you. Turning you into something you're not."

Was she serious? "Nothing is poisoning me but you." He stepped away from her, needing to increase the space between them. "Maybe you should be afraid, Avalynn."

She stepped closer, the defiance in her every movement igniting a fresh wave of anger within him. She pressed her hand against his chest, just over the pendant. It was all he could do not to recoil.

"Your necklace," she said, her voice soft but insistent. "I'd like to see it again."

His gut roiled. His hand shot out, seizing her wrist. "Why?" he snapped. "Do you want to take it from me, the same way my birthright was taken?" His heart pounded as the pendant pulsed against his chest, feeding his rage.

"No," she said, her voice trembling. "I don't want to

take anything from you. But that necklace has changed you. I think it has dark magic, Mateo."

"Dark magic?" The accusation rolled over him like a tide of broken glass. A bitter laugh escaped his throat. "You are desperate." He released her wrist, shoving her hand away as though her touch might burn. "You don't want me to have power."

"It's not power," she shot back. "It's dark magic! You're not yourself anymore. You're angry, cruel—"

"I'm becoming who I was always meant to be, and you can't handle it!" He felt a twisted satisfaction as she took a half step back. His hand moved to the pendant, gripping it through the fabric. Its touch felt warm and alive. The pulse beneath his fingertips both comforted and unsettled him.

"That's not true," she said, shaking her head. Her voice softened. "The Mateo I know—the Mateo I love— would never say these things. He wouldn't hurt family and friends. He would have never put away his father's cross."

Her words hit harder than he expected, cutting through the haze. For a fleeting moment, he felt something else—guilt, even regret. But the feeling was smothered by the pendant's steady, insistent beat against his chest.

"Maybe you never knew me," he said, his voice low and venomous. He turned away, fists clenching at his sides. Every nerve in his body blazed, the flame fueled by something he couldn't control.

She didn't give up—never did before. "*Izel*, the dragon, told me about that necklace," she said, stepping closer. "It's not a piece of jewelry, Mateo. It's changing you. It's feeding on you, twisting everything good about you."

"Enough!" The word exploded from him like a thunderbolt, raw and jagged. He yanked the pendant free from his tunic, letting it hang in the open. The etched tree caught the fading light, its glow unnatural, almost hypnotic. The S on the other side seemed to writhe like a living creature. "This is mine, Avalynn," he growled, his voice trembling. "From my birth family. It's the only thing that's ever been truly mine."

Her gaze fixed on the pendant, her lips parting in a silent gasp. He saw fear in her eyes. It made his chest tighten, though he didn't know why.

"It's from Raelor," she whispered. "And it's controlling you." Tears welled in her eyes. "Please, Mateo, please. I'm begging you, let me help you."

For a moment, her plea almost reached him. His grip on the pendant faltered. A flicker of doubt crept into his mind. Raelor? But then the warmth of the pendant surged again, stronger this time. He clenched his jaw, shoving the necklace back beneath his tunic.

"You can't help me," he said, his decision final. "No one can."

He turned away, his steps heavy as he walked toward the forest. Her voice called after him, but he didn't stop. He couldn't. Only the pendant's steady pulse grounded him now, pulling him further into its embrace.

CHAPTER TWENTY-TWO

Keeth barreled toward Avalynn with his axe raised high over his head. Lirien and Gareth followed as well as a group of others dressed in green; they must be Valians.

"It's me! Avalynn!" She raised her arms and waved. It was dark now, and she needed them to see her before she met an axe.

The group approached at a slow trot. Keeth lowered his weapon, his gaze darting across her face. "You're alive and unharmed!"

"I am." She nodded.

Lirien and Gareth looked around. "Where's Mateo?" Lirien asked. "We thought we heard his voice."

She swallowed, sorrow striking her heart. "He was here. But he left." She pointed up the path. "We had an argument, and he went that way."

Keeth started off, but Avalynn latched on to his arm, pulling him back. "Let him go. He needs to cool off." *Izel* had told Avalynn to trust herself. Right now, trusting herself meant filling them in on everything. "Besides, I need to talk to you all."

Her eyes landed on Engrendorn. Her mouth fell open. The fae warrior was here? "Engrendorn?" She blinked, studying his face and the others' who had beautiful dragon-scale markings etched into their skin. "Sun, Moon, and Stars, is that really you?"

"Avalynn, meet Dorn," Keeth said, making a formal introduction. "He is a leader here." He raised a brow as if speaking an untruth. "He says he has lived here all his life."

"You know," Lirien muttered. "The Bramble way."

"The missing companion." Dorn tipped his head. "Welcome to Frost Vale, Avalynn."

She blinked, then smiled. "Thank you... Dorn." Now, she finally understood what it meant to cross the border into the Wild North and forget your identity. Yet Engrendorn, or Dorn, looked happy.

"Please, Avalynn," he said. "Come this way to our village."

Frost Vale unfolded like a wintry vision woven with silver and shadow. Thatched huts with steep, frost-covered roofs dotted the landscape, their edges glowing in the cold twilight from suspended magical orbs. The orbs emitted a soft silvery light, illuminating the pathways between the homes and casting long shadows over the frosted ground. Avalynn recognized the same orbs as the ones from Stromm Palace—a magic she had thought unique to the royal bloodline and the palace grounds.

The air hung thick with the mingling scents of

woodsmoke, roasting meat, and something herbal wafting from a bubbling pot at the heart of the village. A large bonfire crackled in the center, surrounded by villagers clad in dragon-scale cloaks. They moved with a quiet grace, their silver hair and eyes catching the orbs' light, their dragon-marked faces and hands mirroring Dorn's. They made no effort to approach, merely nodding as Avalynn and her companions passed.

Dorn led them through the village toward its edge, where the huts were sparser, the air quieter. Thin patches of snow crunched underfoot, though the chill never reached her. Her gaze drifted to the horizon where Skywatcher Mountain loomed, a haze spilling down from its peaks. Was that hazy warmth what kept the vale from freezing? Like the tufts of vapor *Izel* had breathed on her?

"This is yours while you're here," Dorn said, motioning to a modest yet larger hut tucked against the settlement's outer edge. Smoke curled lazily from its chimney, and a small firepit surrounded by logs waited outside. Someone had prepared the flames, the embers glowing beneath a lattice of logs.

"Thank you, Dorn. This is quite lovely."

"You are most welcome. But please know, you and your companions must leave tomorrow." He bowed. "I hope you understand."

"Oh, I see. Well, thank you for the evening's hospitality." Avalynn returned the bow, though her focus lingered on the scales etched into Dorn's skin. The same artistry adorned every villager's face and hands, marking them as dragonfolk.

He handed everyone a flask of water, then they left them alone.

She settled onto one of the logs, extending her hands toward the warmth. She rubbed her face, exhaustion settling into her bones, then took a sip from the flask. The drink warmed her throat and stomach, though it did little to thaw the twisting inside her.

The fire crackled, its flames casting dancing shadows on her companions' faces. Her gut clenched tight with everything she had to say to them. They were Mateo's friends, not hers. Would they listen? Would they believe her? More importantly, would they help her?

"I have much to say, and I need you all to please listen." She studied their faces, hoping they'd come to her aid. "Mateo and I fell in love during the Summit Range hunt."

Lirien's jaw clenched, and his hands tightened into fists. "And?"

"I know, I know. I betrayed him, Lirien, but I had no choice. I did it to help him survive. But then..." An incredulous laugh escaped her lips. "In a cruel twist of fate, we ended up reversing roles."

The fire crackled and popped. Mateo's friends stayed quiet, waiting for her to finish. "Since then, Mateo has changed. I don't know if you all have noticed."

Gareth made claw shapes with his hands, held them to his stomach, then forcefully pulled his hands up and out, brow furrowed and mouth open.

"Angry," Avalynn said with a nod. "I thought it was because of what I did to him, crossing the finish line first, but there's much more at play."

"Like what?" Keeth asked, leaning forward.

"He's been magicked. By the Stromm necklace that hangs around his neck. The dragon who took me, *Izel*, told me. It was something I had already noticed, but I didn't understand it."

Keeth shifted in his seat, grasping his knees. "I have seen him touching it when no one is looking." He eyed the others. "I thought he was forming an attachment with his lost family, but I see the truth too. He's drawn to it like a siren's song. It glints with a sinister glow during the night."

"There is more," Avalynn said. "Remember how Bramble mentioned Faevenly's decay?" she asked, raising her brows. "Well, the realm is being poisoned. The origin is coming from the Sublands' water."

Lirien sprang to his feet. "Always the Sublands! So much hate for us!" His breath came out in bursts. "Your prejudices run deep, Ice Princess. You would do well to mind what you say."

Rising, Gareth dusted off his seat pants. He clamped his hands around Lirien's shoulders and shoved him back down onto the log. Gareth plopped in a seat facing Avalynn. He made a fist with his hand and struck his chest with a downward motion, mimicking a cough with his mouth.

Shivers raced down Avalynn's spine. "Stars above. Dragon's Bellow," she muttered. "You're right. It must be related."

The enormity of the implication fell on the group, and no one spoke for a few long seconds. The Dragon's

Bellow sickness was being spread in the Sublands on purpose.

"Look, I don't like you. I never will," Lirien seethed. "But I love the Sublands and everyone in it. If malicious royals insist on spreading death, then we need to stop it." Lirien swiveled toward Keeth. "You are a Stromm guard. You must pick a side."

Avalynn's exact thoughts, but she appreciated Lirien had said it first. They couldn't afford to have Keeth working against them.

"Let me think." Keeth rubbed his forehead with his thick fingers. "My order is to protect the lord prince." He rubbed a few more times before lowering his hand. "If that necklace harms him, then it must be destroyed. We can figure out this business with Faevenly's decay after its destruction."

Avalynn nodded, studying the dwarf's grizzled face. She searched for any hint of hesitation but found none. He'd stand with them, at least for now.

Her eyes drifted to the darkening sky. Nightfall swallowed what little light remained. "It's the first sunset," she murmured, a chill slipping down her spine. "We have two more to get that necklace off Mateo and get out of here. The mission for pyrosia and dragons be damned."

Lirien's eyes blazed. "I don't care what it takes or who stands in our way." His jaw tightened. "Mateo doesn't deserve this darkness. That cannot be his fate."

Avalynn understood the fire in Lirien. He, Mateo, and Gareth loved each other like brothers. She could never forget that.

Dorn and Zalarae approached the group with filled

bowls. Despite the gloom, Avalynn and the group ate the food offerings without haste. They hadn't had a decent meal in days and needed the nourishment for the road ahead. The savory root vegetable soup carried the perfect blend of seasonings, the meat roasted to perfection.

"What is our plan for the morning, then?" Keeth asked with a beefy burp, wiping his mouth with his sleeve. "After tonight, we only have two more days."

"At first light, we follow his tracks," Lirien said, setting his empty bowl aside. "We jump him and bounce his head off a rock if necessary to get that damned, cursed necklace off."

She prayed to the Sun, Moon, and Stars the task would be that simple. But that prayer brought on a chuckle. Yeah right.

CHAPTER TWENTY-THREE

High Queen Lysandra Stromm paced the cramped dungeon room. Her royal slippers padded against the rough stone floor. The damp air clung to her skin and clothing like an unwelcome second layer. She tugged her cloak tighter around her shoulders, although the waiting, not the chill, gnawed at her.

Her jaw clenched as her eyes darted around the dimly lit chamber. A single torch flickered weakly on the far wall, casting uneven shadows dancing like mocking specters across the room. The stale, earthy stench of stone long forgotten by sunlight filled the room.

She despised this place. The dungeon was beneath her station in every sense—filthy, hidden, and unfit for a queen. Yet it remained the only place where she and Raelor could meet in absolute secrecy. No one else knew of this room. It was carved deep beneath the Stromm Palace dungeon and connected by a hidden underground tunnel that led to the palace's secret stairwell, which spiraled up within the walls to her private chamber. Even her mate did not know of the place. The fool couldn't be trusted with such critical secrecy.

Her pacing quickened, her gown brushing the coarse walls as she turned sharply at each end of the narrow chamber. The hem would need to be burned after this. She must not allow this place's grime to touch her chambers.

Where is he?

Her hands curled into fists at her sides, nails digging into her palms. Raelor was never late. Had something happened to the witch? She'd heard rumblings of the other houses scrambling to find a witch of their own. Had they succeeded and taken out her trusted adviser? A sharp crackle from the torch startled her, and she scowled, cursing under her breath.

But then a ripple of energy prickled the air, and her head snapped toward the doorway. A shiver ran down her spine, though she hid it, schooling her features into an icy mask. His magic always preceded him, a whisper of power that sent a thrill through her no matter how many times they met.

Raelor stepped into the chamber, his tall frame cloaked in black, the edges of his robes trailing like shadows in his wake. His unblinking crystal eyes gleamed like distant stars as they locked onto hers. The air grew colder, the dim torchlight faltering as though shying away from his presence.

"You're late," Lysandra snapped, her arms folded across her chest, her voice designed to wound.

Raelor bowed his head. "Apologies, my queen. The

palace bustles as we prepare for war. Coming here required my discreet arrival."

Lysandra's nostrils flared, but she tamped her temper down, straightening her posture. "Thank you, Raelor," she said, her tone clipped. "You know how much I appreciate discretion."

He nodded his agreement. She gestured impatiently toward the crude wooden table at the center of the room. The chair scraped against the stone floor as Lysandra seated herself, folding her hands tightly in her lap.

"Report?" she demanded, her gaze never leaving him.

He leaned forward in his chair. "The palace forces have grown," he began, his tone measured. "Five hundred foot soldiers from the outlying villages have pledged loyalty in return for palace favor. I ensured their oaths were binding. They will bolster our strength."

"Continue." Lysandra nodded, though her lips remained pursed.

Raelor's long fingers tapped the table, "The other houses have searched for witches of their own. Although none have been successful, I can taste their desperation. If one is found, it will bow to me, I assure you."

"Good," she snapped. "And what news do you have of Mateo?"

Raelor's tapping ceased. His pale fingers stilled, and for the first time, he hesitated. "It's most troubling news," he said as his eyes darkened. "It comes from Master Keeth."

"What news?" Lysandra's eyes narrowed, her body stiffening.

Raelor leaned forward, his voice a low murmur.

"Master Keeth was crafty enough to send a raven. He and Mateo have joined Avalynn and two Sublanders. Together, they head for the Wild North. They are probably already there."

The table shook as Lysandra's palm slammed against its surface, the ripple echoing through the chamber. The torchlight flared before dimming.

"Avalynn!" she shouted. "That insolent girl has always tried to ruin this house!" She rocketed from her chair, pacing the room like an unrestrained predator. "That girl is a plague." Her voice dropped to a growl, her fists clenching at her sides. "She must not succeed in swaying my son."

Raelor observed her in silence, his head tilting slightly as though pondering her rage. "She will not. The magic of the pendant holds."

"What if it falters?" Lysandra halted midstride, turning to face him. "We must be prepared for any scenario." Her usual poise cracked.

Raelor's expression hardened, his eyes piercing hers with a chill. "My magic will not falter, I assure you." He let the words hang before continuing. "But if you so desire, I can send a force after her. Something that will ensure her demise."

"Something stronger than the thunderstorm?" she asked, her lips curved into a satisfied smile.

"Stronger," he said.

The shadows in the room gathered around her like loyal subjects. "Do it. At once."

Raelor nodded, a smirk gracing his lips. "Consider it done, my queen."

Lysandra turned toward the door. She paused at the threshold, glancing back over her shoulder. "Thank you, Raelor. Your loyalty is invaluable."

"You will always have my loyalty, my queen," he replied, his voice as smooth and unwavering as the dark magic he wielded.

She nodded, a calmness settling over her. As she traversed the orb lit tunnel, a sense of triumph bloomed from her chest. Everything was falling into place. The pendant would keep Mateo under her influence, Avalynn would be dealt with, and her prisoner—her leverage—remained alive.

Nothing would take the Stromms down.

The thought carried her through the dank, oppressive corridor as she emerged into the secret palace stairwell within the walls. Ascending in silence, she entered her private washroom. She eyed her tub filled with warm water and rose petals. She stripped out of her dungeon-scented gown and tossed it on the marble floor. She slid into the tranquil water.

Her enemies would fall. Every last one. And the Stromms would reign supreme.

"Mother?" Lysandra turned to see Lily at the doorway. "May I come in?"

She wore a sparkling pink dress with gold trim. Her long silver hair flowed down her back. Lysandra's heart swelled with pride at how much like her Lily was, in spirit and fire, with the same determination and sharp wit. And always so amenable and obedient. The way she liked it.

"Yes, my lovely princess." She motioned to the comb on the stool by the tub. "You may comb my hair too."

"Okay!" Lily took the comb and sat on the edge of the tub. She began pulling it through the queen's dark tresses.

"Were you so proud when I helped my brother find that dragon book in the library?" She giggled.

"Oh, indeed I was," the queen said. "You were quite helpful to me, my darling."

Lily's combing slowed. "Will he be okay? My brother? He has been gone for a while, and I'm worried."

"My dear, there is nothing to be worried about. He is a Stromm. He will be more than okay." With Keeth by his side and the pendant around his neck, she had no other choice but to believe whatever obstacles he faced, he would escape victorious.

"You are right, Mother," her daughter said with renewed pep. "He is as clever and brave as he is lovely." She laughed again, and the queen smiled.

While Lily worked her hair, the queen daydreamed about her son's triumphs. Everything was falling into place.

CHAPTER TWENTY-FOUR

Mateo walked away from Avalynn at a brisk pace. He spotted a lighted orb along the path and snatched it, holding it out as he increased the distance between him and her and the other Sublanders. He didn't need them. They were holding him back with their narrow minds. They could never understand what it meant to have Stromm power. *Pfft.* Not even Avalynn understood when she had lived as one of them. She never wore the pendant. She never belonged. He was better off without them. The sooner he got a dragon and returned home, the better.

He swung the orb back and forth, searching for the red-orange petals. His chest swelled knowing his mother would honor him when he returned with a dragon. She'd host a royal celebration, erect a statue in his likeness, and all of Faevenly would know his name. Those who defied him? Death by fire. Especially Selene Baffin and any that stood with her.

With every step away from the vale, the chill in his bones grew. The warmth of the dragon's breath had long gone. He glanced up at the crescent moon and bright stars. Setting out during the night was not his most brilliant move. His destiny would have to wait until tomorrow.

He huddled within his cloak, his gaze now searching for a cave for the night. Swinging his light, his eyes adjusted to the forest shadows. He spotted a patch of darkness. He walked closer, finding a clearing and, just beyond, a cave opening. He ducked in. The small space welcomed him with an earthen warmth. Settling into a spot of leaves in the back, he brought out his chain. His fingers stroked the pendant.

Avalynn's claim of dark magic repeated in his mind, sparking rage. The presence in the pendant connected him to his family. It was real love. Now that he'd found them, nothing and no one would come between them.

Including Avalynn Strong.

A poking connected at Mateo's back. Followed by another. His eyes snapped open to a pair of dark beady eyes. "Hey, now," he said, shooing the shy rabbit away.

He sat up and rubbed his face, eyeing the cave opening. Daylight had broken, and he needed to move. He left his underground refuge. The bright sun warmed him, and his spirits lifted. Today would be a good day. He circled the clearing, eyeing Skywatcher Mountain behind him. The sun rose in the east; he found due north and started walking to where the dark steely-gray dragon had flown.

The thought of failure nagged at him, a premonition he couldn't shake until he pushed it aside. His focus required finding pyrosia and nothing else. Keeping his eyes trained ahead, he stumbled upon a small brook. His thirst kicked in, and he knelt, cupping his hands and drinking deeply. The icy water jolted his senses but did little to quell the shaky feeling inside. He stared at his reflection, distorted by the ripples. The fae prince stared back, looking tired—his gray eyes ringed with shadows and his jaw tight with worry.

The fault for his horrid condition lay with Avalynn. And the other lowborns too.

He slapped the water and rose to his feet. If he didn't return with a dragon... His stomach twisted, picturing the Stromm gates breached, the palace halls filled with invaders, and his family falling one by one. The legacy of the Stromms crushed beneath treacherous boots. And him—cast out, abandoned, reduced once again to a lowborn nothing. Not in this lifetime.

He clutched the pendant hanging from his necklace as he kept walking. "Get a grip," he muttered, shaking his head.

As the day waned, despair crept closer. But as doubt took hold, his eyes caught a flash of orange in the under-brush ahead. He froze, his heart pounding as he recognized the pyrosia plant's petals. He rushed forward and dropped to his knees. Sun, Moon, and Stars, he'd found it! He plucked the petals, gathering handfuls and stuffing them into his pouch until it bulged. When it overflowed, he stuffed his pockets.

Relief surged through him, and for the first time in a long while, hope blossomed in his chest. He stood and gazed at the darkening sky. He still had time to use the pyrosia and call the dragon.

But first, he needed strength from his family. He pulled out his pendant and wrapped both hands around the treasure, his fingers trembling. The tree engraving and the curved S radiated comfort that seeped into his hands and through his chest like a long-lasting family embrace. How dare Avalynn see anything sinister in the gift. How dare she try to take his family away from him.

Mateo envisioned himself riding the steely-gray dragon and slaying his enemies. All around him, burnt corpses of those who'd stood against him littered the earth. A death sentence they all deserved.

Closing his eyes, a heavy stillness descended as if the world itself paused for him. "I call on the strength of my ancestors," he whispered, his voice resolute. "Please be with me as I call on the dragon."

The pendant hummed, its heat pulsing like a heartbeat. He opened his eyes, brought it to his lips, and kissed it. He laid it against his tunic and took a pyrosia petal from his pocket. He had no idea what to do without tools or fire, so he rubbed it between his palms.

When the petal was reduced to several small pieces, he blew. The remains swirled in the air, dancing up high into the sky. Watching them drift away, he touched the pendant.

"Come on, dragon. I'm ready for you."

With his chest heaving and his pulse racing, he waited. Then, slowly, the earth shifted beneath his feet with a shiver. The ground trembled with an ancient and primal energy. A cracking reached his ears. He glanced down to see a thin fracture snaking through the frosty dirt, spreading outward like a spiderweb.

He turned his face skyward as a low rumble echoed, a guttural sound so deep it must've come from the Passing Place. It rolled toward him like distant thunder, building and insistent. The vibrations beneath his boots intensified, first subtle, then stronger, as if the land shifted and adjusted to some unseen force.

Mateo knew what it was. He was ready.

CHAPTER TWENTY-FIVE

Avalynn emerged from the Valian hut at first light. She found Dorn preparing a fire in the middle of the village. He said they'd give a blessing before setting out to find Mateo, a ceremony they called *Tletl Xochitl*. Dorn explained it as a fire blessing.

Keeth, Gareth, and Lirien sidled up next to Avalynn. "Well..." She nodded toward them. "Let's join our hosts."

"They'd better not burn me," Keeth grumbled.

They stood behind Dorn and watched him stack the wood with care, each log brought to him by a member of the village. Upon finishing, Zalarae and the others sprinkled around dry leaves and jagged sticks. With everything in place, Dorn struck two black rocks together, sending sparks into the pile. Flames leaped to life, orange and gold tongues reaching out to the new day, illuminating Frost Vale's frost-dusted ground.

With the villagers gathered around, the humming began. It rumbled low and resonant, a sound that rose from the frozen earth. It thrummed in Avalynn's chest, a rhythm that felt as old as the Wild North. The Valians stamped their feet in unison, a deep cadence harmonizing with the song. The flames danced higher, responding to the music.

Keeth raised a brow at Avalynn. He shuffled back a step but kept quiet. Lirien and Gareth stayed planted, curious and mesmerized by the ceremony.

Dorn and Zalarae stepped toward the fire. Their movements stopped the humming and stomping, leaving only the fire's crackle.

Zalarae addressed the group. "We gather around the Valian flames seeking blessings for our visitors as they seek their companion, Mateo Stromm," she said, her voice melodic while delivering the blessing. "May the strength of Frost Vale guide them, and may the dragons watch over them."

Dorn reached out, plunging his hands into the fire.

Avalynn gasped, trading surprised glances with Keeth and the others. No one expected that.

As if reaching into a stream, Dorn brought out cupped hands filled with smoldering ash. With graceful steps, he approached them. Starting with Avalynn, he smeared the ash over the back of her hands. He bowed his head, then moved to Keeth, and then down the line. Zalarae followed with a stick. She drew intricate, scale-like patterns onto Avalynn's skin that glowed in the firelight.

"With this mark, you carry the strength of our kind," she announced. "Let your heart burn bright with courage, and may the dragons lend their power to your journey."

"Thank you." She nodded, staring at her hands. Were the markings permanent? She would have asked, but she didn't want to be rude. She'd find out later.

Zalarae moved on, mirroring the gesture and blessings with Keeth, Gareth, and Lirien. When she finished, the Valians began humming again, softer this time, and Dorn and Zalarae stepped back. The fire burned lower, embers swirling into the air like fleeting spirits until the fire died out.

After the last flicker, the Valians surrounded the four companions with hugs and well wishes. Avalynn wasn't sure what had just happened, and it didn't matter. Her heart swelled and she thanked them for their blessing. They needed all the help they could get with Mateo.

With fruit flats, water, and replacement daggers for Lirien and an axe for Gareth, they left Frost Vale. Avalynn took care not to smudge her new markings, not right away. She liked the dragon scales.

"Is this permanent?" she asked no one in particular as they increased the distance between themselves and the vale.

"Only one way to find out." Keeth spat and rubbed his hand with his sleeve. The markings spread out with a smear. "Nope."

"I wouldn't have minded," Lirien said with a shrug, leaving his markings alone. "This dragon marking is impressive."

"How do you think the Valians keep their markings?" Avalynn asked, considering the markings on Dorn's and the others' faces didn't look ash-born.

"I've seen markings like that made with a special ink coloring. But I'm betting it's some sort of dragon magic," Keeth replied.

She reached for her sword's hilt at her back. The dragon markings reminded her of the blue etchings on her blade. Maybe the Valian's markings were like that—magical.

With no snowfall, they picked up Mateo's tracks with ease and soon found themselves far away from the vale. The tracks led south for a long while, then veered to a cave.

"He must have spent the night here," Avalynn said, crouching down and examining the small opening.

But beyond the cave threshold, they lost all signs of Mateo.

While Gareth and Lirien scoured the ground for tracks, Avalynn scanned the horizon. Her sharp eyes caught movement in the distance. A dark swarm grew larger against the pale-blue and purple sky. It moved with unnatural speed.

"Hey, everyone. What's that?" She pointed, her voice tense.

The others looked up. The flock approached at a furious pace, a blur of crimson wings and black talons, their shrill cries growing louder.

"That's no ordinary flock," Keeth said, his jaw tightening. He gripped his axe, knuckles whitening.

"Bloodhawks," Lirien hissed, drawing his daggers.

"Sharp talons and powerful beaks. They don't hunt like this unless someone controls them."

Sheer panic raced through Avalynn, followed by anger. She narrowed her eyes, drawing her sword with a swish. There was only one witch who held true malice toward her. "Magic," she said, her tone edged with certainty. "Raelor's magic."

The first hawk dove, a sleek missile of feathers and fury. Avalynn slashed upward, her blade cutting through its chest. Blood sprayed across her hand as the bird fell at her feet.

The flock cawed, descending all at once.

"Scatter!" Keeth roared.

The air erupted with chaos—wings beating, talons slicing, and beaks snapping. Keeth swung his axe in a wide arc as three bloodhawks dove at him. Two fell, but the third clawed at his shoulder before he batted it away.

Avalynn spun her sword in a deadly blur, cutting down a diving hawk.

"Get down, Avalynn!" Lirien hollered.

She ducked as a pair of attackers swooped in tandem, their cries sharper than blades. Her sword arced upward, cleaving one and then meeting the other between the eyes.

Gareth fought beside her, his axe splitting one blood-hawk in half. A fluid motion and he took care of the second one.

"There's too many!" Keeth shouted over the cacophony, blood covering his face and hands.

"Keep slashing!" Avalynn yelled. She hacked at a

careening hawk but came up short. Its talon scraped her hair, narrowly missing her scalp.

Lirien darted through the melee, his daggers flashing as he stabbed a hawk mid-dive. Blood splattered across his tunic as he spun to catch another as it lunged at Gareth's back.

Gareth let loose a guttural roar, swinging his axe and sending feathers flying. But a hawk slipped past his guard, its talons sinking deep into his neck. He let out a choked cry, his axe falling from his hands as blood poured from the wound.

"Gareth!" Lirien hollered, rushing to his side. He plunged his dagger into the bird and yanked it free, tossing the bloody corpse aside.

Avalynn and Keeth fought to finish the remaining hawks. With a final, brutal swing of her sword, Avalynn cleaved the last one in two. The battlefield fell silent, save for Gareth's ragged breathing.

Lirien held his hands against Gareth's neck. Blood seeped through his fingers, staining the ground with red streaks. He ripped off his shirt and pressed it to the wound. "Stay with me," he whispered, his voice trembling. "Your mother will be so mad if you don't come home. And really mad at me for letting this happen."

Keeth ripped a strip of cloth from his tunic. He and Lirien wrapped it around the bloodied makeshift binding, securing it to Gareth's neck as tightly as they could.

"I need to get him back to Frost Vale," Lirien said, his voice cracking.

Avalynn didn't hesitate, the sight taking her back to

the hunt and Eiric's wound. Since he had survived a similar injury, Gareth could too. "Yes, go."

With a stricken expression, Lirien eyed Keeth. "Help me get him across my shoulders."

Lirien knelt to the ground, and Keeth helped heave Gareth onto his shoulders. With Gareth snug and in place behind his back, Lirien looked at Avalynn. "Get Mateo and get across that boundary. No matter what it takes. Gareth and I will meet you on the other side."

"Lirien—" Avalynn started. She knew how much he and Gareth disliked her, and she didn't want to leave them like that. "I promise I will do everything I can."

He nodded. "I know."

Avalynn swallowed hard. She moved closer to Keeth, who looked as torn as she felt. Together, they watched Lirien run back to the vale, Gareth limp across his back.

Tears flooded her clogged throat. Keeth scooted closer and patted her back. "He'll get him there, and those Valians with their magic will fix Gareth right up."

She took a deep breath, letting Keeth's words sink in. The dwarf was right. Lirien was fast, and Dorn and Zalarae would know what to do. She had to hold on to that.

With the sun dipping lower, they needed to hurry. Time was running out. She steeled her resolve, rubbing her blade on the icy grass and wiping off her face with clumps of frost. Keeth did the same. When they finished, she set her sights north. If Mateo was headed in that direction, there was no reason why he would've veered off.

She eyed Keeth, relieved to have him with her. "Let's go."

They raced forward, determined to find Mateo. The cold air stung Avalynn's lungs, each breath a sharp reminder of the ticking clock behind their backs. Her boots pounded the ground. Pulse racing in her ears, she drove forward, pushing back the burn in her legs.

The landscape blurred around her, wind whipping at her face as she ran. Where was he? Her mind screamed his name, her heart hammering as if it could summon him through sheer force of will. Shadows stretched long beneath the lowering sun, turning the terrain into an endless maze. The dread gnawed at her. What if they were too late?

Her gaze swept the horizon, her heart hammering inside her chest. Then, through the hazy distance, she spotted a figure. Her heart leaped—Mateo! Relief surged through her, but it was fleeting. Her breath caught in her throat. The massive, steely-gray dragon streaked across the sky, its powerful wings slicing through the air. *Izel* had said his name was *Teyocel*. Destruction bringer. He barreled straight toward Mateo.

"Keeth! He's heading for Mateo!" she shouted.

"I see it!"

She surged forward, leaving Keeth to follow in her wake. She brandished her sword. "Get down!" He made no sign of hearing her. "Mateo, get down!"

Avalynn tackled him from behind. They crashed to the ground, her momentum sending them skidding across the icy dirt. Mateo's shout of frustration mingled with the roar of the huge dragon circling above. He twisted beneath her, his eyes wild with fury as he locked onto hers.

"What are you doing?!" he asked.

"I'm saving you!" she shouted, her voice strained as she tried to pin his arms.

"You're ruining me!" His venomous glare scorched her on the spot.

"Stop it, Mateo!" She lunged for the pendant, but he rolled away, narrowly escaping her grasp. "That thing is destroying you!"

He pushed himself to his feet, his chest heaving. He shoved the pendant behind his tunic. "You have always wanted my power!" he spat.

"Give it!" Keeth roared, charging with his axe raised high.

Mateo sidestepped Keeth's attack, his hand lashing like a viper. The punch to Keeth's throat sent the dwarf crumpling to his knees, gasping.

Mateo stood over him, fists clenched, his expression twisted. "Stay down, Dwarf!"

A deafening screech tore through the darkening air. Avalynn looked up at the flashes of silver and purple scales streaking across the sky. *Izel*. With her three dragons in formation, they descended like bolts, their roars shaking the earth.

Teyocel reared back, his massive wings churning as he prepared to engage.

The dragon battle erupted in a frenzy of flaring fire and metallic clashes. Avalynn's heart raced as she watched *Izel* and her dragons dive at the larger beast, their coordinated attacks forcing him to retreat.

"Mateo, look!" she shouted, pointing to the aerial fight. "This isn't you! That pendant is—"

"Enough!" His voice cracked like a whip. He spun to face her, his eyes narrowing. "You've taken everything from me. And now, you've ruined my chance with my dragon!"

"Don't you want to know what happened to your friends?" Keeth asked, axe in hand as he approached step by step.

Mateo's gaze faltered. He glanced about in a daze. Keeth was getting through.

"Gareth was mortally wounded." The dwarf crept closer. "Lirien races with him to the vale now. He might not survive."

With a shake of his head, Mateo uttered, "Gareth is wounded?"

Avalynn gritted her teeth and launched herself at Mateo. Keeth jumped into the fray as well. They wrestled Mateo, grappling for the pendant beneath his tunic.

"Let go!" Mateo hollered, thrashing beneath their combined weight. "You don't understand what this means! You'll destroy us all!"

"We're trying to save you, idiot!" Keeth growled, his hands clawing at Mateo's wrist.

Fire and roars filled the skies. Avalynn pulled at Mateo's collar. "Please," she pleaded, her voice cracking. "Let me help you!"

Mateo growled. With a sudden surge, he threw them off, sending them sprawling.

The gray-scaled dragon's bulky form blotted out the fading sunlight. Mateo staggered to his feet, his eyes locking on to the beast. "It's not over," he muttered, almost to himself.

Before Avalynn could move, *Teyocel* swooped low, his massive talons snatching Mateo from the ground. He didn't resist; instead, he clung to his scaly talon as the dragon carried him skyward.

"Mateo!" Avalynn screamed, her voice raw. She scrambled to her feet, reaching toward the retreating figure. But it was too late. The dragon and Mateo disappeared into the horizon, leaving nothing but the fading echoes of the beast's roar.

Avalynn dropped to her knees, her chest heaving. Keeth limped to her side, blood seeping from a gash on his arm. "We lost him," she whispered. "And he still has the pendant."

Keeth's jaw tightened, his expression grim. "We'll get him back. No matter what it takes."

"How?" she muttered.

He shook his head. "I don't know. But nothing is ever over until it's over."

With *Teyocel* gone, the other dragons touched down. Their scales were marred with fire stains. *Izel* approached. *"You have done what you could, Avalynn Strong."*

She wiped away her tears. "It wasn't enough." The sun dipped lower, and Avalynn felt the moments slipping away like sand through her fingers. "But we still have one more day."

"You and your companion may come with us for refuge for the evening, if you wish." Tufts of warmth drifted from her dragon nostrils. *"You will be safe with us."*

"You talking to it?" Keeth whispered as he leaned in closer.

Avalynn faced him. "She says we can go with them for the night."

His mouth fell open, and his bushy brows shot up. "Nope. No way. I cannot take another plunge through the skies. We dwarfs are made for land." Then he muttered, "Even if it is warm up on the mountain."

A low rumble, like a laugh, came from *Izel*. "*Use your sword. It will warm you both. We will check on you when the sun rises.*" She backed up, joining her younglings, and with a whoosh, they took off.

Avalynn watched the dragons soar off into the horizon, becoming smaller with each wing beat. She looked at Keeth. "She said I can use the sword to warm us."

"Alright then." He clapped his hands together. "What do we need to do?"

She wasn't sure, but they needed a fire, and they needed it fast. The cold was beginning to creep in, seeping through the layers of her clothing. The harsh mountain air bit at her skin. And she couldn't shake the image of Lirien running off with Gareth on his back.

"I know," Keeth offered. "Let's do things the old-fashioned way, eh? We can start with kindling."

It was a good idea. "Yes, let's do that." She needed the dwarf's reliability now more than ever because she could barely think.

She scanned the area for anything to build a fire. There were a few scattered bushes not far away, their dry leaves clinging to brittle branches. She pointed. "Those bushes will do."

"My thoughts exactly," he agreed. "Come on."

They trudged to the bushes. They snapped the branches and pulled the leaves, then dragged them together and made a small pile like an overgrown nest. When everything was stacked well enough, she glanced at Keeth. His face was pinched with frustration and discomfort, his eyes darting from the fireless pile to the horizon. They were stranded with nothing but cold and uncertainty for company.

"Now, do your thing," he said, motioning to the sword at her back. "Like you did in the meadow."

Her thoughts zoomed to the meadow. She reached behind her and pulled the sword free from its sheath, enjoying the familiar weight of it in her hands. The cold wind stung against her face, but her mind was focused, intent on unlocking its power.

"You should probably move back," she warned, envisioning a flame bursting out and lighting his bushy brows on fire.

He spit. "I ain't scared of it."

That wasn't what she had meant, but she left it alone. Keeth Graddor was going to do what he wanted to do.

She stood before the pile of kindling. She placed the sword's tip in the middle and poked the stiff ground. She leaned in. Bearing down, she pressed the blade into the earth. She held it firm for a few seconds and mentally searched for the sword's power. "Help us," she whispered, her hands trembling. "We need fire."

The blade pulsed. A soft, steady hum vibrated through her fingertips. The blue light of the blade flickered to life, brightening until it shone in waves, casting a pale-blue glow across the makeshift nest. She watched as the energy surged, running down the length of the sword and spreading into the soil. Her heartbeat quickened as the blue energy enveloped the kindling like a fog, a steady pulse that seemed to ripple through her entire body. She concentrated harder, holding her breath as the hum grew louder. The tip of the sword vibrated, and in an instant, a spark ignited in the dry leaves, bursting into a warm flame.

Avalynn's heart leaped in her chest, and she smiled. She was getting the hang of this. The fire crackled to life, its warmth spreading outward, the flames dancing in the chill mountain air.

Keeth exhaled, stoking the flames with a long stick. "You've got a talent there," he said, shaking his head. "There's no mistaking that."

She pulled out the sword. "Thank you, Keeth."

She didn't know exactly how it worked, and at that moment, it didn't matter. The warmth was real, and it was enough to keep them alive tonight. As the fire crackled and the shadows grew longer, she let out a sigh of relief. The sun sank below the horizon, casting the world into darkness. She might have lost Mateo, for now, but she still had her sword, a fire, and Keeth Graddor at her side.

And one more day.

CHAPTER TWENTY-SIX

The dragon's wings whipped up a final gust as he swooped into the mountain's jagged opening. Mateo's stomach lurched at the descent, swirls of dirt and rock scattering across the cavern floor. They glided over a plateau of obsidian stone, smooth and glossy like spilled ink, then jolted to a halt. The beast unfurled his claw, and Mateo tumbled out. He steadied his breathing, then found his footing and righted himself. A tremor vibrated through his boots as though the mountain lived and breathed. The stench of mud and the bite of metal crammed his nose.

The dragon folded his sprawling wings and coiled his tail around himself. His body settled with a grace that belied his immense size. All around, treasure lay scattered—coins, weapons, and gemstones, the items dulled by ash and dust.

The dragon's eyes, two pools of molten lava, watched him with unsettling stillness. Mateo hid his gulp. He resisted reaching for his pendant. He needed the dragon to know he was the Stromm prince, next in line to rule Faevenly. His name carried power and status. The dragon would do what he wanted.

"*Do not speak, little prince. Your thoughts are loud enough.*"

Mateo's breath caught; the deep and serrated voice, like the grinding of stone, slid into his mind like a blade. He'd heard it earlier when the dragon plucked him away after their dash across the frost meadow, though this time it was louder. But he hadn't known the dragon could hear him think.

He staggered back. "You can hear my thoughts."

"*I am Teyocel. I can hear your thoughts. I can taste your fear.*" His lips curled, exposing rows of sharp, glistening teeth. "*I can smell the pyrosia, but you don't need that with me. Now relax, boy. You are not the first to tremble before me.*"

"I'm not trembling," Mateo snapped, his voice harsher than he'd intended. He straightened, forcing himself to meet the dragon's gaze. "I am Mateo Stromm of House Stromm of Faevenly." The heavy air pressed against him from all sides. He cleared his throat. "You know why I'm here."

Teyocel lowered his head, his serpentine neck coiling as he brought his face level with Mateo's. His breath, hot and tinged with ash, washed over him. "*You seek my fire, my claws, my strength. But you come bearing gifts already... that trinket around your neck.*"

The pendant's pulse quickened. Mateo resisted the

urge to flinch, clenching his fists at his sides. *"It's not yours."*

"Not yet," Teyocel said, his mental voice amused. *"Let us speak plainly. You wish for my aid in defending your family, your palace, your bloodline. Do you think me so easily purchased?"*

Mateo took a step forward, his jaw tightening. "I offer you the chance to rise above this mountain, to fight alongside me. The provinces will fall to their knees when they see you. You could tip the scales in a war that will be remembered for centuries. Eons even."

Teyocel's laughter rumbled through the cavern, shaking loose a cascade of pebbles. *"A fine speech for one so young. But power, Prince Mateo, cannot be bartered for with future tales. It is taken, seized with sacrifice."*

"It is no laughing matter," Mateo growled.

The dragon's eyes burned brighter, pinning Mateo in place. *"You wish for my fire? My claws? Then give me something in return. My soul is bound to the Wild North, tethered by ancient magic. But there is a way..."* The dragon's stare narrowed. Puffs of heat escaped his nostrils. *"Share with me half of your soul. With that bond, I will be free to leave this mountain and fight by your side. When you are done with me and your enemies are slain, I will return your soul to you."*

Mateo's heart raced. "Half of my soul?" He forced a scoff. "Do you take me for a fool? I'd be at your mercy."

Teyocel's red eyes danced. *"You already are. But let me reassure you—I have no interest in keeping what is not mine. The bond will break the moment I return here. A mere temporary price for my aid."*

Mateo's mind churned. The pendant's heat seeped into his thoughts, muddying his judgment. He knew better than to trust the dragon, but the image of his family —of the Stromm Palace falling to ruin—burned within. He couldn't defend his bloodline alone.

"Fae do not lie. Do dragons lie?" he asked. It was a fool's question. Fae were cunning and did not need to lie. Was it the same for dragons?

"We do not."

The answer was no surprise. "And if I refuse?" he asked, his voice sounding hollow.

Teyocel's grin widened. *"Then I remain here, bound to this frosty land, and you walk out to face your enemies alone. Your choice, little prince."*

The pendant throbbed, its pulse merging with his heartbeat. Mateo's lips moved before his mind caught up. "Fine. I accept."

Teyocel's tail lashed the ground, sending a wave of dust shooting into the air. The dragon's mental voice turned soft, almost soothing. *"Wise choice. Step closer."*

Mateo hesitated, then closed the distance between them. *Teyocel's* claw reached out, a single talon pressing against his chest. The sharp tip pierced his skin, and a searing pain tore through him like fire racing through his veins. His breath hitched, his vision blurred, and the world around him dissolved.

Teyocel withdrew his claw, and he collapsed to the ground, weightless and unmoored. Time unraveled, losing its hold. Mateo felt himself fragment, as though pieces of his essence had scattered into the void. He was no longer bound by the confines of his body—no longer sure of where, who, or even when he was. He floated, suspended in an ethereal state, stripped of identity and meaning. He was nothing more than a speck, adrift in a vast, incomprehensible expanse, the pain a distant echo in the fabric of his unraveling mind.

His breaths came in rapid bursts, urgent and panicked. Suddenly aware of his hands, he brought them to his chest. He held on, waiting for his breathing to return to normal. What had happened? *Teyocel* sat on his obsidian stone. His red stare locked on him. He pulled himself up to his feet. He watched the dragon's scales pulse brighter, his body larger and more vibrant. What had he done?

"The bond is made," Teyocel said, his powerful voice resonating. *"I will fly with you, prince."* The dragon's crimson eyes blinked.

Mateo nodded, though unease coiled in his gut. "Do we fly now?" he asked, ready to leave the Wild North and fulfill his destiny.

A low, menacing chuckle came from *Teyocel*. *"Yes, Prince Mateo. Now we fly."* He extended his wing. *"Climb to my neck and hold on. And when you speak to me, use your mind."*

With pride blooming in his chest, Mateo stepped onto the dark scales. His boots slipped against the ridged texture, but he steadied himself with a hand against *Teyocel's* neck. The scales there were finer and more tightly knit, their edges sharp enough to nick his skin if he wasn't careful.

He climbed higher, avoiding the jagged spines that ran along the dragon's back, mindful of keeping his footing secure. When he reached the nape, a ridge of bone jutted out like a natural saddle. Swinging his foot over it, he settled into place, gripping the dragon's neck with his legs and clamping on to the dragon's spine for balance.

"*Comfortable, prince?*" *Teyocel* asked as if amused. "*Ready to ride the storm?*"

Using his mind, he said, "*I'm ready.*" His knuckles whitened as he gripped the spine tighter. He leaned forward. His heart pounded as the dragon stretched his wings, their vast expanse scraping the cavern walls.

"*Then hold fast.*"

The dragon shifted, his muscles flexing beneath Mateo. With a powerful leap, he launched himself from the obsidian platform. The cavern walls blurred. Wind howled around them as they hurtled toward the jagged opening. Mateo's stomach dropped, and his eyes squeezed shut as the dragon tilted into a sharp dive before leveling out.

The Wild North spread below them. An endless expanse of snow and jagged peaks glowed under the setting sun. "*The sun,*" he thought. "*When I arrived, it was in this same position. How can it still be if we have been in the cave?*"

"*A day has passed.*"

Terror seized Mateo. His soul... During the exchange, he had lost himself. Had he lost time too? Would all this be for naught like Avalynn had warned? "*Quick! I must make it through the boundary before the sun sets.*"

The wind tore at Mateo's face as *Teyocel's* powerful wings beat against the icy air, each stroke propelling them closer to the boundary. Skywatcher Mountain loomed below, its jagged peak catching the fading sunlight. Was Avalynn there? Or had she already crossed over?

A guttural roar split the air, and Mateo twisted. *Izel* and her brood hurtled after them like death seekers, and Avalynn crouched low on *Izel's* back. She was relentless. "*Lose her!*"

Flames poured from the attackers. The fire scorched the air, the heat prickling his skin even at this distance. *Teyocel* swerved sharply to avoid the searing blast. "*Izel* is hard to shake," *Teyocel* growled. "*Hold tight.*"

Mateo gritted his teeth and dug his fingers into the dragon's ridge. "*Do what you must!*"

With each movement, *Izel* stayed on *Teyocel's* flank. She flew so close he thought they'd collide midair. Avalynn's hair whipped in the wind. She leaned forward, as if urging the dragon closer.

"Drop the necklace, Mateo!" Her voice cut through the chaos, carrying on the wind like a warning echo.

He found his pendant and clutched it. Not a chance he'd ever let it go. The heirloom pulsed against his hand, its energy fueling him. "*Get rid of her!*"

"*If you wish.*"

Another plume of fire erupted, narrowly missing *Teyocel's* neck. The beast folded his wings and plummeted in a dizzying freefall. Mateo's stomach lurched; he clenched his thighs, his grip digging into the dragon's back. The maneuver worked. *Izel* overshot them, her fire scorching empty air.

Teyocel leveled out, and *Izel* was back, her brood closing in on both sides. This time *Izel* didn't attack. She flew alongside them, close enough for Mateo to see the fire burning in Avalynn's eyes.

"Drop it, Mateo!" she shouted again.

Mateo's lip curled. "Not in this lifetime."

Avalynn's gaze hardened, and before he could process what was happening, she leaped. Her body arced through the air, but the jump fell short. Mateo's instincts kicked in, and he reached out, his hand catching hers in midair. She dangled precariously, her weight nearly pulling him from his perch.

Teyocel roared in protest. *"Release her! She is dead weight!"*

Mateo's mind raced. His grip tightened on her wrist.

"Pull me up!" Avalynn shouted.

Below, the jagged peaks of Skywatcher Mountain waited like teeth for meat. He glanced at the horizon. The sun was a sliver now, dipping below the world's edge. If he dropped her now, he could make it to the boundary. Avalynn would remain here, if she lived, and the Wild North would claim her. She'd forget who she was. Forget him. Forget everything. Did he want that?

Her striking blue eyes pleaded with him. Their moments together flashed through his mind like a beautiful memory from long ago. He could save her. They could cross the boundary together and face whatever came next.

But the pendant's pulse throbbed against his chest, whispering promises of power, victory, and destiny fulfilled. She had betrayed him once. She would do it again. She hated him and his Stromm family. That would never change.

Time slowed as he met her gaze, her eyes wide with fear.

"Don't do it!" she cried, her voice cracking.

Mateo's jaw clenched. His heart hammered as he made his choice. "Goodbye, Avalynn."

He let go.

Her scream was swallowed by the wind as she plummeted into the darkness below.

Teyocel surged forward with a triumphant roar, the boundary nearing with every beat of his wings. Behind them, *Izel* shrieked, her brood crying with her. The mountains fell away, replaced by open skies and the promise of victory. And in the distance, a lone wolf howled.

Mateo's hand hovered over his chest, his fingers brushing the pendant. What he'd done pressed against him, heavier than a mountain. But he didn't look back. They soared through the boundary, and the skies went dark.

"Where to, Prince?"

"Summit Range, Stromm Palace." His lips curved into a smile.

He had done it.

THE
RECKONING

CHAPTER TWENTY-SEVEN

The wind howled against Mateo's face as *Teyocel's* wings cut the night's crisp air. Beneath him, Faevenly stretched out like an oil painting—rolling hills, jagged cliffs, and, finally, the grandeur of the Summit Range mountains rising to meet the sky. His chest swelled. This was his home, his legacy. And now, his moment.

The palace was tucked at the bottom of the range. He couldn't see it with his eyes yet, but his mind envisioned it. He and *Teyocel* would touch down in the gardens. Everyone would clap and cheer for House Stromm's savior. His mother and father would be overjoyed, and Lily too.

They might even worship him.

He leaned forward, his hands steady on the ridges of *Teyocel's* neck. The dragon's gray scales hummed under his touch. Its powerful muscles rippled with every beat of its wings.

Teyocel's deep voice rumbled in his mind like a calm storm rolling across the horizon. *"Warriors surround the palace."*

Mateo narrowed his stare, unable to see that far. *"Get closer. But not enough to be seen."*

Teyocel descended, and the palace grounds came into sharper focus, unfolding like a grim tale. Warriors were encamped a stone's throw from the palace. Tents clustered tightly with horses tethered nearby and weapons stacked in readiness.

Mateo's gaze shifted to his home, now surrounded by barricades and trenches that marred the once-pristine grounds. The signs of preparation stood as both a testament to Stromm resilience and a reminder of their vulnerability. They were outnumbered.

"Do you want them gone, my prince?"

Did he? His pulse quickened as he studied the encampment below. Tents sprawled like an invading blight upon the land. The Baffin, Lind, and Brunt banners fluttered defiantly in the breeze. These warriors from the rival houses had no loyalty to the Stromms. They had no place within his kingdom. They were invaders. They planned on decimating everything his family had built and Mateo had newly acquired.

He could end them. Now. *Teyocel's* fire would consume their tents, their armor, and their plans. All of it reduced to heaps of ash. The intoxicating thought surged within him, satisfaction curling at the idea of wielding such power. But it wasn't power for power's sake. This was his birthright. He had a moral duty to protect his bloodline. He would show the world that Mateo Stromm was no longer a pawn but a mighty force to be reckoned with.

And yet, something held him back from his base instinct. His gaze flicked to the palace, where Stromm warriors stood behind barricades, their faces hard. They were prepared to defend their king and queen and fight until their last breath. But what kind of kingdom would remain if he razed every house in Faevenly other than his own? Who would he rule? Where would he find subjects?

He needed to be careful. An impulsive show of destructive power could alter his destiny. The Stromms needed more than a vengeful prince; they needed a strategist and a leader worthy of the dragon beneath him. Mateo knew what to do.

"Burn the ground around them," he said. *"Make them run, but let them live—for now."*

Teyocel's growl rippled with the promise of ruin. *"With pleasure."*

Mateo leaned forward, gripping the dragon, as the beast descended. Let them see his capability. They'd tell their families and friends that Mateo Stromm had returned and was ready to rule.

The warriors snapped their heads upward, freezing with fright. Horses neighed, their reins snapping as they bucked and tore free, bolting in all directions.

"Show them," Mateo commanded. *"Make them regret stepping foot on Stromm land."*

Tucking in his wings, *Teyocel* dove. The air screamed around them as they plummeted, the ground rushing closer. Before impact, the dragon unfurled his wings, and a powerful downbeat sent a shockwave throughout the camp. Warriors sailed off their feet. Tents buckled and then collapsed.

"*Fire,*" Mateo said.

Flames erupted from *Teyocel,* searing across the earth in a wide arc. Grass and soil ignited, the heat warping the air and sending smoke plumes skyward. Warriors scattered, their shouts and screams blending. Horses galloped wildly, their cries piercing the air as they vanished into the surrounding forest.

Mateo watched it unfold from *Teyocel's* back, his jaw tightening as conflict churned within him. The sight of Stromm enemies brought to their knees filled him with a dark satisfaction, a vindication for the rebellion the other houses had stirred. Yet, a tiny part of him wondered if this was too much.

Teyocel circled back, his wings stirring the smoke below into eddies. He watched, letting the chaos linger before patting his neck. "*Enough.*"

Circling the skies, the deadly dragon roared once more. A final warning that echoed across Summit Range. Mateo took a last look at the devastation, the fleeing warriors, and the smoldering earth. "Let them remember this day," he muttered aloud, more to himself than to *Teyocel.* "Let them remember who they must face."

"*They will not forget, my prince.*"

He guided *Teyocel* toward the palace and the wide-open space behind the gardens. Guards rushed toward him, weapons out, and faces pale with fear.

Mateo swung down from *Teyocel's* back. He landed

lightly on his feet and held up a hand. "Do not be afraid. This is my dragon. A Stromm dragon."

The guards lowered their weapons. They stepped back and bowed. Some looked relieved, others wary, their eyes darting to the dragon behind him. Whispers rippled amongst them like wind through dry leaves. "He's here. The prince has returned—with a dragon."

"Stand back for the king!" a guard shouted.

In full battle regalia, the king approached through the throng, imposing as ever. His armor gleamed, the Stromm crest etched into his breastplate. Mateo touched his tunic where the pendant rested. Triumph filled him unlike any he'd ever known.

He straightened his posture, meeting his father's eyes. This was the moment he had craved for so long—proving himself worthy of the blood running through his veins. But beneath the triumph, Mateo's soul stirred. Had he done enough? Had he gone too far? Would his father see a son reclaiming his place or a threat to the throne he guarded so fiercely?

"Mateo. My son." The king's voice carried the weight of command. But his eyes reeked of envy, betraying that he wished he'd captured and submitted a dragon to his will like Mateo.

"Father." His chest tightened under the king's scrutinizing gaze.

For a moment, they stood frozen, two pillars of pride. The king stepped forward, and with a firm grip, he clasped Mateo's shoulders. "You've come home. And not a moment too soon."

Behind the king, the queen emerged, her flowing

purple dress contrasting the king's armor. Her dark hair was pulled into an intricate braid. Her piercing gray eyes, so like Mateo's, locked onto him. The king's expression was guarded, but hers resembled an open wound.

"Mateo," she whispered. She closed the distance between them. Her arms flung around him in a fierce embrace. To her, Mateo was no warrior or dragon rider. He was her beloved son.

He hesitated, but only for a moment. Her trembling form broke through the walls he had built, and he returned her embrace. "I am home, Mother."

"Thank the Sun, Moon, and Stars," she said, her voice thick. "I thought—" She pulled back to look into his eyes. "I thought we'd lost you."

"I'm here, my queen," he said, his voice softer than intended.

She studied him with a tilt of her head. "But you've changed," she said quietly, almost to herself. "You've been through so much, my son."

He pulled away, his expression hardening. Avalynn's face as she hurtled to her death flashed in his mind. He'd never forget the anguish filling her eyes as he made his choice. He couldn't afford to let his family know what had happened. Couldn't reveal the conflict that had brewed within him. What he had done, and who he had left behind. Not now, not ever.

"What I've been through doesn't matter now. What matters is that the Stromms will not fall. Not while I'm here."

The king stepped forward, his gaze narrowing. "The dragon." He nodded toward *Teyocel*, who watched from a

271

distance, smoke curling from his nostrils. "Where did it come from?"

Mateo's jaw tightened, his father's question pressing on him. How could he explain *Teyocel* without exposing everything he'd done and become? The bargain weighed heavily on him—a price far too great and a secret too dangerous to share. If they knew he'd surrendered half his soul, they'd view him as tainted and less than whole. Not a Stromm, but something... other.

His fingers twitched toward his pendant, but he held back. Its weight against his chest grounded him, a reminder of what he had endured and what he would bear alone. No one needed to know the depth of his journey or the truths he had unearthed in the Wild North. That knowledge would remain his shield, his weapon, and his burden.

"*Teyocel* came to me," he said, his voice distant as though the answer itself was immovable. The simplest truth of what had transpired. Anything more would invite questions, which would lead to truths he did not wish to reveal. Not yet. Perhaps not ever.

"Enough of the questions," the queen said, moving her arm around Mateo's shoulder. "My son, the prince, is home." She eyed the guards and raised her arm. "He has saved us all!"

The crowd shouted and then erupted in cheers. Hooting and hollering rang out like a victory cry and rolled across the mountains. Finally, the recognition Mateo deserved.

The queen ushered him toward the palace. A messenger rushed forward, bowing low for the queen.

"Your Highnesses. Prince Mateo. The envoys from the other houses request an audience. They've reconsidered their battle stance."

"As they should." Mateo smirked.

The queen's brow rose "Well, well. How the tides have changed." She exchanged a glance with the king. "We will entertain the invaders in the morning. Let them spend a night with their ruins." She smiled at Mateo. "We will show them what it means to stand against the Stromms."

He strode with his mother toward the palace. Behind him, *Teyocel* let out a thunderous roar, the sound reverberating like a claim of dominion. "*I will be in the mountains, my prince.*"

"*Thank you, Teyocel.*"

With a whoosh, the dragon launched skyward, his wings slicing the air as he soared toward the distant peaks. Mateo watched him go, a raw and dangerous reminder of the force now bound to him.

The clatter of the crowd echoed behind as he entered the palace, but Mateo's focus remained ahead. His path was one of power and peril. Every step carried him further from the lowborn Sublander he'd once been.

There was no going back now.

CHAPTER TWENTY-EIGHT

Mateo moved through his bedchamber, his fingertips brushing against the edges of carved furniture, ornate tapestries, and heavy drapes that framed the room. The fire crackled in the hearth, casting shadows on the rich wooden walls. The earthy crispness of pine lingered in the air, mingling with the hint of polished marble beneath his boots. His steps were measured, hesitant. The pendulum of victory and uncertainty swung wildly in his chest.

So much had changed in so little time. The Wild North. *Teyocel.* The fire outside the palace walls. The cheers of the guards and warriors. He clenched his hands at his sides, then released them. The pendant beneath his tunic hung heavier than it should, pulsing with the weight of his choices—choices no one else could understand and others he didn't understand himself.

He crossed to the window and pushed aside the thick curtains. Quiet darkness stretched over the palace grounds. Somewhere beyond the stillness lay the remnants of the day's chaos. The charred earth. The scattered warriors. The proof of his might. His future. Further out, his dragon rested somewhere in the Summit Range mountains, waiting for his next order.

He let the curtains fall closed and moved toward the fire, its warmth a stark contrast to the cold knot forming in the pit of his stomach. Tomorrow, they would hear from the other houses. Selene Baffin would make an appearance, no doubt. From the beginning, he had no illusions about her and her house's intent. They would feign diplomacy, spouting empty words of apology for encroaching on Stromm land. Yet their eyes would be searching for weakness, for him to falter. He would never let that happen.

A knock sounded, and Maid Penny entered, holding a stack of royal threads. "My lord prince," she said with a bow. "It is most splendid to see you again."

"Hello, Penny." He smiled. Her honest simpleness grounded him and made him feel almost normal, as if he carried fewer wounds.

She held up the neatly folded bundle. "The queen has requested you wear these for the audience with the rebel houses tomorrow. She calls them regal and powerful."

"Of course. Thank you," he muttered.

She set his things at the foot of his bed. "The queen also requests your presence in her chamber before you retire for the evening." She clasped her tiny hands in front, fidgeting with her fingers. "Shall I escort you?"

He had wanted nothing more than to indulge in a

warm bath and fall asleep in the plush linens. But his mother undoubtedly wanted to discuss more details of his journey. With a sigh, he said, "No, Penny. I will see myself there."

She bowed before leaving. "Thank you, my lord. I shall return at sunrise."

"One more thing, Penny," he said. She paused at the door. "I have pyrosia petals that need proper storing." He motioned to the petals he had placed on the table beside his bed. He didn't need them for *Teyocel*, but he didn't want to destroy them either. They might still have some use yet.

"I will see it done." She nodded.

He made his way out of his bedchamber, down the corridor, and to the royal quarters. Exhaustion lingered in every muscle. Pain throbbed in his temples. Whatever the queen wanted to say, he hoped it would be short. He needed rest.

He knocked, and Marina swung open the door. She bowed low. "My lord prince." She motioned him in. "Please have a seat while I inform your sires you are here."

He sat down in the chair beside the fire. The same spot where the queen gave him the pendant. He touched his tunic where it hung. Should he tell her how much it meant to him? How it had strengthened him during his darkest moments in the Wild North?

She swept into the room in a silver evening robe. The king, in matching attire, trailed after her. "My son, thank you for coming." She sat across from him while the king remained standing. "We know you are weary, but your father and I thought it best we discuss things before our audience with the traitorous houses in the morning."

Recounting the fragments of his journey filled him with unease. All he'd endured threatened to unmoor his careful composure since returning. Some truths were best left buried. Still, there were things they needed to know.

"Where would you like to begin?" he asked, masking the wariness that tugged at him.

"The beginning." The queen glanced at the king, who lowered himself onto the sofa beside her. "You set out to the Wild North with Master Keeth to find the dragons. You were successful, but where is Master Keeth?"

"He remains in the Wild North." If Keeth, Gareth, and Lirien had made it out of the boundary before the third sunset, they'd show up sooner or later. Until then, he would assume that they had not and that they had stayed.

"Why is that?" The queen's brow shot up.

He leaned forward. "A magical boundary protects the Wild North. Those who enter must leave within three sunsets. Those who stay beyond that time lose their memories."

Her eyes widened. "Is it visible? This boundary?"

"Only to the most careful eye." He drew in a deep breath. Time to tell them whom he had crossed the boundary with. "I journeyed with four companions— Master Keeth and my friends from the Sublands, Lirien and Gareth, as well as Avalynn. Unless they are seen again, we must assume they stayed."

The queen reached for his knee. "So you found the pyrosia and were the only one to make it out?"

"That's right," Mateo said.

"Oh my son." The queen nodded with a soft swallow. "That must have been so difficult."

"You persevered. The Stromm way," the king said. "We are proud of you, son." His arms folded across his chest. "But what of Avalynn and her Only One sword?"

Mateo didn't want to discuss the other dragons, the Valians, Engrendorn, and certainly not Avalynn. "We shall not see her again." He rubbed his aching temples. "Or her Only One sword." He had seen it strapped to her back when she fell. He shifted in his seat. "Let us talk about tomorrow."

"Of course, my son." The queen straightened her posture, putting on her queenly airs. "The Baffins are the leading house standing against us and challenging the hunt results. Your father and I plan to announce the hunt as forfeited and void. No winner, no loser."

Mateo raised an eyebrow. He wasn't expecting that but was glad to know the Sublands would be spared. He was a Stromm, and he wanted nothing to do with the Velas anymore. But he didn't desire unnecessary harm to come to them. Let them survive as they always had. "That is fine with me. Anything else?"

The king rose and slammed his hand on the fireplace mantle. "Every house will be punished. But the Baffins deserve special consideration. They must be made into an example of what happens when we are challenged."

Mateo's chest fluttered with dark satisfaction at the idea of that despicable Selene Baffin being dragged before him, her once proud demeanor stripped away. She had mocked him, schemed against him, and sought to break him. Now, he held the power, and the tide had shifted without return.

But it wasn't just vengeance. It was justice. The Baffins led the rebellion against the Stromms. Selene, with her silver tongue and treacherous cunning, had welcomed being the face of her house and representing the other houses. Letting her go without punishment invited chaos and signaled weakness. He would remind the Baffins, and everyone else, of what it cost to defy him and House Stromm.

"To the dungeons with each steward, and Selene as well," he said, his tone decisive. "And we schedule a public execution within the fortnight."

"We are in agreement." The queen nodded, glancing at the king.

Mateo rose. "If that is all, then I will see you both in the morning." With a quick bow, he turned and left.

Tomorrow would be the start of a new era. He was ready.

CHAPTER TWENTY-NINE

Mateo stood in front of the mirror, adjusting the collar of his silver shirt. The fabric shimmered in the morning light streaming through the window. Its hues echoed the scales of *Teyocel*, a subtle but clever touch he knew his mother had orchestrated. It wasn't just clothing. It was a statement, a reminder to all of the bond he now carried with the dragon and of the strength of the Stromms.

The soft click of the door opening drew his attention. Maid Penny entered with a bundle of dark fabric draped over her arm. "Your coat, my prince. Still warm from the tailor's hands."

She held it up, and Mateo stepped closer. At first glance, it was a deep, shadowy gray, the same color as his trousers. But when the sunshine touched the fabric, subtle stitched patterns became more visible. It was as if he wore a coat of dragon scales. He loved it. More than regal, it was fearsome. The design reminded him of the markings on the Valians' faces and hands—symbols of power and resilience.

With Penny's help, he slid his arms into the coat, the shoulders settling perfectly. The tailored fit and unique detailing made him feel invincible. He glanced at his reflection again, seeing not a prince but something more. A future king. A powerful figure who commanded dragons and kingdoms alike.

"You wear it well, my prince," Penny said with a smile before leaving him alone.

Mateo moved to the window. Somewhere out there, *Teyocel* roamed the Summit Range peaks. Could he hear Mateo's thoughts from this distance? Surely. They were bound now, in soul and mind.

He closed his eyes, focusing on the magnificent dragon. *"Teyocel, can you hear me?"*

The response resonated deep within him. *"I haven't stopped hearing you, my prince."*

Of course. The bond was always there, steady as Mateo's heartbeat. *"I face my enemies today."*

"Do you require assistance?"

He hadn't considered an appearance by *Teyocel*. But hearing the dragon's mighty roar at a well-timed moment might prove most advantageous. *"Yes. Stay close. Await my command."*

"Of course, my prince."

Mateo left his bedchamber and strode down the corridor. He slowed when he neared Avalynn's door, but he refused to stop. She was a memory now. A reminder of what he must do to his challengers, a promise of betrayal's steep price. Never again would he allow himself to trust blindly. He had learned his lesson with Avalynn Strong.

Pushing her from his mind, he hurried downstairs to the receiving room. Entering, he found the king and queen, dressed in silver, on their day thrones fashioned of Stardust Oak, the sparkling wood. Lily wore silver too and sat beside the queen. She smiled widely when she saw him and waved her little hand.

He took his seat beside the king. He studied the room while Stromm Palace officials and advisers entered, including Raelor. The witch wore all black and stationed himself behind the queen.

The head maid, Elizabeth, approached the queen with a quick bow. Tall and thin, she wore all white with a silver sash, her lavender hair braided down her back. "My king. My queen. Are you ready for the traitorous invaders?"

"Yes." The queen nodded with regal composure, glancing at the king. "Show them in."

Elizabeth curtsied and departed, her footsteps fading into the silence of the grand hall.

The massive doors creaked open. The stewards of House Brunt, House Lind, and House Baffin entered, their heavy armor still marked with the scorched streaks of dragon fire. Selene walked behind them with a few other maidens. Guards surrounded the group.

Mateo's gaze locked onto the steward of House Baffin, who stood closest to Selene. So this was her sire. The resemblance to Selene was unmistakable—fiery red hair, the same haughty tilt of the chin, and no doubt just as deplorable.

His stare moved to Selene. Her long hair hung loose over her shoulders, a stark contrast to the plain blue dress she wore. The gown, modest and unadorned, seemed a deliberate choice, signaling humility. Her eyes were puffy and bloodshot, a telltale sign of her sleepless, tear-filled night. She looked terrified, humbled, even contrite. Still, Mateo wasn't convinced.

He kept his posture casual, but his gaze was like that of a predator studying its prey. He waited for the king to dole out the punishment.

"Look at you," the king snarled, his voice menacing. "You stand here before the High King and High Queen of Faevenly, the prince and princess, as traitors to our realm and House Stromm. You dared defy us, inciting rebellion against your sovereigns, and in doing so, you have brought shame to your houses."

The king's hands curled into fists. "You wear the marks of your folly on your armor, scars of a battle you could never win." He pounded his fists on his armrests. "And now, you come before us—disgraced, broken, and unworthy of the air you breathe in this chamber!"

The stewards resembled lost travelers in a storm, their faces pale, their eyes darting everywhere. Fear clung to them like a second skin, each twitch and shallow breath betraying the terror they suppressed. Mateo's gaze lingered on their dragon-scorched armor, a pitiful display of failure.

Yet amid their trembling forms, he noticed Selene's posture shift. Her chin rose, and her eyes narrowed. Her every movement gnawed at him like splinters under his skin. Pride? Resilience? Whatever it was, it wasn't the humility he'd expected. It wasn't enough. Not after everything.

"My king, is there anything we can do to—"

"Silence!" the king shouted to Lord Baffin, his voice ringing like a hammer striking an anvil. It was so forceful the sniveling traitor backed up a step as did the others.

"Get ready, Teyocel."

"I am, my prince."

The queen patted the king's hand, then rose. The room held its breath as she moved forward, her presence commanding absolute attention. This would be good.

"Lord Baffin of Sand Bluff, Lady Selene of Sand Bluff," she began, her voice cold as frost. "Lord Lind of Cuesta, and Lord Brunt of High Meadow. You stand here as traitors to the crown, conspirators who dared to sow discord and invite ruin upon this realm and House Stromm. Your actions have not only betrayed your oaths but have placed countless lives in jeopardy."

She paused, her condemnation pressing down on the accused like a suffocating shroud. Mateo's lips curved into a smirk, a flicker of pride sparking within him. The queen—his mother—was outdoing herself. Her measured words, icy composure, and the way she wielded authority like a blade were masterful. This showed the power of House Stromm.

"Almost time," Mateo said.

"I am in position."

With her head held high and shoulders squared, she said, "The results of the Summit Range hunt are forfeit and void. As for your crimes against House Stromm and all of Faevenly, and for the stain you have left upon your houses, I hereby decree your punishment—public execution. Let your fate serve as a warning to any who dare to defy the rightful rulers of this kingdom."

"*Now.*"

A thunderous roar broke out. The walls rattled. The chandeliers swayed, their crystal edges clinking with the sound's tremor. Mateo's chest swelled as the ground beneath him trembled, the force of the roar rippling through the very bones of the palace. The roar was not just a sound—it was a warning, a promise of what would come. He glanced toward the window, and for a spine-chilling moment, the shadow of *Teyocel's* form passed over. Like a dark omen, it blackened the sky, as if the sun had disappeared.

Gasps rang out, mixed with hollering. Maids and maidens fell to the ground. The stewards crouched together in a huddle. But Selene's nostrils flared. Her eyes narrowed. She wasn't afraid. How dare she! After all she'd done—after the betrayal, the chaos she helped unleash—she had no right to appear anything but crushed. Contrition should have hollowed her out by now. Instead, she stood there, still maintaining her dignity, and that was intolerable.

The roaring ceased, and the queen motioned with her hand. "Guards," she called, her tone sharp as steel. "Escort the prisoners to the dungeons until the time of judgment."

But Mateo wanted more. Needing his wrath to be felt, he stepped forward. "My queen. I have something to add."

"Of course, my prince," the queen said, lowering herself into her seat.

Mateo leveled Selene with a death stare. Execution would not be enough for the likes of her. She needed to suffer all the days of her life. "The king and queen are wise in their punishment. Traitors do not deserve to stand amongst us... except for one." He lowered his chin, his lips curled. "Selene Baffin, you will not be executed. Instead, I punish you to a lifetime of torment. You will live every day in the aftermath of your betrayal, never knowing peace and never feeling safe. The very air around you will remind you of your traitorous ways. The consequences of your actions will always be at your heels. You will hurt in every way imaginable. May you suffer your choices until your last breath."

He let the silence stretch, his words hanging like a guillotine's blade, poised and ready to fall but hovering for eternity.

Her lips trembled; her eyes welled with tears. "My lord prince," she choked out. She fell to her knees. "I beg for death alongside my father. I implore you to let me enter the Passing Place by his side."

Finally, Mateo got the reaction he craved. "Beg all you want. Your punishment has been declared."

"The prince has spoken. Now, guards!" The king slammed his fists against his armrest. "Take them away."

Mateo's fingers twitched at his side. He longed for the touch of his pendant, the same pendant that hung around the necks of his mother, father, and sister, but he kept his hands still. He had been nothing more than a lowborn, a Sublander with nothing to call his own. He had been overlooked and had fought for every scrap of respect. Those days were long gone now, swept away by the rise of his true blood.

He was no longer the boy who had lived in the shadows. He was a prince, with a future to carve out. The kingdom would soon know the depth of his resolve, and he would not allow anyone—least of all Selene—to ignore the power he now wielded. He was no longer a servant to fate; he shaped it himself.

"What else do you require, my prince?" Teyocel rumbled in his head.

He wasn't ready to release his dragon. Not now, maybe not ever. He was doing fine without half his soul. *"Let me think about that."*

CHAPTER THIRTY

Lysandra paced the length of her private study, the whisper of her soft slippers against the polished marble floor the only disturbance in the room. The glow of the candelabras mixed with floating orbs showcased the ornate filigree carvings adorning the walls. The scent of aged parchment juxtaposed with that of fresh-cut gardenias and roses hung heavy in the air. Her hands, strong and slender, were clasped in front of her as she mulled over the state of her kingdom.

She had sworn to protect her Stromm legacy, an oath she would never fail. With her son's cunning and the raw might of his dragon, House Stromm had risen triumphant, as she knew it would. The rebellion had been snuffed, and the stewards of the opposing houses had met their end beneath the blade. Selene stayed imprisoned. Order had been restored. Power had been punctuated. Despite the resounding victory, an unease gnawed at her, coiling in the pit of her stomach like a sleeping serpent waiting to strike.

Her dreams kept reminding her of Avalynn Strong, the Only One as some had claimed. Rumors still circulated about her and that mighty weapon. She lurked in prophecy, a warrior foretold to end the Stromm reign. Mateo had assured her that Avalynn and her blade were gone, erased from fate's chessboard. So far, Mateo's claims held true. No rumors, no sightings. Not even Raelor detected her. Yet, in the deepest recesses of her mind, doubt lingered inside her like a festering wound.

Could she trust that Avalynn was truly gone? Could she afford to?

Lysandra's pacing quickened. For all her victories, she knew better than to believe in things unseen. Sure, Avalynn had vanished. But silence could be deadlier than a dragon's breath. She had no intention of being caught unprepared.

Marina entered her chamber. "My queen." She bowed low. "Raelor is here, along with your guest."

"Finally," she murmured. "Ensure my bath remains prepared for when I return." She shuddered. "You know how I feel about that place."

"Of course, my lady."

With a swish of her royal gown, she hurried to her washroom and ducked into the hidden stairway behind the floor-length mirror. She descended the narrow steps, making her way to the secret door that led to the hidden tunnels. She stepped through the dank corridor without delay until she arrived at the dungeon's connecting room.

When she entered the room, the stink of decaying soil and dust assaulted her nose like a punch. Her vision darkened before adjusting to the low light of the single torch. Raelor came into view, leaning against the stone wall. Arms crossed, his crystal eyes shining brightly. He motioned to their guest, who sat blindfolded at the rectangular table.

Lysandra smiled at her favorite puppet.

She lowered herself into the plain seat, then motioned to Raelor to remove the blindfold. His long fingers slipped beneath the fabric and tugged it free. Lysandra leaned forward, her gaze fixed on Verona. The Sublander blinked against the sudden light, her eyes settling on the queen.

"Ah, Lady Verona," Lysandra said smoothly, resting her hands on the crude wooden table. "Thank you for accepting my invitation for a meeting."

"There was no invitation," Verona snapped, her nostrils flaring as she straightened in her chair.

"Semantics, my dear." Lysandra chuckled, tapping her fingernails on the wood. "You're here now, and I have a task for you—one that will secure your loyalty and... perhaps... your brother's freedom."

"What do you want this time?" she asked through clenched teeth.

The queen tilted her head, her voice mockingly sweet as she replied, "I want you to travel to the Wild North and find Avalynn Strong. Dead or alive, I want her and her sword returned to this palace. Brought to my feet."

"What game is this?" Verona's eyes narrowed, her jaw tightening. "I thought your son ended her."

She shrugged. "So goes the claim, but I desire proof and I want that sword."

Verona's stare tightened. "And if I do this, you will release my brother from the dungeon?"

Lysandra's smile widened. "Yes, of course. Do this for me, and Adrius will be released and returned to you."

Verona's cheeks puffed, and then she exhaled. "Fine," she spat out, the rebellion in her eyes clear as daylight. "I will do it."

"But let me make myself clear." Lysandra leaned forward, tone shifting to icy warning. She wanted no room for misinterpretation. "If you cross me, your brother will meet the blade. His blood will stain the stones beneath the palace."

With a swallow, Verona nodded. "And what of the Dragon's Bellow? The Sublanders are still suffering. At least let me stop poisoning the waters." She slammed her palms against the table. "We have no more healing seeds!"

The queen's fingers stopped their rhythmic tapping. She raised a brow to Raelor, who pressed his hands down on Verona's shoulders. "You must do something about that temper. And your disregard for my royalty."

Verona's nostrils flared. With a pained look in her eyes, she murmured, "I humbly request permission to stop poisoning the waters, my queen."

Lysandra continued tapping. She'd been receiving reports of the waterways suffering beyond the Sublands. It was an unintended result of her plan to cripple the region. Allowing Verona to cease the operation should reverse further harm.

"Request granted. Your people are broken. And I"—she gestured to herself with an elegant sweep of her hand —"I am quite pleased with the results."

"You are a monster," Verona seethed.

"I have been called much worse." She smirked and sat back. "Now, see to your task. Remember, your brother's fate rests in your hands. Fail, and you will learn exactly the monster I am."

She rose, dusting off her hands, and turned to Raelor. "Spell her so that she speaks nothing of this conversation. Then see her out."

He smiled and nodded. "Yes, my queen."

As Lysandra climbed the stairs to her chamber, a satisfied smile curled her lips. The rebellion had been crushed, the stewards executed, and Selene Baffin imprisoned. House Stromm reigned supreme, exactly as she had planned. Her pawn, Lady Verona, would set out for the Wild North to bring back that cursed sword and that detestable Avalynn, breathing or not. But Verona's brother? She chuckled. She had no intention of giving him up. At least, not alive.

Her crowning achievement, Mateo, filled her heart like a blazing torch in the darkest night. Her beloved son and greatest legacy, who now had a dragon at his command. He had proven himself, yet she would not leave anything to chance. That pendant—the anchor of her control—would never leave his neck. She would see to it, no matter the cost.

As for those responsible for taking her beloved Mateo from her? She would uncover the truth, no matter how long it took. And whoever had dared to commit the vile act of switching Mateo and Avalynn would suffer consequences so severe they'd curse the day they had crossed her.

She reached her washroom, and her resolve pulsed stronger. She would break anyone who stood against her and her bloodline. No matter the cost, no matter the foe, Lysandra Stromm would stand unshaken, her crown gleaming atop a throne of ash and ruin if it had to.

Nothing, not Avalynn Strong, not dragons, not even fate itself, would bring down her or House Stromm.

Conclusion of *A Shadow Falls*
Continue the epic saga of Avalynn and Mateo
with *A Legacy Forged*

Subscribe for Rose Garcia's updates here:
https://rosegarciabooks.com/newsletter

NOTE FOR THE READER

Thank you so much for reading *A Shadow Falls*! It was so important for me to get this story right after such a powerful start with *A Storm Rises*, and I hope I did that for you!

I honestly didn't know how I was going to top the gut wrenching betrayal and epic twists from book one. It's one of the biggest reasons why it took me a bit longer to write this book. Where could I go after leaving Avalynn in the Sublands with her world turned upside down? What depths could I plunge Mateo further into after leaving him in Stromm Palace staring at the flames and thinking "everything is on fire, and so am I?"

For Mateo, – more fire!! He would never embrace his Strommness, so I had to literally "make" him step into the legacy of his bloodline. Luckily, I had the evil queen and her devious witch more than eager to take on the task of pulling Mateo into the shadows. Not to mention *Teyocel* who's going to make everything so much worse for Mateo in book three. EEP!

For Avalynn, - more heartache!! She was the big betrayer after all. She needed to suffer the consequences of her actions. Not just from Mateo's family and friends, but from her own guilt. Will anyone ever trust her again? Can she realize the meaning of the prophecy of the Only One now that she doesn't even know who she is anymore? ACK!

This book challenged me in ways I didn't expect. It took me deeper into the world of Faevenly, into the minds of these characters, and into the darker corners of their struggles. There were moments where I questioned everything—where the story was going, whether certain scenes would land the way I wanted, and if I was truly capturing the tension and emotion that made A Storm Rises so powerful. But in the end, I trusted the journey, and I hope you felt that through every page.

I would be remiss if I didn't give a huge shoutout to my critique partner, Keith Grady! (aka, Keeth Graddor!) As always, he is the wind beneath my words, helping me soar to new heights with my craft. He's amazing!

Another huge shoutout to an incredible reader I met at the Giddings, Texas Word Wrangler Book Fair, Kyle Shimpock! When he found out I had a deaf character, Gareth, in A Storm Rises, he shared with me that he is the leader of the Deaf Ministry and interpreter at Flatonia Baptist Church. (https://flatoniabaptist.org/index.php/project/asl/) He graciously agreed to look over and review the parts of the book that feature Gareth. His feedback was so valuable! With his help, I'm excited to do more with Gareth in book three!

I could go on and on about A Shadow Falls and the evolution of the story and the characters, but I'll save that for some blog posts and newsletters features. I just hope you enjoyed the book! If you did, it would mean the world to me if you left a review or shared your thoughts with others. Your support helps so much, and I can't wait to bring you the final chapter of this trilogy in A Legacy Forged!

With all my love and gratitude,
    Rose

ALSO BY ROSE GARCIA

BLOODLINES LEGACY SERIES

A Storm Rises, book 1

A Shadow Falls, book 2

A Legacy Forged, book 3 (coming soon)

FAE BLOODLINES SERIES

Fae Away, book 1

Fae Fractured, book 2

Fae Hunted, book 3

Fae Rising, book 4

FINAL LIFE SERIES

Final Life, book 1

Final Stand, book 2

Final Death, book 3

First Life, book 4

ABOUT THE AUTHOR

Rose Garcia is a USA Today bestselling author and screenwriter. She believes that no matter how dark the world may seem, there is always a sliver of light if you look hard enough. This theme permeates every aspect of her being and threads itself through the fabric of her stories.

A lawyer turned writer, Rose writes Young Adult fantasy with Hispanic characters, complicated romance, powerful families, and dynamic friendships. She is known for bringing richly diverse characters to life as she draws on her own cultural experiences.

Rose lives in Houston with her husband and two needy fur babies. If she's not writing, she's either reading or watching a show. She might even be eating tacos because tacos are life!

For more on Rose, visit www.rosegarciabooks.com.

Join my FB Group!

www.facebook.com/groups/TheRoseBudSociety

Subscribe to my NL!

www.rosegarciabooks.com/newsletter

facebook.com/AuthorRoseGarcia

instagram.com/rosegarciabooks

tiktok.com/@rosegarciabooks

bookbub.com/authors/rose-garcia